Sapphyre

Sapphyre

Book One of the Runestar Chronicles

Jason Komito

Published 2014 by Creativia
Book design by Creativia (www.creativia.org)
Second Edition, Edited by Simone Beaudelaire

To Mitchell,
Whose imagination dwarfed the world I created here
With a special thank you to Mom and Dad
I love you

Chapter 1

THE Dragon's Flagon, an inn in a town of two hundred thirty people, is crowded on this cold night. Located off the Great Southern Road in the southwest corner of the continent in the hamlet of Tondor, it has a reputation of being welcoming to travelers and for serving cold ale and hearty food. There is a fire keeping the patrons warm while mutton and corn are cooking in the kitchen. Ornik is behind the bar as usual, serving up his good humor along with the fine ale that is renowned throughout the region. He has seen every type of character in his establishment, which he has been running for almost forty winters. Travelers are frequent as the Great Southern Road is just to the west of town, and the port city of Meer is only forty or so leagues to the southwest. He has seen barbarians from the north, dwarves from the Myth Mountains, dark-skinned foreigners from across the Sea Of Tears, soldiers who patrol the entire Kingdom of Martell, and countless other strangers he cannot put a name to. He has no problem with any of them as long as they don't cause trouble and have enough kendra to pay the bill.

The inn is full since the roads have become dangerous, and bandits are becoming more brazen in their attacks on travelers. The autumn season is cruelly frigid and sleeping outside without a fire is not the most pleasant experience. This influx of travelers seeking shelter has led to the diversity of the crowd on this night. The regulars from the town make sure the sixty-five-winters-old owner gets no trouble from the strangers. Rarely does a fight break out. The occasional brawl arises when there is a discrepancy at one of the two stasshire tables or if there's a cheat at the dice game.

The serving girl with blue streaks in her blonde hair is tiptoeing around the patrons with a pitcher of ale in each hand. She maneuvers between two tables when a drunkard makes the mistake of grabbing her bottom as she passes by. Without losing a step, she spins to her left, gracefully places the pitchers on the table, and in one fluid motion reaches down to her ankle and unsheathes her dagger. Before the drunk patron realizes what is happening, the serving girl finishes her spin and is face to face with the man while her dagger point is firmly pushing into his crotch. As she's about to speak, Ornik screams from behind the bar, drawing attention to the spectacle. "Sapphyre, please don't do it. We don't need another eunuch leaving this tavern thanks to you."

All eyes are now watching Sapphyre. The embarrassed drunkard has both hands up signaling surrender as she allows the dagger to linger a moment longer. She slowly withdraws her weapon and with an icy stare retreats backwards to the raucous laughter of the crowd.

The attention shifts to the dice game as Ashcon, the stranger with the yellow eyes, is on a lucky streak. The crowd surrounding the game is growing. Sapphyre had noticed the stranger and his black-clad friend upon their entrance hours earlier right before the evening meal, after which they secured a room on the second floor.

Skenn, Ashcon's companion, is one of the largest men Sapphyre has ever seen. He stands almost seven feet tall and has broad shoulders and huge hands. Garbed in black, billowing robes, he has no problem slipping into the shadows and remaining nondescript despite his size. Ashcon is thin with dark skin, no facial hair, and his slanted yellow eyes angle downward toward a sharp, pointed nose. Although he is not extremely good-looking, Sapphyre has to admit he is somewhat handsome and conducts himself with an aura of self-confidence. While his companion in black has no obvious weapons, the gambler has two swords hanging from his belt and two dagger hilts protruding from his boots.

The dark-clad giant has situated himself in the corner by the fireplace and is enjoying a mug of ale while fixing his attention on the dice game and his friend on a lucky streak. Sapphyre is in the process of delivering some mead to a member of the dice game when she notices the large stack of kendra in front of the somewhat handsome stranger, who seemed to always be in control of the dice. She pauses to watch a few rolls and sees that each time he throws a winning combination, what looks like a small tattoo of a cat's eye on his neck glows yellow before each toss. As she looks around the dice game, she senses that no one else sees this phenomenon and wonders why. After realizing she's been staring and has been derelict in her duties, she retreats back to the bar to continue with her service.

As the evening turns into early morning and the games come to a close, the tavern slowly empties and the patrons who are staying the night retire to their respective rooms. This is true of the lucky dice player and his companion. They head to the second floor to count their winnings and get a night's respite from their travels.

As the door closes behind them, Ashcon turns toward it, holds up his hands and gestures to the door. An octagon tattoo on the wrist of his left hand glows blue as his spell of warding is put in place. Activating this spell via his Rune of Warding enables the two companions to engage in conversation without the fear of being overheard. The Rune of Warding is one of the dozens of designs all over his body, which engage a certain power when activated. The fact that there are few people alive who can actually see these runes leads to the current conversation.

Skken, knowing the ward is in place, turns to Ashcon with concern in his eyes and is about to speak, when Ashcon holds up his hand and says, "The serving girl saw something. If we are to assume she saw my Luck Rune, then we have much to discuss."

Skken replies quickly, "There is no doubt as to what she saw. While you were busy taking these people's kendra, I was carefully observing her demeanor in reaction to the dice game. At first, she outright stared at your neck and, once she realized that no one else could see it, she became nervous. If she is your seeker, Ashcon, the enormity of that possibility cannot be ignored."

Ashcon sighs audibly and while disarming himself, turns to Skken. "We cannot assume anything, Skken. I admit it is unnerving to know she can see the runes, but let us not jump to conclusions."

"So, when do we apprehend her?"

"Calm down, Skken. I don't think we will need to apprehend anyone. We need a few questions answered. That is all. Let us retire as tomorrow looks to be quite an interesting day."

Skken reluctantly agrees and prepares to drift off to a restless sleep.

Sapphyre finally finishes her cleanup duties and heads to her quarters for the evening. After putting her dagger under her pillow and washing up, she reclines and ponders what she has seen this night. She considers sneaking up to the second floor and eavesdropping on the two strangers, but thinks better of it. All of her instincts tell her that she must learn more of the yellow-eyed man with the glowing tattoo, but has to decide on the best course of action. She has always followed her instincts and tonight will be no exception. As she lies down on her bed and drifts off to sleep, she begins to think about fate and how it brought her here.

Chapter 2

S APPHYRE'S earliest memories go back to when she was five winters old and living on the streets, doing what she could to fill her belly and keep safe. Orphans and homeless children are a common sight in the city of Thorenn, the capital city of the Kingdom of Martell, located in far-east Arstevia. It is the largest city on the continent and home to the Imperial Palace, as well as the main port on the eastern seaboard. The city is broken down into districts, with the biggest being the Emerald Center, where most of the trade takes place. This is where you can purchase various foodstuffs, weapons, clothing, gems, and almost anything worth a kendra. It is bustling during the day, but once the sun goes down and the shops close up for the evening, it's a ghost town. Dock Bay is where the sailors congregate and is crowded with inns of ominous repute and whorehouses for seafaring travelers. Granite Loop is home to the laborers, with family restaurants scattered throughout. Skid Way is the dark side of the city, where thieves congregate and the authorities turn a blind eye to all happenings. The gambling houses provide entertainment for the masses and dozens of taverns line the streets. The Guild of Slight controls Skid Way. Almost all illegal activities go through that organization. There are a few other notable gangs in the area, and there are always new groups challenging the rule of the Guild of Slight, only to find themselves destroyed when they gain too much power. The Royal Compound is where the truly rich reside, as well as being home to the Imperial Palace and the barracks for the large Imperial Army. The Royal Compound is fenced in and patrolled by the Imperial Guard to keep out the undesirables.

Sapphyre surely fits into the category of "undesirable" and has only seen the Imperial Compound from afar. It is while she is looking at the magnificent castle from a rooftop in the deserted Emerald Center just past midnight that she is approached by the first person to have a real impact in her life.

"It is beautiful, isn't it?" asks the stranger, who startles Sapphyre to a point where she almost falls off the roof. "Please calm down as I mean you no harm." The stranger appears to be a young teenager. He takes a piece of berry cake out of his pocket and hands it to Sapphyre as a gesture of friendship. She hesitates to take it from him. With a light smile, the young man breaks it in two, starts eating his half, and hands the other to Sapphyre.

She grabs it with her small hands and starts devouring the delicious treat. She nods a thank you. As she looks at the young man, she sees in him a sense of strength and a calmness that puts her at ease. He is about five feet ten inches tall, tall for his apparent age, which Sapphyre guesses to be at about twelve winters. He has long black hair, large oval brown eyes, and a small scar beneath his left eye. His garb is similar to most of the young people who wander the streets of Thorenn; however, his clothes are absent the filth that covers most of the downtrodden homeless of the capital city. She doesn't spy any weapons on him and that is not alarming, as she has no weapons of her own. As he finishes his half of the tasty morsel, he extends his hand and introduces himself. "My name is Katrivus, Kat for short, and it is a pleasure to make your acquaintance."

"Sapphyre," she replies softly and accepts his hand, "and thank you for the cake."

"I've seen you around here before. You need to be more careful when you're stealing bread in the middle of the afternoon. You don't want to be thrown in the jailhouse, believe me. I've had to break out of there once and they are not kind to pretty girls."

Sapphyre, still very much hesitant to engage in conversation, just nods.

"So you steal during the day, engage in frivolous dreaming from rooftops at night, and steal sleep in garbage heaps and abandoned lodgings when you can. That doesn't seem like the proper way to spend one's time," whispers Kat.

"I do what I have to do to survive."

"I also do what I must to survive, Sapphyre," says Katrivus as he stands up and kicks a pebble off the roof. "I lived for a long time just the way you do until I realized that if I kept going it alone I would die on the streets. So I formed a group, and now we have a place to stay. We have food to eat and have over fifty kendra saved." He pauses for a moment and continues. "Do you know of the Black Pearl in the Row?"

Sapphyre nods yes.

"My people have a place in the basement there," continues Katrivus. "There are fourteen of us at the moment. The proprietor lets us stay there in exchange for the occasional favor. It's not much but it's warm and dry. Please accept this formal invitation to join the Pugs. If you decide not to come, please forget we ever met and good luck to you."

Sapphyre stands up and looks at Katrivus who is taking short steps backwards to the roof's edge. "Why are you doing this? Why do you want to help me?"

"Like I mentioned, I've seen you around. And I need more people in the Pugs," Katrivus replies smiling. With that, he jumps off the rooftop and disappears into the dark of the night, leaving Sapphyre on the roof pondering her thoughts. As the night turns into early morning, Sapphyre shuffles down the ladder on the side of her favorite escape and searches for a place to sleep for a few hours.

The following day is cold and wet and Sapphyre finds herself walking the streets of the Emerald Center as the various shops are opening for business. She notices one shop owner being especially careless as he unloads goods from his wagon and she slides into a corner to observe. The man is taking his time going from the wagon to the inside of his shop and back, leaving plenty of opportunity for a thief to snag a bag while his attention is elsewhere. The hour is early, with not too many people out and about. Sapphyre decides to make a move. The man grabs a wool bundle from the back of his wagon and retreats into his shop, and at that moment Sapphyre slides in silence to the opposite side of the wagon and waits patiently for the man to head back outside. She sees the man grab another sack and as he is turning to enter the building, Sapphyre reaches up to steal a bundle. As she touches the top of the sack, a hand grabs her hair from behind and throws her to the ground with such force that her breath is knocked out of her. The man then puts a foot upon her chest and yells, "Hey, Floren, I nabbed myself a little whore thief!"

Sapphyre tries to struggle, but it is of no use as the large man has her small frame pinned down to the wet pavement. Floren then comes out of the shop and reaches down with one hand, grabbing Sapphyre by the hair, and slapping her across the face with enough force to draw blood. "You think you can steal from me, you little brat? I don't know if I'm going to hand you over to the authorities or if I'm just gonna sell you m'self!" He brings Sapphyre to her feet, and as his face comes inches away from hers and she can smell the mead on his breath, he whispers, "You're a pesky little thing, aren't you? She'll fetch a nice price with this long brown hair and them dark brown eyes, won't she, Stormm?"

"She will," he responds smiling. As the two men engage in a small bit of laughter, a dagger flies through the air and lands in Stormm's throat, forcing him to release Sapphyre as he clutches the bloody wound with both his hands. As soon as the man drops to his knees, four boys emerge from the shadows with clubs at the ready and surround the shop owner. Katrivus removes the dagger from the dying man's throat and pushes him onto his back. The air emerges from the gory wound with a gurgling noise while his mouth gasps ineffectually for breath. Red bubbles froth around his throat and trickle from his lips. Slowly he begins to suffocate on his own blood.

Floren is in shock and starts to inch away when he is struck in the back of his knees from behind by one of the club-wielding boys. He falls down to the ground, bent over in pain. Katrivus whips his head up by his hair and puts his dagger only inches from his eye. "If you'd like to live, you will not only keep your mouth shut but you'll gladly hand over to us the remains of what you have on this wagon." He then cuts the man from his eye to his mouth, deep enough to leave a scar. "Let this scar serve as a reminder of our little meeting today. Bother this girl again and I will cut out your tongue. Do you understand?"

Floren nods in understanding and Katrivus kicks him in the back as the four other boys take the contents from the wagon. Grasping the shaken Sapphyre by the arm, Katrivus leads her away.

That night, as Sapphyre is eating in the basement of the Black Pearl Tavern, discussing the terms of her membership in the Pugs, she feels a sense of family for the first time in her short life. After eating her fill and bathing for the first time in many weeks, she falls asleep on her bed of straw with tears rolling down her cheeks.

Over the next three winters with Katrivus and the Pugs, Sapphyre learns various ways to earn a profit and is trained to use a dagger and pick a man's pocket without him feeling a thing. Kat's skills are advanced beyond his fifteen winters. He teaches everything he knows to the aspiring thief. She is a quick study and after only a few winters in the service of the Pugs has gained herself the respect of the small brotherhood.

At night, when they are not out stealing, Katrivus and Sapphyre engage in conversation about all aspects of life. Kat does most of the talking. Sapphyre is quite happy to listen to the young man pontificate with passion about the empire he plans to build. He talks about his admiration of the Guild of Slight and how they have used their power to control most of the gambling in the city and even have politicians in their back pocket. He talks of philosophers and entrepreneurs, of trade and commerce, and it all fascinates Sapphyre. When she inquires as to how he knows so much, to her amazement he responds it's from reading books on history. This is something that is foreign to Sapphyre, as she has never known anyone who was able to read or write.

That is when her education truly begins. Katrivus spends hours at a time teaching Sapphyre. He steals books just so he can read them to her and have her read them back to him. Sapphyre buries herself in her studies and if she was a quick learner with a dagger, she is even better with the written word.

Katrivus warns her, "The less people know about you, the better, so there is no need to advertise your ability to read and write. The knowledge you can gain from appearing ignorant is beyond measure."

As the Pugs gain in power and size, they expand their operations beyond petty theft. The kendra they acquire over the winters enables them to purchase a small hovel in Dock Bay, believing if they situate themselves by the pier and away from Skid Way, they will keep from being discovered by the Guild of Slight. Some of the older members of the Pugs even get legitimate jobs on the docks for the purpose of finding out information. One of these acquired tidbits lead to another monumental point in young Sapphyre's life.

The rumor was that a barge would be arriving from the far northern continent with goods of unimaginable value. Assailing the ship would be out of the question, as it would be guarded at all times. Katrivus decided that they should obtain a copy of the shipping manifest and see where the goods were being distributed.

After obtaining the inventory list, they peruse it and come up with a plan of action. Katrivus, looking over the list, quietly summarizes, "Most of the goods are being sent to the Imperial Palace, and that will be out of the question. A handful will be immediately put to sea again and we can't risk our contacts on the docks to attempt those. There are goods being distributed to the wealthy citizens of our own capital city." With a grin on his face he decides, "That is where we shall make our move."

The largest quantities of goods were being bought by Steele Monthall, a newly rich member of the populace with a taste for young boys. His pomposity and his extravagance, along with his newly acquired wealth, have left him less than popular with the aristocracy of Thorenn. His peculiar sexual preferences also make him an easy choice for the Pugs, as the authorities, while they won't ignore the theft completely, will be less than diligent in their duties to assist him.

The ship was due in to dock at daybreak, and the goods were to be distributed immediately for security purposes. As fate would have it, there was a royal gala marking the anniversary of the birth of the prince regent at the Imperial Palace that evening, and all the nobility was expected to attend. Steele Monthall would never give up the opportunity to hobnob with royalty, so there was no question that he would be gone from his estate that evening.

Katrivus, Sapphyre, and two other experienced members of the Pugs would lead the operation. Steele Monthall's estate was located inside the Imperial Compound in the western section, only two blocks from the west gate. They would wait until the celebration was in full bloom, and then two members of the party would enter through the back of the estate and pick the lock of the door leading into the library. Their surveillance showed that the servants' quarters were off the library, to the left of the kitchen on the main floor. Most of the servants would be tending to their charges at the Imperial Palace, so the burglars expected only three or four to remain on the grounds.

As Sapphyre and Katrivus stand lookout on the street in front of the mansion, the two boys pick the lock and are in the house within seconds. Forty-five seconds go by and the back door is opened slightly, the sign that it is safe to enter. Sapphyre and Katrivus silently enter the house and one of the boys signals to them that the servants are bound and gagged and will be no threat. Sapphyre and Kat go upstairs in search of the booty while the other two remain downstairs to keep watch.

Two shipping boxes are untouched on the floor of the upstairs study, and Katrivus takes out his dagger to open them. Inside are smaller boxes, and the two thieves are confident that they contain goods and jewels of various size and value. Since they couldn't very well walk away with a horde of boxes, they decided ahead of time they would transport the treasure in the pouches concealed on their person.

As they pull the small containers out of the larger one, Sapphyre notices something that stops her in her steps. She reaches out to Katrivus and whispers, "Do you see a glow emanating from any of these boxes?"

He replies, "No" and continues emptying the shipping containers.

Sapphyre grabs his arm, "We can't take all of them."

"What are you talking about, Sapphyre?"

"Some are evil. I can't explain it, but I see an aura coming from some of the boxes. The one in your left hand glows brown and has a distinct, awful smell."

Katrivus looks at her warily, "Sapphyre, you're just..."

But Sapphyre cuts him off. "Kat, listen to me!" she whispers. "You must trust me." She holds a small box in her left hand. "This box has a light blue aura and has a magic to it, but a good magic. Most of the boxes have no aura at all. Please, Kat, leave behind the boxes I ask you to."

He gives her a long, considering look, but at last replies, "If you insist, Sapphire, I will," says Katrivus.

The two thieves continue opening the boxes and transferring the contents into their pouches, less the few Sapphyre orders them to put aside. As Sapphyre reaches the bottom of the crate, she finds a box that is larger than the rest. It has a bright green aura to it, brighter than the others. She opens it and gasps. Katrivus turns to see what brought about the reaction, and he too is stunned as to the beauty of what lies within. Sapphyre withdraws a dagger with a shiny blue twelve-inch blade, sharper than anything she has seen before. The hilt is embedded with diamonds, emeralds, and rubies.

"Katrivus, look," she exclaims, holding the dagger for her friend to see. "It's the most beautiful dagger I have ever seen."

He looks at the small weapon before responding. "Take it for yourself. We have enough here to make everyone happy."

Smiling, Sapphyre grabs the scabbard from the bottom of the box. The two thieves then casually walk downstairs, join the other two Pugs, and escape into the night.

After stowing the goods from the haul, Sapphyre asks Katrivus to take a walk with her. She leads him up to the rooftop where they met the first time. "Thank you for allowing me to keep the dagger, Kat."

"No problem. It seems drawn to you. How long have you known about your gift of detecting magic?" he inquires.

"Tonight is the first time it's ever happened. I guess we don't travel in circles where magic is in abundance," she says.

"True. Let's keep it between us. We can use this ability of yours to our advantage." The two then sit in silence admiring the bright lights coming from the palace where the gala is still in full swing.

The next five winters are abundant ones for the Pugs. The riches gained from the Monthall heist enabled them to grow their operation and even led to the purchase of a ship. They were starting to get noticed by the Guild of Slight, but did their best not to infringe on their operation. Katrivus knew it was just a matter of time before action would have to be taken, but for the time being, the Pugs enjoyed the riches of their spoils.

The coming summer celebration of StarSight excited the populace of Thorenn, as they expected thousands of visitors from all over the kingdom. Everyone would profit from the influx of strangers, from the desirable inns inside the Imperial Compound, to the shady taverns down at the docks. The Guild of Slight even imported working girls from all over the region to fill the whorehouses with ladies for every taste. The celebration of StarSight took place once every nine winters, and the influx of magic users to the kingdom made it a monumental event in the lives of the common folk. There were wizards, witches, shamans, sorcerers, sorceresses, priests, shamans, mages, and more. All types of magic users were represented, except for the warlocks, of course.

Sapphyre, just turning fourteen winters old, has never experienced the celebration and is absolutely in awe of what she sees. The magic users keep her attention, their auras glowing with all the colors of the rainbow. She even notices the imposters who have no glow as they try to trick the populace with bogus readings and fake trinkets. There are fortune tellers, mages selling robes of power, and necklaces foreign stones she has never before beheld, emanating magic. As Sapphyre wanders about the grounds, she happens upon an old woman sitting in a carriage decorated with bright feathers of all colors. The beauty of it transfixes Sapphyre. When the old woman signals to her, she steps up.

Once inside the carriage she realizes that the old lady is blind, however she is staring directly into Sapphyre's eyes. Looking into the unseeing gaze, Sapphyre feels a sense of warmth and trust she has never before withheld. Tears start streaming down her face for reasons unknown to her, but the sense of déjà vu is so strong that Sapphyre asks without thinking, "Are you my mother?"

The woman smiles and replies softly, "No, my child. I did know your mother and your father. Please give me your hands."

Sapphyre then places both her hands into those of the old woman and instinctively closes her eyes. As she does so, a vision appears to Sapphyre. It is a vision of her as an infant, submerged in a pool of brilliant blue, the old woman glancing down at her lovingly. Suddenly the vision changes and she is staring at a middle-aged couple, the man standing approximately six feet in height with no distinguishing characteristics except for his eyes. The man's eyes reveal an intelligence that goes beyond the comprehension of mere mortals. The woman is the most beautiful Sapphyre has ever seen. She stands a demure five feet tall with a tiny frame and has the most striking bright blue eyes the girl has ever beheld. The most distinguishing characteristic of this woman is her hair, which is a rich blond with a blue streak extending from above her right eye down through the entire length. Sapphyre melts at the sight of these two and understands immediately they are her parents. Instead of feeling anger or resentment toward the couple she has never met, she feels an outpouring of love and affection that causes her to sob uncontrollably. Suddenly, the woman removes her hands and the vision ceases.

Sapphyre looks at the blind woman who has tears streaming down her own face and a radiant smile of someone half her age. Sapphyre feels tears running down her cheeks as well and senses a change within her. The woman holds up her hands. Sapphyre sees a reflection in the air in front of her and gasps. Her hair is no longer dark but blond with streaks of light azure, and her eyes have changed from brown to sparkling blue.

She is about to speak when the old woman cuts her off. "There is much I cannot tell you. Those were your parents and they loved you dearly. You were placed in my care due to circumstances that you will one day become privy to." Sapphyre again attempts to interrupt but the old woman holds up her hand to stop her and continues. "I knew the day would come when you would first become aware of your magical ability. That indicated it is time to start the fulfillment of your destiny, child."

She then reaches down and picks up a bowl containing a sky-blue liquid and hands it to Sapphyre. She puts three feathers of different colors into the bowl. The floating feathers form the shape of an arrow with a glowing blue tip. Sapphyre stares at it, wide-eyed. "You must always trust the feathers. They will point you toward your destiny," says the woman as she hands the bowl to Sapphyre.

Sapphyre looks down into the bowl and sees that the feathers are pointing west, and she realizes she must leave Thorenn and head in that direction. She looks to the old woman for acknowledgement and receives a nod in response. She is about to put the bowl down in the carriage but the old woman gestures for her to take it. The old woman then touches Sapphyre on the cheek and she knows it is time for her to exit the carriage. Sapphyre nods and descends the short steps to the gravel below. She turns to bid farewell to the woman, but when she spins around, the woman and the carriage are gone.

Taking a deep breath, Sapphyre walks slowly to a large flat rock leaning upon a leafless tree on the outskirts of the main square and sits down. She takes her left hand and reaches over her right shoulder and grabs her now blonde hair and turns toward it in wonder. Her eyes are drawn towards the blue streak and she combs her hair through her fingers. She closes her eyes and takes a deep breath and brings up the image of her parents in her mind. Sapphyre stands up confidently and opens her sparkling blue eyes energized with the prospect of learning her true identity.

With an ethereal calmness that even surprises Sapphyre, she heads back home and searches for Katrivus but can't find him anywhere. One of the younger Pugs tells her that Kat left on his ship on business and would be gone for quite some time. Sapphyre wishes she could bid him a farewell, but decides she must leave at once. She leaves a long note for Kat, packs her belongings, binds the dagger to her waist, puts the bowl and feathers in her pack, takes a little under half of the kendra she and Kat have hidden away and leaves the only place she has ever known, heading west toward her destiny.

Chapter 3

THE smell of baking biscuits and frying bacon stirs both Skken and Ashcon awake. The sun is just making its way over the horizon as the companions finish dressing for the coming day. "So what's the plan Ashcon?" Skken impatiently inquires.

Ashcon sits on the edge of the cot and sighs, "Let's set a simple trap for her." He stands up and paces in short steps with a devious look on his face. "We will pose to leave the inn for a bit in search of a tradesman and have her tend to our room."

Skken smiles slightly with his head down as he polishes Grizzclaw, his prized saber, which has been blessed by the Star Gods. "So we come back, catch her in the room, grab her and go?"

"No, I think we'll question her here. And be nice," Ashcon chides. "Don't scare her too much."

Then he looks around the room and walks toward the small bedside table. Ashcon reaches down, withdraws the smaller of the two daggers from his left boot and places it on the table beside his cot. He puts his hand upon the dagger and closes his eyes. A rune in the shape of a horn on his left calf shines green and then fades, as Ashcon withdraws his hand. "We'll know when she's in the room. Come, let's eat," states Ashcon as he walks briskly to the door.

They are sitting at a table for two when Sapphyre brings water and bows slightly. "Girl," inquires Ashcon. "Is there a leatherworker in this town by chance? My mate lost his saddle and we're hoping to replace it as soon as possible."

Sapphyre nods yes in response. "His shop is on the other side of town by the well."

"Thank you," says Ashcon, and waves his hand, shooing her away. "Bring us hot food."

"A saddle?" whispers Skken, grinning slightly.

"Makes sense. She doesn't need to know you ride bareback."

Sapphyre returns to the table with rashers of bacon and steaming hot biscuits with gobs of butter. She puts the plate between the two men and Ashcon removes a two-kendra coin from his purse, holds it between his fingers, and hands it to her. "We are staying another night. When we are gone, go to our quarters. There are leggings that need cleaning and I want them done by this evening." Sapphyre nods, takes the coin from the fingers of Ashcon and hurries away.

Sapphyre can't believe her luck and she smiles as she patiently waits for them to leave the inn so she can go their room and take a look around. She watches as they exit and approach the stables. She waits until she sees the men retrieve their horses and start toward the other side of town before she runs up the stairs to their room.

She puts the key in the lock, turns it until she hears the familiar click, and opens the door with a sense of foreboding. She giggles to herself quietly, realizing she has nothing to be nervous about, as she was invited after all. She eyes some dirty leggings on the floor as she closes the door behind her. Glancing around the room she spots a wide-brimmed black hat upon the mantle, a few belts on the floor, empty glasses by the bed and a dagger on the bedside table. The dagger has a slight green hue to it and Sapphyre looks at it wide-eyed, inquisitively reaching to grab it. As she twirls it in her hand, on the street below, Ashcon glances Skken as he turns his horse around and says, "She's in the room."

Sapphyre slips the dagger out of the scabbard and sits down on the edge of the bed. The weapon itself is nothing special, with a clean, sharp blade, yet it definitely has some magic quality to it. Sapphyre is looking down at the blade, wishing she had the ability to tell what type of spell enchants it, when the door suddenly opens and Skken and Ashcon enter quickly and close the door quietly behind them. Sapphyre jumps up, startled. Ashcon smiles a toothy smile, holds up his hands to his shoulders, and says, "Sorry to surprise you. Please." He gestures with his hands to the chair beside the bed. "Sit down."

Sapphyre sits down as Skken moves toward her. He holds his huge right hand out and eyes the dagger still in her grasp. She hands the dagger to Skken without a word and places her hands on her lap with her head down toward her chest.

Ashcon takes the seat opposite her and Skken retreats to the other side of the room where he lights the two small torches affixed to the wall. "What is your name?" inquires Ashcon.

"I didn't do anything wrong!" replies Sapphyre defensively. "You told me to come here. I'm sorry I touched the dagger. Please don't tell Ornik." Tears start to form in her eyes.

Ashcon holds up his hand and says, "I'm not telling anyone anything, and you're right, you did nothing wrong." Sapphyre relaxes a little in her chair and Ashcon continues. "I just have a few questions I need to ask you. Will that be ok?"

Sapphyre nods slowly.

"What is your name?" inquires Ashcon once again.

"What's yours?" she replies quickly.

"Ashcon," he says. "That is Skken." He points in his direction.

"Sapphyre," she responds.

"Where are you from, Sapphyre?" asks Ashcon.

"Here and there. I've been here for over two winters, so now I say I'm from here."

Ashcon, not known to be a patient man when he is seeking information, activates a rune above his left eyebrow that glows bright orange in the shape of a single flame. While it's glowing, the two torches that Skken lit earlier burn brighter and illuminate the entire room. Ashcon deactivates the rune and the light returns to its normal state. His attention is focused on Sapphyre's eyes. She is staring in awe at the area of his Sun Rune, which affirms their suspicions of her ability to see the markings. Fazed by this, Ashcon rises from his chair and turns to face Skken. Skken nods and Ashcon walks toward the door, activates his rune of warding, and then returns to sit down facing Sapphyre.

"Please tell me exactly what you saw. Both now and downstairs last night." He looks at her and continues. "It's very important. Please, don't be afraid."

Sapphyre raises her head and glances across the table. "I saw a tattoo of a flame above your left eye. And last night I saw a tattoo of an eye on your neck when you threw winning rolls," she replies honestly.

"Thank you for being so forthright." He stands up, pushes his chair in and continues. "They are called runes, not tattoos. Skken can see them, and occasionally I run into another who has the ability. But never one so young and not in quite a long time." Skken walks toward Ashcon holding up his hands, apparently thinking that Ashcon is giving up too much information. Ashcon nods and gestures for Skken to remain where he is.

"Have you ever met any magic users before?" asks Ashcon.

"The inn is right off the main road. Yes, I've seen magic users before."

"Do you notice anything about them like you do about me?"

Sapphyre pauses. Her eyes creased, she ponders the question. "No," she replies softly, not wanting to reveal her ability to detect auras. Then she attempts to distract them with a bold question. "Where are you from?" Sapphyre asks.

Ashcon looks at her. Amused, he smiles and replies, "I come from a town a few hundred leagues to the northwest of here." He glances at Skken and continues, "Sapphyre, we need to find out why you can see my runes."

Sapphyre looks up and back and forth between the two men. Ashcon stands up and turns to Sapphyre. "Skken and I need to talk privately." He holds up both of his hands, palms out toward Sapphyre, and moves them in a circular clockwise motion. Small orbs glow a faint blue on each palm. As he puts his hands back down to his sides and turns toward Skken, Sapphyre realizes she can no longer hear the men, though they are less than four feet away. Sapphyre utters her name out loud and, relieved to hear her own voice, sits back and watches the conversation she can't hear.

Skken turns to Ashcon. "Is she your seeker?"

Ashcon moves his head sideways. "I don't know but we obviously need to find out. We can't take her to the temple without a summons."

Skken replies, "Maybe this is an exception. To confirm your seeker."

Ashcon interrupts. "There is never enough reason to attempt to enter the temple without a summons."

Skken says, "So, then what?

"We need to find Sorenthor," Ashcon replies, alluding to the infamous Lost Seeker.

Skken sighs in response and replies, "Fine. Where do we start?"

"We know he goes to Thorenn for supplies. Someone there would know how to contact him or how to locate him. He's the only one who would be able to confirm or deny," says Ashcon.

Skken gestures toward Sapphyre. "What if she won't go? Do we just take her?"

"Yes," Ashcon immediately replies. "Hopefully that won't be necessary."

Ashcon turns back toward Sapphyre, holds his palms out, and moves them counterclockwise. Two red orbs glow briefly. Ashcon says, "Sorry about that, Sapphyre, but it was necessary. You are a very unique individual and in order to figure out just how special you are, we are hoping you will join us on a journey."

Sapphyre looks up warily. "To where?" she inquires.

"We will be heading east. We need to go see a man named Sorenthor. He'll be able to tell us why you're able to see my runes," replies Ashcon.

"Why is it so important to know?" Sapphyre inquires.

"There are very few people alive who can see what you can, Sapphyre," says Ashcon with a subtle tenderness to his voice. Ashcon does not want to confuse the young girl so feels no reason to bring up seekers. He places his hand in hers and asks quietly, "Will you come with us?"

Sapphyre, still confused by all that has transpired, replies, "First I would like to know what you are."

Ashcon looks at Skken, who is shaking his head from left to right, and then he turns toward Sapphyre. Releasing her hand, he rises and asks, "Have you ever heard of a runestar?"

"No."

"Most beings your age haven't," Ashcon says as he paces with slow steps. "I have runes all over my body that give me certain abilities. We don't have the time to really delve into all that is a runestar at present, but rest assured, I mean you no harm." He stops in front of Sapphyre and gazes into her blue eyes. "My powers were bestowed upon me by the Star Gods themselves and I am sworn to protect the light and the stars. You must consider all you have learned and make a decision, Sapphyre. I pray you will come with us, and on my honor, Skken and I swear to protect you."

Sapphyre has been able to see a light green aura surrounding Ashcon ever since she touched the dagger earlier, but feels no need to reveal that yet. She stands, looks at Ashcon, and states, "I know you not, and you may be without honor, which would negate your oath." She looks down at her feet and back at Ashcon who does not reply. "I must ponder this. When do you leave?"

"We depart in two days' time."

"Very well. You will have my answer before you gp."

Sapphyre leaves their room and heads to her small quarters. She retrieves the bowl with the liquid and the three feathers. Ever since she arrived at the tavern almost two winters ago, the bowl has revealed the same thing on a daily basis.

The feathers all join together in the center of the bowl. Their tips touch together and glow a bright blue. She recalls the surprise she felt when she saw the feathers take that shape for the first time, knowing she had arrived at a predestined location after spending so much time on the road.

This is the only time since then that she is truly wondering what the bowl will reveal. As she sets the bowl on her small table and drops the feathers in, she closes her eyes and wonders what fate has in store for her. As the feathers turn in the bowl and start to form an arrow facing east, she thinks of the old woman in the carriage instructing her to always trust the feathers. Sapphyre opens her eyes and smiles as the tips begin to glow blue.

Chapter 4

NORTH of the Myth Mountains, hundreds of leagues from the Dragon's Flagon, Drak'thonn is awakened from his slumber by a thought from the Zagador. He hesitantly pushes himself off of his Bed of Perpetual Ice and places his two feet on the floor. At once the pain sets in, a pain he has come to treasure as a reminder of his lifelong quest. Once he is no longer touching his magical bed, his skin returns to smoldering ash.

It has been over seven hundred winters since the fateful day that changed his life forever and his body became living fire. He always had dark skin, but now it is black as night and resembles burning charcoal. Drak'thonn is huge, standing almost seven feet tall with a body of solid muscle. His face has the remnants of what was once an eye but is only scar tissue now, leaving him with one seeing eye. His nose is melted down to just the two nostrils above a hideously deformed mouth. He is an expert with every known weapon, and the Zagador have granted him the power to control fire. As the anointed leader of the Dark Horde, his power over his followers who worship the Zagador is absolute.

He is not one to have servants, although there are thousands who would cherish that honor. Drak'thonn hears the orc sentries outside of his quarters as he slides on his body armor and attaches his mithril axes to his belt. He starts walking, leaving a trail of fire footprints on the ground, and the doors open on his approach as the astute guards part them for their leader. It will take most of the day for Drak'thonn to make it to the Temple of the Dark Gods from the Skeed Towers where he resides. He takes his large mount from the stable and makes his way to answer the summons of the Dark Gods, knowing that Zidi will be awaiting him upon his arrival.

Zidi is one of the high council members of the Dark Horde and is second in power to Drak'thonn. He is a warlock of unimaginable power and maintains his residence in the Temple of the Dark Gods. He is invaluable to Drak'thonn as he is the only one who can summon the portal to reach the Zagador.

Zidi is bald with charcoal skin, hollow eyes, and thin lips. He is so skinny he resembles a bag of bones. He is always garbed in a black robe with his staff and nothing else. The staff is made of connected human bones, and the handle is a human skull with a pearl dagger embedded in it. The pearl dagger is enchanted by the Zagador and contains the power to call the portal. As the religious leader of the order, he inherited the DarkFlame Staff upon his ascension seventy-seven winters ago. His time is running out and the staff will pass on to the next leader upon his demise.

Drak'thonn enters the Temple of the Dark Gods and approaches Zidi, who is already beginning incantations with his staff at the ready. He greets Drak'thonn and tells him he is not privy to the information the Zagador will entrust to him, but that they are anxious to meet right away. Drak'thonn nods to Zidi, removes his weapons, and positions himself on his knees in front of the Great Seal below the DarkFlame Staff. As Zidi continues the spell, the seal starts to glow and amber and black fire shoots out and covers

Drak'thonn, who disappears into the realm of the Zagador for only the third time in his life.

He is greeted by one of the Zagador, as the Dark Gods do not have individual names. The Zagador decided on the appearance of a female being, one that is unfamiliar to Drak'thonn. Drak'thonn assumes a kneeling position in front of the Zagador, as she begins to speak. "The time has come to fulfill your destiny, chosen one," the Zagador says. "Your brother and his guardian have been joined by a third and the prophecies are now in play. The time has come to prepare for the invasion of the kingdom and the destruction of both your brother and his newfound charge."

"As you wish," replies Drak'thonn, relishing the opportunity to exact revenge on Ashcon and the Star Gods.

"The form in which you see me now is that of a dreggan. They reside on the northern continent and will join you and aid you in your quest. They are powerful warriors and number in the thousands. The females of their race lead them, and you will take the leader as your bride upon their arrival in two moonsigns. After you have destroyed the kingdom and killed Ashcon and his companions, the two of you shall reign forever as king and queen of the eternal night that will come to pass after you succeed in your mission."

"As you wish."

"Over the next few moonsigns you will be joined by other allies to expand your ranks. Each of these allies will prove most valuable to you and have powers to aide you. They will all acknowledge your sovereignty over them without question. You are to make the leader of each of these factions a member of your high council."

"As you wish."

"We wish you luck in your quest, chosen one. We expect you to be ready to invade the kingdom and begin the search for your brother within six moonsigns," says the Zagador. The Dark God then disappears and Drak'thonn is transported back to the temple.

He stands up and turns to Zidi, and with a new-found fire in his eyes, says with purpose, "Prepare a high council meeting for the end of this moonsign. We have much to discuss." As he prepares to exit the temple, he looks into Zidi's hollow eyes and states, "The time of destiny is upon us. Vengeance will be mine."

Chapter 5

WHILE Selentha is mounting one more human slave – a handsome and muscle-bound specimen who has inexplicably given her enormous pleasure – a calling never before heard disturbs her. The voice in her head gives her alarm, but also fills her with a feeling of power and security. She dismounts the slave and decapitates the man with one swipe of her clawed hand. She flings the body with little effort out the window onto the courtyard below.

She drops to one knee without realizing why, and a vision comes to her. She knows without a doubt that the vision is from the Zagador, the Dark Gods that the dreggans have prayed to for eons. The vision shows her leading her people south to the lower continent to seek out someone named Drak'thonn, the leader of the Dark Horde. She must follow Drak'thonn in his quest to destroy his brother and his companions. She must also lead her army with Drak'thonn and invade the Kingdom of Martell and then, upon her victory, plummet the world into eternal night. In exchange for the services of her people, she will marry Drak'thonn and become queen over the entire world.

The dreggans are creatures built for warfare and domination. Selentha is the queen and leader of the dreggans, humanoid creatures with powerful legs and thighs three times the width of the average human. They stand on average seven feet tall and have hands with retractable claws. Their faces are strangely passive and don't match the body, but they do give off a sense of intelligence. The dreggans are brute-force fighters who wield maces to complement their retractable claws. Their skin is akin to mail armor and their legs give them interesting battle tactics and the ability to travel great distances.

The dreggans have always had female leaders, and Selentha is well respected amongst her people. She will always lead her army into battle and will always be protected by the eleven members of her War Stack regardless of the situation. She rules alone with an iron fist. Selentha has secured her position through war and one-on-one battle. She has had enough victories that she cannot be challenged and will rule until death. Upon her death bed, she will name a successor who must prove herself worthy of leading the dreggans.

The female dreggans rule the society and the army. They are members of her War Stack. The male dreggans are smaller in stature and play a lesser role in society. The smallest males, below five feet, become eunuchs and are in charge of the healing arts. A crippled female dreggan of enormous respect leads them. The dreggans are in control of the majority of the small northern continent, long ago having defeated the humans who inhabited the land, making them slaves who are used for the dreggans' enjoyment and to manufacture weapons of war.

After absorbing the enormity of the message from the Zagador, Selentha calls the War Stack to order. The meeting usually takes place in the council room, but Selentha, feeling that this particular meeting is of the utmost importance, calls for it to take place in the Chamber of the Dark Gods.

Human slaves are sent to gather the members of the War Stack and summon them to the chamber. As the members prepare for the meeting, Selentha has some of the male cooks prepare roasted quail and sweet wine. Selentha decides to wear the garb of the Liaison of the Dark Gods as opposed to her usual battle armor to illustrate the importance of this gathering.

As the torches are lit in the circular chamber, the members of the War Stack enter and take their assigned seats. Unlike most societies, there is no second in command to Selentha. Each member of the War Stack is of the same rank and each defers to Selentha on all counts. There is no democracy when it comes to dreggan society. It is a dictatorship run entirely upon the whim of the queen. If she so wishes she can condemn anyone to death for any reason whatsoever, or banish anyone to the desert of the far north. There are no trials and no rights afforded anyone.

When the members of the War Stack finally take their seats, she issues her order to bring out wine to all the members. As the human slaves distribute the wine, Selentha declares, "As our Dark Gods have promised, we are going to war once again!" The assembly responds with thunderous applause and raises glasses in joy. One member of the War Stack is so overjoyed at the prospect of killing that she lashes out with her claw at one of the human slaves in the room and disembowels him with one thrust of her arm. As his entrails are falling onto the floor, the other members of the War Stack howl with laughter.

"I have had a vision from the Zagador!" exclaims Selentha. The members of the War Stack all drop to their knees in silence as the true name of the Dark Gods is uttered out loud. "Rise and I shall tell you what will transpire," continues Selentha. They once again take their seats. "All of you are to amass your squadrons at once as we shall sail to the southern continent where our next victory awaits. Leave only a small contingency behind, as we will need large numbers in our new quest." She calmly looks around the chamber, assessing the looks on the faces of her War Stack. She heaves her chest in pride at the willingness of her warriors to head into a battle they know nothing about. In the world, there are none so eager to engage in battle as the dreggans. Selentha knows they will do exactly as she says without question, so she sees no reason to give any of them a reason for the upcoming conflict. She continues, "We sail for the southern continent in three days' time. We will take all but eleven frigates. I order you to bring one healer for every ten warriors and enough human slaves to provide for easy passage. We must be on the southern continent in one moonsign." The War Stack members are shocked at the number of warriors Selentha wishes to bring on this excursion, but none would dare question her motives. "This meeting of the War Stack is over," exclaims Selentha. She then orders the slaves to bring out the roasted quail and more wine for everyone to enjoy. As she rips the flesh off of the bone of the bird and follows it down with sweet nectar, she reclines in her chair, closes her eyes, and dreams of having the entire world as her kingdom.

Chapter 6

THE first three days of the journey eastbound are thankfully uneventful. The companions have been traveling parallel to the Continental Pass and perpendicular to the Great Southern Road, staying off the main thoroughfare to avoid detection. On the morning of the fourth day, as the sun is rising in front of them, Skenn signals Ashcon and Sapphyre to remain silent and points northeast. Ashcon closes his eyes, and Sapphyre sees a light blue aura emanating briefly through his shirtsleeve on his right arm. He opens his eyes, holds up six fingers, and points to the northwest. Skken heads in that direction. Aschon signals Sapphyre to remain silent and takes her hand, moving briskly east parallel to the road and just south of it. Ashcon spies two trees and a shallow ditch a short distance to their south and directs them to it. After tying off the horses, Ashcon directs Sapphyre down into the ditch. He then removes from his pack what looks like a compact crossbow and attaches three small ten-inch arrows with mithril tips. Ashcon carries the small bow up to his shoulder and aims northeast. Sapphyre is lying beside Ashcon looking in the same direction but sees nothing but forest. A dark green glow flashes from Ashcon's trigger hand and three successive shots in the flash of an eye exit from the bow. As the first arrow enters the forehead of one of the bandits, Skken emerges behind another and without a sound slices his throat from ear to ear with Grizzclaw.

Before the first man hits the dirt, the second man has a bolt hit him square in the neck and he drops down dead. As the bandits are trying to figure out where this attack is coming from, Skken releases four daggers simultaneously from his hip to take down his second target. As another stunned attacker turns his head to his dead comrades, the third arrow hits him square in his left eye, killing him on the spot. Skken turns toward the last of the six bandits and lowers his saber, preparing to ask for surrender. The bandit feigns submission, but as he is putting his weapons down on the floor, he launches his right arm up and a dagger shoots out toward Skken. He expected nothing less, and deflects the dagger with his offhand sword while at the same time advancing on the bandit. Sweeping Grizzclaw around in a hook he slices the man's head from his body with ease.

Ashcon starts to climb out of the ditch and reaches down to help Sapphyre up. "Bandits" is his one word response to the question that Sapphyre was about to ask. "Skken has a knack for sniffing out trouble," Ashcon starts to explain. "We've travelled together for many winters, Sapphyre. Over time we've developed an understanding and rarely do we need to speak to know what the other is thinking. They were waiting in ambush just a bit northeast of here. We decided to make sure they wouldn't be doing any more killing of innocents." The two continue north to the outskirts of a makeshift campsite where they see Skken waiting for them. "Wait here, Sapphyre. The scene will be a little gruesome. We'll be back shortly."

Ashcon leaves Sapphyre with the horses and continues to the campsite, where Skken has already started looting the bodies. They find a total of two hundred Kendra and a few weapons that can be sold or traded. They gather all the provisions, return to Sapphyre, and get ready to continue east.

"There is a town with a tavern about twelve or so leagues to the southeast. We'll get a hot meal and sleep in a warm bed," says Ashcon as he mounts his horse.

Sapphyre looks down at her hands as she grasps the reigns of her small mount, somewhat surprised they aren't trembling from the killings that just transpired. She falls a few feet behind both Ashcon and Skken looking at their backs and wondering if they took joy in killing the bandits or if they were just immune to it. She thinks back to the short battle she couldn't see and visualizes their actions. They sniffed out the bandits and immediately took action, at the same time ensuring Sapphyre's safety by keeping her out of harms way. Afterwards they went about looting the corpses with a job like efficiency and never did either crack a smile or make a joke about what transpired. After waiting a few moments, Sapphyre asks her horse to speed up a bit and secures herself between the two companions and smiles comfortably to no one in particular.The three continue the trip in silence and right after sundown they approach the small village. The town is similar to most small towns in between the cities in Arstevia. It is made up of a few farmhouses as the townsfolk tend to provide for themselves. This particular one has a small dirt road leading up to it and a bridge extending over a picturesque creek with a small waterfall on the eastern edge. There is a smithy situated next to the bridge, and a few small homes scattered throughout the town center. One of these small houses has a stable attached and as they head in that direction, Sapphyre sees the sign reading "Ale Mug" and assumes it's the tavern Ashcon mentioned.

"Ashcon, achturn ameili tu natchu stekannifun!!!" screams the bartender as the three travelers enter the tavern.

Ashcon replies with a huge grin, "At least she wasn't your sister, you scoundrel!!!"

The two friends embrace and the proprietor leads the group toward a table in the back left corner of the establishment. "Ale is on the way, and the wife will cook something special in the kitchen. Later we will meet in the common room for a pipe and some catching up," the proprietor says as he scurries toward the small bar.

Sapphyre takes in the surroundings and notices the difference between the Ale Mug and the Dragon's Flagon. There are only five other patrons and there doesn't seem to be a second floor. She is looking at the small fireplace and relishing the smell of cooked meats emanating from the tiny kitchen when the dwarf bartender returns with three mugs of ale. Sapphyre is not much of a drinker, but realizing it would be rude not to accept the hospitality, takes a small sip of the bitter beverage.

Crawkford is off the beaten path, a few leagues south of the Continental Pass. A dwarf named Alwin and his wife Craty run the Ale Mug. They don't get many visitors, but the travelers that do visit are the discreet kind who travel off-road. The couple have learned to be excellent listeners and are a good source of information.

As the two companions are catching up, Craty emerges from the kitchen with a huge slab of venison, potatoes, and a big flask of gravy. "Don't be shy," Craty quips as she starts filling the guest's plates with steaming hot portions.

"Thank you so much," says Sapphyre as she eagerly starts cutting at the succulent meat. Craty responds with a smile and a nod and heads back to the kitchen, dragging Alwin behind her. The three companions eat in silence, thankful for the meal and the ale.

After dinner, Alwin says, "Let me show you to your room so you can get comfortable. Then you'll meet me for a pipe and a mug."

They follow Alwin around the corner where there is a long hallway with six doors, and Sapphyre thinks to herself that the building seems a lot bigger on the inside. The three enter the last door on the right where there are three cots situated along the far wall and two washbasins in the back. Ashcon removes his belt with his two swords, lays them on the first cot, and then walks to the basin and washes his hands and face. Sapphyre places her small bag on the second cot while Skken stands immobile by the door. Ashcon walks toward Skken after washing up and signals to open the door so they can head back. As Sapphyre follows Ashcon toward the door, he turns to her and says, "Sorry, Sapphyre. Alwin tends to be an old fashioned type and the after-dinner drinks and pipe are for the men only."

"So what am I supposed to do?" she inquires.

"Get some rest. We will leave early on the morrow." Ashcon and Skken then exit without another word, closing the door behind them.

Once the two men turn the corner back into the common room, Sapphyre leaves the room and walks stealthily in the same direction. She assumes that the last door on the left before reaching the common area should be on the other side of the fireplace and provide a good place to listen in on the conversation. She uses her lock-picking skills from her former life to open the door and moves over to the fireplace where she situates herself on the floor and smiles as she hears voices.

"The news from around the kingdom is not good but not dire either, old friend," says Ashcon. "The king is doing as kings do, and there is relative peace in the region. The smaller towns are feeling the brunt of some new taxes, which are being levied to build larger barracks for the Imperial Army. The bandits have become more aggressive on the road, and it takes kendra to hire more men to police the roads." He takes a long swig of ale and fills in Alwin on the encounter with the bandits they had earlier in the day.

Alwin replies with agreements and then starts telling the two men what he has learned as of late.

"The rise in banditry can be attributed to what is going on inside Thorenn between the Pugs and the Guild of Slight."

"The Pugs?" inquires Skken as he takes a long toke off his pipe.

"Aye," replies Alwin. "A fairly new but strengthening thieving guild. It is the first real challenge to the Guild of Slight's power in over a hundred winters. If your occupation is that of a thief or bandit, you have two choices of who to work for: the Pugs or the Guild of Slight. The Guild of Slight has had a freeze on hiring for over ten winters and the Pugs are very particular on who they take into their ranks."

"So, if that's the case, the bandits have to take to the road and do what they can outside Thorenn," says Ashcon.

Alwin continues as he takes a long swig of ale and wipes his bearded mouth with his dirty sleeve. "The Pugs have been cornering the trade routes out of the far northern markets of Starkk, Prospekt, and Thull. As you know, these lands have been widely avoided due to the distance to travel and the weather conditions travelling so far north –" plus having to deal with barbarians. The Pugs have recruited former pirates, sailors, and navy men to join their ranks and provide the transport to those faraway lands. There are only two islands that are reachable by boat on the route between Thorenn and the northern lands and these islands are under the firm control of the Pugs. No other ship is permitted to land. It is virtually impossible for anyone to make the trip without having to stop on one of those two islands. The barbarians have what seems to be unlimited supplies of mithril ore for weapons for the dwarves, silks of extraordinary quality for the Thorenn women, gems and diamonds for all nobility, and unlimited ice-cold pale ale. They only require food, so the Pugs generally trade shiploads of rice and grain for shiploads of exotic goods. It has brought them extraordinary wealth and very powerful allies. Rumor has it they have teamed up with Dockhelm Lumber to provide more ships."

Ashcon stands up, heads to the bar to refill his mug, and asks, "How did the Guild of Slight allow this to happen? They're normally so brutal with people who try to get in on their action."

"Apparently the Pugs are rather resourceful," answers Alwin. "They started working in Dock Bay as opposed to Skid Way and stayed out of the businesses that the Slight are involved in. They don't own any whorehouses or gambling hells, so they stayed away from the main sources of revenue for the Guild of Slight. They are, however, in the business of loan sharking, and with the coin they've made they can charge a lower interest rate than the Slight. That's where the real contention has come in. The Pugs have accumulated some serious wealth in a relatively short time. Kendra buys politicians. Politicians provide protection."

Skken nods in acknowledgement and finishes his mug of ale in one big gulp.

"Their profit margin is such that they have much to go around to secure allies in the government. It is my estimation that they will either join with the Guild of Slight, or Slight will take measures to destroy them."

As Sapphyre is sitting by the fireplace listening to the increasingly loud voices, her mouth is agape hearing of the power of the Pugs. Katrivus always discussed with her his vision of a global empire that revolved around trade. He always believed that he who controls trade controls the world. She is astonished that Katrivus has accomplished what he has in such a short time. As the men start reminiscing once again about old times, Sapphyre retreats back to her room and spends quite a while drifting off to a restless sleep.

Chapter 7

KA'ALSHENE, the high priestess of the Temple of the Stars, is amazed at what she has just learned from the Star Gods: the long awaited prophecies are now in play. As Ka'alshene ponders these latest developments, she sits down in quiet prayer within the temple to contemplate how to fulfill her latest obligation.

The high priestess Ka'alshene is the highest-ranking member of the Temple of the Stars and speaks for the Star Gods. She is the foremost authority on runestars and seekers and it is her responsibility alone to decide whether a seeker is deemed worthy enough to receive an audience before the gods and ask to be granted title of runestar. She is fair of skin with blond, almost white hair that tapers down to her lower back. She is short in stature, standing only about four feet five inches tall, with sharp features and eyes of sparkling green. It is rumored she has been alive for over a millenium, although she resembles a woman of only twenty-five winters. She levitates six inches off the ground as opposed to walking, and is always seen wearing a yellow and white robe with the Halo of Stars resting an inch above her head.

She has been charged with assisting Ashcon and Sapphyre in their quest to find Sorenthor, the Lost Seeker; however, she cannot help them personally. Her status as high priestess prohibits her from interfering directly with the subjects of prophecy. After much prayer and thought, she decides her best course of action is to contact Talon and have him aid the two companions in their travels.

As Talon is sleeping soundly in his bunk in his room in the lower levels of the most pres-tigious of the Guild of Slight's barracks, he is awakened by the heat emanating from the locket worn around his neck. He rises from his slumber, slips on his shoes, and sneaks through the hidden doorway leading out the back of the guild hall. Using his keen eyesight, he makes sure no one has noticed him leave before starting to make his way to the Sacred Wood to communicate with the high priestess.

Talon is a seventeen-winters-old member of the Guild of Slight and the youngest officer on the Board of Slight. He is an established pick-pocket and is very close to receiving his commendation for assassination, which will only further his standing. Talon has impressed the elders of the guild with his uncanny ability to bring in almost five times the revenue of the average member. He is also an agent for the High Priestess Ka'alshene.

Talon is five feet eleven inches tall with dark hair that he keeps cropped very short and striking green eyes. Although there is a distinct bump on his nose, he is considered handsome. He is in excellent shape, as is required by the guild, with catlike reflexes and a keen sense of imminent danger. You won't see him if he doesn't want you to, as he is a master at blending into the current situation. This is due to his uncanny abilities as well as the Cloak of Shadow bestowed upon him by the high priestess many winters past.

He spends almost an hour meandering around outside Thorenn in the vicinity of the Sacred Wood, a walk that would take no more than ten minutes using a direct route. Once his is convinced he was not followed, he makes his way to the middle of the Sacred Wood by the Lake of Bliss, and removes one of the feathers from inside the locket. He closes his eyes and slips the tiny feather into the clear water, creating ripples visible in the moonlight. The shimmering vision of the high priestess comes into view and Talon sits down, closes his eyes, and silences his mind. Although the discussion takes place entirely via thought, the ritual is necessary for communication.

"Hello, m'lady," says Talon.

"Greetings, Talon," replies the high priestess. "Please forgive the lack of pleasantries, but I have a most important task for you."

"There is no reason to apologize, m'lady. I live to serve."

Her lips curve upwards into a small smile as she continues. "There will be visitors coming to Thorenn before the end of this moonsign whom you must assist. The party will consist of two men and a young girl about your age. They will make themselves known to you as they will be inquiring about the location of the one you know as the Lonely Hermit."

Talon sighs audibly as he reflects on what he knows of this strange man. The Lonely Hermit visits Thorenn twice every eight to ten moonsigns to pick up supplies and rarely stays in town for more than one night. He doesn't visit the taverns or the whorehouses and never haggles on the price of his goods. The rumor is that he has a dwelling somewhere north of the Myth Mountains.

The high priestess continues. "They know of him by the name Sorenthor. You are to aid them in their quest."

Talon interrupts her. "May I inquire as to the identity of these strangers?"

Ka'alshene has thought about how to answer this question, as Talon, although brilliant and devoted, is still an inquisitive teenage boy. She answers with authority, "You may not. Just understand that you have never done anything as important as what I am ordering for you to do today."

Talon replies, "Yes, m'lady. I meant no disrespect."

"I am sorry to be so blunt with you, dear one, and no disrespect taken." The high priestess has learned to have an enormous amount of patience when dealing with him. Over the years, she has forged an almost maternal relationship with the young spy. "Clear your mind now, Talon, as I must impart a vision to you," the high priestess continues.

Talon has had to enter this trancelike state on many occasions in the past when dealing with the high priestess, and has mastered the exercise. Once he enters this state of mind, a vision appears before him in his mind's eye. It is a map of the continent of Arstevia with a star marking a specific location. He notices familiar landmarks on the exquisite chart. The star is located north of the Myth Mountains and northwest of Thorenn. It seems as if the location is almost due north of the Dragon Tooth Pass and west of the barbarian land of Thull.

"The star marks the location of the Lonely Hermit's dwelling. It is up to you, dear one, how to reach this land with the three travelers. You may not transfer the map I have imparted to you to parchment; therefore, you must go with the three strangers and lead them. At any time throughout your travels, you may view the map by simply closing your eyes and clearing your mind."

"I will do as you order, m'lady," says Talon.

"I have no doubt you will, my Talon. Take care of yourself and may the Star Gods shine upon you always," continues the high priestess as her form in the water dissipates to nothing.

Talon secures the locket around his neck, rises from the earth, dusts off his pants, and starts walking back to town, contemplating this latest turn of events.

Chapter 8

THE discussion during the meeting of the Board of Slight this early morning is very heated. The topic is one that has been hounding the guild for quite some time: how to handle the Pugs. Trey is leading the conversation, as he always does, being the head of the Guild of Slight for the last fifteen winters. He is a benevolent leader and commands the utmost respect from the other members of the board, even those who were passed over for his position when it became available. This is due to the overwhelming prosperity they have known under his rule and guidance. Not only have they exponentially increased their wealth, but their power has grown tremendously as well. Trey's keen sense of business has brought them strong allies within the government, and there have been virtually no arrests of any members of the guild in the past five winters.

The board meets in the guild house common room and the nine members are the only people allowed to be present on the premises during such gatherings. No one would dare to breach this protocol, so they have no fear of being overheard.

"There are many options open to us regarding the Pugs and I want to discuss all of them before making any decision," Trey states.

"The only decision in my mind is to destroy them completely and do it now!" exclaims Kross, one of the oldest members of the guild, and one whom many defer to.

Chants of "aye" can be heard while a few hands pound in agreement.

"That is certainly an option," replies Trey as he gets up from his chair and starts walking around the long oak table where the board members are seated. "It is not our only option, however, and I would like to hear from those opposed."

Shantir, the eldest member of the guild, speaks up. "Why not make them an offer to join us? The profits from the shipping alone will be worth the effort. We can also then go back to charging a higher interest on our loans since the competition no longer exists."

Kross raises his voice, "Why should we do this, Shantir? We have ten times as many members as they do, and we have been established for hundreds of winters. If we simply bow down and allow another group of thieves who have been around for only twenty winters to dictate our policy it will show weakness. I say we kill them all and simply take it from them!"

"We can't just kill them all, Kross," rebukes Trey. "Even we can expect backlash from the authorities if we do something on such a grand scale."

"Then kill Katrivus and let the body die after the head is gone," counters Kross. "Without Katrivus, they lose their contacts with the barbarians and the government contacts they've amassed recently. The rest of the membership will have no choice but to join with us. We will have saved face by destroying our enemy and at the same time increase our power and revenue."

"Or we can try and cripple them." interjects Talon for the first time this morning. The heads turn to the man as he continues. "We can talk to our contacts in the government and have them raise the tariffs on their goods, decreasing their profits. We can persuade Dockhelm Lumber that it is in their best interest not to do business with the Pugs."

Kross counters, "But that will not destroy them, Talon. And who's to say they won't simply smuggle in all of their goods to avoid the tariffs or bring them to a different port of call?"

"I think the point here is to not only destroy the Pugs but at the same time take over their operations," says Nitios, a quiet but powerful member of the guild. As the members nod their heads in agreement, Nitios continues. "Although I see the reasoning behind your idea, Talon, I'm afraid I must agree with Kross. If we assassinate Katrivus we can take over with little opposition."

"It is time for a vote," says Trey, although everyone at the table knows what the outcome will be. Trey always allows a vote on important guild matters even though he has veto power and can dictate policy. "Raise your hand if you are in favor of the assassination of Katrivus." Six of eight hands are raised, as Trey does not take part in the voting. The only two people not voting for this measure are Shantir and Talon. "It is decided," continues Trey with his gaze set on Talon. "Although you are opposed to the measure, Talon, I trust you will do as the board has voted."

"Absolutely," replies Talon without hesitation.

"Then you will gain your commendation for assassination, Talon. It is your charge to be the one to kill Katrivus," states Trey. With excitement in their voices, the board members congratulate Talon, as this commendation will further cement his status as an elite member of the Guild of Slight.

"Thank you, Trey. It will be my honor to fulfill this duty," says Talon honestly. Although Talon does not agree with the killing of Katrivus as the best course of action, he has no problem fulfilling the obligation.

"This meeting of the Board of Slight is called to rest. No one will speak of our decision outside of this room. We all trust in Talon's ability to get the job done." He then addresses Talon, "After you have decided how you will go about the assassination, I would like you to meet with me before you take action. Is that understood?"

"Of course," replies Talon.

"Then I expect to hear the specifics of your operation within three days' time," says Trey as he stands up and exits the room, signaling the end of the meeting.

Chapter 9

THE trio bids farewell to Alwin and Craty as they prepare to continue the long journey toward Thorenn. Craty hands Skken a bag filled with dried beef and crusty bread while Ashcon and Alwin embrace. As Alwin walks with them to the stable to retrieve their horses, he has a suggestion for Ashcon. "It might be worth a quick stop in Stagg on your way to Thorenn."

"I'm not familiar," Ashcon replies. "Where is Stagg?"

"It's about halfway between here and Thorenn, forty leagues north of the Continental Pass," answers Alwin. "There's a tavern there called the Slaughtered Boar run by a dwarf named Horace. He's a member of the Guild of Slight and runs some of their smaller operations in a few of the hamlets surrounding Stagg. He is a lifelong friend and will certainly have some information for you that will prove valuable." As Ashcon and Sapphyre are saddling their horses and Skken is attaching the sack of provisions to the back of his mount, Alwin continues. "When you get there, say 'I have just journeyed from the far reaches of Glumby and can use a tankard.' This will let him know you are a friend of mine. And do try his mead; it is magnificent!"

"I will, my friend," says Ashcon as he sits down upon his horse. He waves to Alwin one last time and they start their march eastward.

It will be about eight days before reaching Stagg, and Sapphyre passes the time talking with the mysterious Skken. "I've never met anyone quite as large as you," Sapphyre begins.

Skken replies with a laugh, "I'm about average height from where I come from."

"And where is that?"

As the wind picks up and blows his robes about, Skken replies, "I am originally from lands north of the Myth Mountains, quite a ways from here."

"How long have you been with Ashcon?"

"Quite a long time," Skken replies evasively.

"You don't talk much do you?" asks Sapphyre.

Ashcon laughs audibly as he hears the exchange behind him. He turns his head about and exclaims, "This is the most I've heard him say in eons!"

"I'm not one with the spoken word, this is true," says Skken stoically.

Sapphyre sighs and mockingly says, "What are you one with then?"

Skken contemplates his answer before replying in all seriousness, "I am one with Grizzclaw," referring to his saber.

"How can you be one with a weapon?"

"It is the only way to be with a weapon. If you are to master the weapon, you must become one with it," he replies matter-of-factly.

The three continue in silence and as noon arrives, they prepare for their midday meal. Skken divvies up the dried beef and bread as they sit in a small circle. While they are chewing their food, Sapphyre decides to show Skken her dagger. She finishes up her last bite of bread, stands up and reaches down in to her left boot, and retrieves the scabbard, holding the prized weapon. As Ashcon and Skken are making sure they leave no signs of their passing and start to untie the horses, Sapphyre approaches Skken and taps him on the shoulder. He turns toward her and Sapphyre, removes the dagger from its scabbard, and hands it, hilt first, to Skken.

Skken reaches for the dagger, astonished by its beauty. "Bless the Star Gods, it is incredible. I don't recall ever seeing one of its likeness," he says as he twirls it in his huge hands.

Ashcon turns to see what Skken is referring to and gasps as the dagger too transfixes him. "Where did you get such a weapon Sapphyre?" he inquires.

"A friend allowed me to keep it," she somewhat honestly replies. She then looks Skken directly in his eyes and states, "I wish to become one with it."

Skken smiles broadly and hands the dagger back to the young woman who takes in her tiny palm and slides it into the scabbard. "Very well. What name have you bequeathed it?" he inquires.

"I have always called it Frostripper," replies Sapphyre.

"A worthy name for such a prized weapon." As they climb astride their mounts and continue their journey, Skken says, "If you truly wish to become one with Frostripper then it will be my honor to train you in its use."

Sapphyre smiles. "Thank you, Skken."

From that moment on, as the trio continue toward Stagg, each night before retiring Skken teaches Sapphyre how to command her precious dagger. Sapphyre is already somewhat proficient and impresses Skken with how fast she learns further intricacies of wielding the weapon. Ashcon does not take part in the weapons training but clearly sees that Sapphyre has a special talent and the dagger a truly exceptional weapon. As the young girl jousts with Skken, the fluid motion of Frostripper leaves streaks of blue and black sparkles in its wake and the blade glows with all colors of the spectrum as it flows through the air. It is truly a sight to behold and as Sapphyre becomes more adapt at wielding it, the blade responds with dancing colors and sparks, seemingly growing in power in accordance with Sapphyre's abilities.

This particular evening is cold and wet and as the temperature continues to plummet, the rain turns into a light snow leaving a thin layer on the hard ground. "Tomorrow we should reach Stagg," says Ashcon as he surveys the land looking for a suitable area to camp for the night. "This way," he says as he leads his horse toward a small open area surrounded by trees with a few leaves still on their branches. Skken tends to the fire and Ashcon and Sapphyre get the blankets out from their packs, preparing to retire. Ashcon looks into the sleeping eyes of the young Sapphyre wondering if she truly is his seeker and thinking back eight hundred winters to the time leading up to when he was sixteen.

Chapter 10

ASHCON and Drak'thonn were born to a farmer and his wife in a town called Seascape just south of the Myth Mountains on the western border of Arstevia along the Sea of Tears. Eight hundred winters ago it was a small village with a population of less than three hundred and the people were either farmers or fishermen. Today it is known as Teeken and is one of the largest cities on the continent and a main port of call on the sea.

Runestars were not legends of the past when the fraternal twins came into the world. They were not abundant, per se, but almost everyone was aware of their existence and many had met one throughout their lives. There were no seekers at that time as the chosen people were born with the innate ability to become a runestar. It was not until centuries later when runestars were becoming extinct that the Star Gods brought seekers into existence.

Every hamlet, with a minimum population of two hundred, had a priest of the Star Gods to look over the village and provide spiritual guidance. The people were pious and although they led a simple life, they entrusted their souls to the Star Gods and prayed to them on a regular basis. One of the many duties of the priests was to participate in the birth of each member of their village and the birth of the twins was no exception. They not only assisted with the delivery and gave the Blessing of the New to each newborn, but they also looked for the telltale sign of the runestar: A tiny rune in the shape of the sun located behind the left ear, known as the Sign of the Sun. The last time a runestar was born in Seascape was so long ago that no one alive at the time could even recall it. If the priest found the rune there was great celebration and anticipation. For it was not until the child's sixteenth winter that he was brought before the high priestess in the Temple of the Stars where he will learn his fate in the presence of the Gods themselves.

The entire village of Seascape payed witness to all the births. The priest and the midwife were inside the two-bedroom house, and the residents were gathered about outside lying in wait. Ashcon was born first followed only minutes later by the larger Drak'thonn. As is tradition, the two brothers were wrapped in sheepskin and handed to their father where he held one in each arm. After introducing the babies to their mother for the first time, he exited the home to the cheers of the local populace. With the priest in tow, the proud father made his way the center of the village. The priest began his incantations as the onlookers lapsed into silence.

Once finished with his prayers, he reached out to the father and took Ashcon into his arms. With tenderness he removed the sheepskin from around the boy's small head. He turned Ashcon over in his gentle hands and peeled back his left ear to search for the sun, and for the first time in this young priest's life, he saw the sign of the runestar. At first he was speechless, and then he regained his composure, lifted the boy up, and stated as he was trained, "By the light of the Star Gods this house and this village are blessed with the Sign of the Sun. May the light shine upon young Ashcon and may the Star Gods favor him and see true to ordain him the title of runestar."

His mother burst into tears of joy while his father pumped his chest with pride. The raucous crowd needed to be quieted by the priest as he reminded them there was a second brother.

As the crowd fell silent, Ashcon was exchanged for Drak'thonn and the priest took him into his arms for the second viewing. If there was anyone breathing at this moment you couldn't hear it. The priest pulled back the sheepskin, turned young Drak'thonn over, took a deep breath, and reached for his left ear. He was stunned to see the same rune of the sun and lifted the boy up. For the second time in less than three minutes, he recited the Sign of the Sun blessing.

As far as anyone knew, never before had twins been born with the sign. The news of the birth spread wide and far. For the first few winters of their lives, priests and followers of the Star Gods who wanted to get glimpses of the boys visited them. Once they reached six winters of age, the fanfare died down and they lived their lives like normal children of the time – the only difference being the study they took part in with the village priest. He taught them the teachings of the Star Gods and prepared them for what would take place upon their sixteenth birthday.

The twins were inseparable for the first ten winters of life. If you searched for one, you found the other. As they got a little older, Ashcon concentrated on studying, reading, and writing while the younger and larger Drak'thonn spent most of his time practicing with weapons and working on his physical prowess. Their personalities differed as well; Ashcon was studious and obedient while Drak'thonn was more rebellious in his youth. He also became increasingly violent as they grew up.

In the cold season of their fourteenth winter, Ashcon and Drak'thonn were walking home after running an errand for their father when three youngsters accosted them, throwing snowballs. While Ashcon laughed and returned with snowballs of his own, Drak'thonn seemed as if he were transformed into a thoughtless drone. He charged the smallest of the attackers and knocked him to the snowy surface with more force than necessary. As Ashcon and the other kids watched in horror, Drak'thonn pummeled the boy with his fists, breaking his nose and relentlessly landing blow upon blow on the helpless and now unconscious victim. Ashcon had to pull his brother off the boy using all the strength he could muster and was barely able to stop the onslaught. Drak'thonn turned on Ashcon in rage and unleashed a vicious right hook to his face sending Ashcon toppling to the earth. The two friends of the hapless victim stared at Drak'thonn in shock, unable to move. Drak'thonn looked around as the realization of what he had done sank in. He turned and took off running in the opposite direction of Seascape. Ashcon lifted himself off the ground and walked over to the still unconscious boy,gesturing to the other two to help take him back to town. While they were carrying the limp body to the priest for healing, Ashcon noticed that the skin on the right side of the boy's face seemed to be smoking as if it was burnt by fire.

After that incident the two brothers spent less time together and while Ashcon diligently worked on his studies, Drak'thonn worked on ways to strengthen his body. Their parents worried constantly about their younger son as he became more distant and detached, plagued with nightmares that kept him from sleeping soundly. He would disappear for days at a time and when he would return, he kept silent concerning his whereabouts.

As the boys were growing up they met regularly with the priest of the village to learn everything they could about runestars. The priest explained to the boys that even though they each had the Sign of the Sun behind their left ear, it was no guarantee they would be ordained as runestars. Upon the boys' sixteenth birthday, the Star Gods would decide that. When Ashcon inquired as to how many people with the Sign of the Sun actually became runestars, the brothers were both astonished to hear that only one in ten with the sign became runestars. That bit of information evoked different reactions from the two brothers. Ashcon became excited and overly diligent in his studies while Drak'thonn became detached and spent less and less time with the priest.

Ashcon was intrigued with the idea of spending his life defending the light and the stars, which is the reason for the existence of runestars. Drak'thonn could not care less about defending good, but instead wanted to know what powers runestars possess and how to attain them. So when the lessons from the priest focused on the powers of the runestar, both brothers were especially attentive.

The priest was leading one of his classes with the two brothers in the small Temple of Seascape when the topic of powers came up. "Runestars have intricate runes all over their body which contain various gifts and powers," he explained. "All runestars share four of the same runes which are common to all. Each runestar has the gift of far-sight, warding your conversation from being overheard, an uncanny ability to detect evil intent, and the gift of persuasion. Beyond these four abilities, each runestar then has runes that are unique to the individual."

Ashcon excitedly asked, "What type of powers?"

"There are many different powers a runestar can obtain. It is decided upon by the Star Gods when they accept you as a runestar, and it is based on your personality and on what the Star Gods themselves wish to attain by your existence."

Drak'thonn interjected, "Can one obtain the power over fire?"

The priest looked at Drak'thonn, sighed, and replied, "The power over fire is not one that can be obtained by a runestar Drak'thonn." The look of defeat on Drak'thonn's face did not sit well with the priest as he continued. "Fire, although helpful in terms of providing warmth and cooking meats, falls into the realm of the Dark Gods. The Star Gods feel that possessing the power of fire can only lead to destruction which is in direct contrast with the wishes of the Star Gods."

Upon hearing this, Drak'thonn stood and abruptly departed from the temple. The priest looked to Ashcon and said, "Your brother does not seem especially diligent in his studies, but do not judge him, Ashcon. It is not your place to judge. That burden falls to the Star Gods themselves."

Ashcon nodded in acknowledgment and asked, "So what types of powers are consistent with the Star Gods wishes?"

The priest smiled and replied, "There are many, young Ashcon. I have met runestars with the ability to communicate with animals and others who can travel as quickly as the wind. What you must understand is that if you are granted the title of runestar your life is no longer your own. You will dedicate it to the light and stars and each rune the Gods decide to bestow upon you will be specifically designed to achieve that goal."

"I understand. Do I have any say in the type of powers that would be bestowed upon me if I am deemed worthy?"

"Yes and no. You will not consciously be able to dictate what powers you will possess but your personality will play a part in what powers the

Gods decide to grant you." Ashcon looked at the priest with a confused look on his face and was about to ask a question when the priest continued. "For example, if you are an extremely gifted blacksmith, the Gods may bestow upon you the ability to forge weapons or armor without the use of a forge or fire. If you are an avid swimmer you may be granted the gift to breathe underwater." This elicited an excited look on Ashcon's face and the priest smiled and continued. "Mind you these are but examples to explain better the answer to your question. I don't expect you to start swimming or working at the smithy."

"Of course not," replied Ashcon, blushing.

The priest decided to change the subject. "If you are to be ordained a runestar you will spend no less than twelve winters at the Fortress of the Invoker to learn your craft."

"What happens there?"

"I am not privy to what takes place at the fortress, although I know it requires diligent study in the ways of the light and the stars. You will learn to control your powers. When you fully understand your role and are deemed worthy to exit the fortress you will be transformed. You will be a tool in defending the light and the stars until the end of days."

"The end of days?" asked Ashcon.

"Yes, my son. Although it is a great honor to be ordained a runestar it comes with many burdens as well. You will outlive all of your friends and relatives, which can be quite trying, as you will be, in essence, an eternal being."

Ashcon looked down at his lap, contemplating this latest revelation. "What if I decide not to take on the burden?"

"If you decide you are not up to the task, you will state so to the Star Gods when asked, and you will live your life in a normal fashion. You will not be punished for declining the burden; however, few have done so." The priest leaned close to Ashcon and said, "Ashcon, my calling is that of a priest and that is how I chose to dedicate my life to the light and the stars. You must decide your own fate and make sure you think carefully as the opportunity to serve does not come along more than once in a lifetime. If the Star Gods decide that you are worthy to be ordained a runestar, do not take that decision lightly. Not many are granted the honor." Ashcon nodded to the priest and the two sat in silence for a moment before the lesson ended.

As the winters went by, Ashcon spent every free moment learning everything he could about runestars from the priest and from books on the subject. The sessions with the priest turned into one-on-one affairs as Drak'thonn decided to opt out of them. When asked why, he simply responded that if it is the wish of the Star Gods to ordain him, it would be so. Ashcon continued as an exemplary student while Drak'thonn continued to spend more and more time in isolation. While Ashcon held no bitter feelings toward Drak'thonn, the opposite was true of the younger sibling. Drak'thonn became increasingly jealous of Ashcon because he was the favorite son of not only his parents, but of the priest and the entire village. Ashcon had no idea his brother felt this way about him. Over the winters, the jealousy ballooned into a hatred Drak'thonn had to fight to keep hidden.

Drak'thonn spent an exorbitant amount of time outside Seascape, sometimes for days at a time, and would never answer questions concerning his whereabouts. Six moonsigns before their sixteenth birthday, Ashcon decided to follow

Drak'thonn on one of his journeys to see where he went and what he did. Ashcon remained silent and seemingly unobserved by Drak'thonn as they headed to the forest a few leagues to the east of Seascape. Drak'thonn saw a deer upon a clearing and quickly notched his bow and let an arrow loose which hit the young buck right above the neck, incapacitating but not killing the animal. Ashcon watched as Drak'thonn grabbed the deer by the neck in his huge hands and dragged him to the center of the clearing. He threw the deer down on the ground and gathered wood for a fire. Ashcon looked on as Drak'thonn started a fire with nothing but his hands. The flames were bouncing up and down imitating Drak'thonn's hand gestures. Ashcon watched in amazement at the realization set in that his brother had control over the fire. He had to hold his hand over his mouth when Drak'thonn grabbed the deer's head, thrust it into the flame, and watched it burn alive in his grasp. Once the deer was dead, Drak'thonn removed his unscathed hands from the fire, threw the rest of the animal into the flame, and sat back with a satisfied smirk on his face, watching it burn. Ashcon slipped away and returned to Seascape prepared to tell his father what he witnessed in the forest.

His father was taken aback by the tale told to him by his eldest son and commanded Ashcon to speak of it to no one. He told Aschon he would address the issue and to give it no further thought. What his father did regarding this incident is still a mystery to Ashcon, but he always assumed that he ignored it, hoping that the visit to the Temple of the Stars in only six moonsigns would put an end to Drak'thonn's destructive behavior.

On their sixteenth birthday, the priest came to the home of Aschon and Drak'thonn to escort them to the Temple of the Stars for the ordainment ritual. Both Ashcon and Drak'thonn bid their parents farewell, Ashcon with sincere hugs and Drak'thonn with distant nods of his head. The priest kissed the cheeks of both parents and led the boys to his quarters where he summoned a portal to transport them to the temple, which was located in far south central Arstevia.

The high priestess Ka'alshene was waiting for the two boys as the three emerged from the portal outside the temple. The two brothers knew the protocol and without hesitation dropped to one knee before the high priestess. The priest situated himself behind them.

Ka'alshene bid them to rise as she floated before them in front of the huge doors to the temple. Ashcon and Drak'thonn took to their feet before her, slowly raising their heads to stare wide-eyed at the breathtaking beauty in light robes, with her face shining under the glow of the levitating halo of stars. She smiled warmly and knowingly, as all who have beheld her before have had the same reaction, whether male or female.

Ka'alshene spoke for the first time, and the boys were taken aback, wondering how the beauty of the voice could surpass the physical beauty. "At tomorrow's first light," she said, looked directly into Ashcon's eyes, "Ashcon will present himself at the temple doors." She shifted her gaze to Drak'thonn. "Drak'thonn, you will present yourself upon the first light of the following morning." They both nodded in understanding as she continued "May the Star Gods shine upon you in your quest." Then she vanished into thin air.

At first light, Ashcon entered the temple and was taken aback by its sheer size. There was marble of many colors and pillars rising hundreds of feet to the ceiling, which depicted a sky filled with bright stars. There was no light source visible but the temple was aglow in a luminous radiance. Breathless, Ashcon eyed the Pool of Shimmering Light in the middle of the temple, filled with a magical liquid transparent in color yet full of substance. The high priestess led Ashcon beyond the pool to the far side of the temple to what appeared to be a large cistern standing almost four feet high and four feet wide at its widest point.

Ka'alshene withdrew an exquisite goblet adorned with various stones, dipped it into the blood-red liquid in the cistern, and filled it to the brim. She gestured to Ashcon to stand beside her, and she handed him the cup. He gripped the glass in both hands and brought it to his chest beneath his chin and held it there, awaiting further instruction from the high priestess.

She nodded to Ashcon, and turned back toward the pool. Ashcon followed her, moving at a slow, deliberate pace. As he was taught in his studies, he took a sip of the nectar with each step. The pool seemed to get further and further away even as they walked directly toward it. The marble ground gave way to sand without warning, and as Ashcon was sinking deeper with each step, Ka'alshene remained above untouched. They were moving with purpose and trepidation, and Ashcon impulsively sipped from the glass while he descended further into the sand. Unable to stop, Ashcon's head submerged beneath the sand. With an ethereal calmness, he opened his eyes. Instead of feeling granules rip into his eyes, it was as if he was under water, clear blue water, so crisp he could see the image of the high priestess hovering above him. The water had another quality to it - one that allowed Ashcon to breathe. As the realization came to him that he was being prepared for the Pool of Shimmering Light, a bolt flashed before him and he was no longer in the sand but lying completely nude on a bed of liquid gold beside the pool.

The high priestess levitated into a prone position three feet above Ashcon and looked down upon him. Ka'alshene opened her left hand to reveal a small leaf, bright green and glistening with dew. She extended her hand toward Ashcon's mouth and placed the leaf onto Ashcon's tongue. He closed his mouth allowing the leaf to dissolve as opposed to chewing it. As soon as the leaf has disappeared, the high priestess was no longer there. She was replaced by the ceiling of stars only inches from his face. The stars were moving in all directions and Ashcon felt as if his body was floating with nothing restricting his movements. He suddenly had control over his muscles again and flexed them in attempts to move around in this zero-gravity environment. Once he regained his physical abilities, he was transported once again and found himself standing at the edge of the Pool of Shimmering Light, the high priestess above the pool directly in front of him.

"It is time," said the high priestess whose voice filled the entire chamber. Ashcon knelt beside the pool and watched as Ka'aleshene called upon the Star Gods to come forth and render judgment. There was a bright flash of light, and Ashcon knew it was time to close his eyes and enter the pool As he steps down,a sense of calmness never before felt by Ashcon took over his body. As the priest instructed he lay down on his back in the liquid, and his body languidly submerged beneath it. Impulsively, he held his breath even though he knew in his subconscious he had no need to fear drowning. When he opened his eyes, he saw the same image he had seen before: Ka'alshene hovering above him in sparkling water of clear blue. He closed his eyes and relaxed all his muscles. A feeling of joy took over his entire being, and he let the presence engulf him.

Without warning, stars started shooting by his consciousness, each probing a different aspect of his mind. He felt it as these rays of light converged on his memories, revealing truths and rendering judgment. His eyes were closed, but he saw the stars from the ceiling of the temple. They flashed brilliant rays of light in every direction. Each one pierced a different layer of his mind, and each of the thousand stars was a different test of character. After what seemed an eternity, all of the stars ceased moving and cast a line of light onto Ashcon's body. As the countless rays of light came to rest on their target, Ashcon's body stiffened and rose from the pool.

A spectacular flash of bright blue light awakened Ashcon. He was no longer in the pool but kneeling in front of what could only be the Star Gods themselves. They addressed him through his thoughts, "Ashcon, you are deemed worthy to be ordained a runestar. You will return to your home, and in one moonsign present yourself to the high priestess. At that point, your training will begin. You will spend no less than twelve winters within the Fortress of the Invoker learning the ways of the light. If you accept this charge and will dedicate your life to the light and the stars, state so now."

As instructed, Ashcon replied with a booming voice, "I will dedicate my life to the light and the stars and defend both until the end of time."

"Rise, my son," said the Star Gods. "Behold yourself in the Mirror of Life and take pride in your newfound charge." Ashcon rose. A mirror appeared in front of him, and his reflection showed his transformation. There was no longer any baby fat on his body, all of which was covered with solid muscle. His skin turned dark and his eyes yellow. His entire body was covered in intricate runes from head to toe. Speechless, he turned toward the Star Gods, who were no longer there. Standing in their place was the high priestess, who welcomed Ashcon with a warm embrace.

"Follow me, Ashcon," she said as she led him to the far end of the pool. "Stand in the pool, only up to your ankles," she instructed. Ashcon walked into the shallow end of the pool and turned toward Ka'alshene. "You are about to feel some of the power you possess. It will be but a brief taste of what you will learn to control."

The high priestess placed her hands on either side of her halo, closed her eyes, and within seconds, her hands were awash in a soft blue glow. She floated in front of Ashcon and placed her hands within inches of his head. She then started to move her hands around Ashcon's body, imitating the intricate designs. As she traced each of the runes, Ashcon could feel the power beneath. As she continued the ritual, Ashcon finally realized the gift with which he had been given. As quickly as it started, it ended. Ashcon opened his eyes to see Ka'alshene in front of him smiling.

"My son," she said warmly, "although your runes are no longer visible to the naked eye, they are still within you and upon you. You will start your instruction in only thirty days' time, at which time your life will truly begin."

As they walked toward the temple door, Ka'alshene handed a pouch to Ashcon. "Go now, bid your brother farewell and return to Seascape. Give the pouch to your father to ease his burden of tending the farm in your absence." She then kissed both of his cheeks, as is the formal greeting amongst those of the light and stars, and led him to the temple's exit. "Until the next moonsign, young Ashcon."

Drak'thonn was taken aback by his brother's appearance. His eyes turned dark when Ashcon embraced him to wish him luck. Ashcon kissed his brother on both his cheeks. As he walked toward the portal back to Seascape, he turned to glance once again at his twin. Little did he know that it would be hundreds of winters before he would again encounter his brother.

Chapter 11

TALON sits alone in the study of the guild house, pondering his latest challenges: How to assist the high priestess by escorting three strangers north and how to best kill Katrivus for the guild. While enjoying a morning smoke, the young rogue signals to the guard at the door. The guard comes to attention. "Find me Ashley and Thorn. Now," Talon barks, and the guard retreats out the door.

Since Talon is working on orders from the board, his requests are tantamount to orders themselves. Ashley and Thorn look like they may have to be reminded of that fact. They storm in looking unhappy to be interrupted this morning.

"What is the meaning of this Talon?" asks Ashley with a slightly raised voice. "I was teaching a class when I received your rather abrupt summons."

Talon replies sarcastically, "I'm sorry, Ashley, but as I'm sure you are aware I am on a rather rigid time schedule, and I need your expertise. If I felt I could handle it alone, I would not have infringed upon your time. Please." He takes her hand gently into his and leads her to a chair. "Sit down. I need your help. I need to know all there is to know about this leader of the Pugs, this Katrivus," states Talon as he paces between the two thieves. He keeps his eyes on Ashley. "His schedule, how many bodyguards, what he eats to break the fast, his favorite ale, everything. You get the picture." Talon says. "Thank you" and nods to the door, indicating her portion of the meeting is over. "Bits and pieces as you get them, Ashley. And everything by this evening."

Talon walks toward Thorn and takes the seat beside him. Once the door closes behind Ashley, Talon says, "What do you know about Katrivus?"

Thorn looks into Talon's eyes, sighs audibly, and sits back in his chair, pondering his thoughts as he frames his answer. Thorn is the leader of the spies within the Guild of Slight and therefore is privy to more information than anyone in the organization. No one, including Trey himself, knows how deep Thorn's spy ring goes. He doesn't want to give up all of the information he has on Katrivus to Talon, although as a member of the board, he knows that Talon is charged with killing him.

"Katrivus is twenty-three winters old and is the leader and the founder of the Pugs. They started out as all the punks do with pickpocketing and petty theft and the like." Thorn slaps his knee with his left hand, laughs, and grabs at his beard with his right. Chuckling, he continues. "Do you remember that old pervert Steele Monthall?"

Talon nods with a sour look on his face. "Well, seems old Steele got himself a rich cargo stolen a few winters back. They say more than thirty thousand kendra worth of goods were taken. There was never any official investigation but word is that the Pugs did that job and that started making 'em big time."

"I know how they got started, Thorn. I need to know about the man. Tell me about Katrivus."

Thorn takes out his tissue, coughs into it, and then continues. "He is very hands-on. The big jobs – I mean, the really big ones – he handles personally. He has two assistants whom he trusts to a point. His study is his sanctuary and no one is permitted inside. His guards stay outside and his assistants have never seen it."

"When you say he is very hands-on, elaborate."

"Just what I mean," says Thorn as he reclines further in his chair. "He's working right now on a contract with Dockhelm Lumber for more ships for expanding routes. I only know because of my contacts at Dockhelm. My contacts in the Pugs have no idea. No one in his entire organization knows the details of his negotiations with Dockhelm. And I must say, they are rather brilliant."

Talon puts his head in his hands as he absorbs the information. "Tell me about the shipping operation."

"Right now the Pugs have control of fourteen ships that regularly make trips to the barbarian lands of the north. The two islands on the route, Cornice and Flotine, are also in their control. They have working relationships with all three tribes of barbarians in all of the ports of call: Starkk, Prospekt and Thull." Thorn stands up and paces as he continues. "Katrivus visits each port of call once every six or so moonsigns."

"How will the deal with Dockhelm Shipping help the Pugs?"

"They will almost double their current fleet. They also have plans to expand their routes and go around south to get to Sloan." This information drew a slight nod of admiration from Talon for the boldness of their plans. "I have word from a reliable source that the Barbarians of the North will not deal with anyone but Katrivus. He has been their contact from the beginning and the rumor is that he has a blood pact of some sort with a barbarian shaman."

Talon stands up and extends his hand toward Thorn. "Please delve a little deeper. I want to know more about this so-called blood pact." Talon sits back down in the study as Thorn exits the building.

Now that the business with Katrivus is rolling along, Talon has time to contemplate his other charge. He sits back, closes his eyes, and clears his thoughts as the map of the lonely hermit's dwelling appears to him. After carefully studying the map, he sees that there are limited courses of action. The library is located far north of the Myth Mountains and west of the populated barbarian lands. The Northern Trail traverses the barbarian lands from the northernmost port city of Starkk, travelling southeast toward RedPost, the last city before the Marsh of Sorrow. It is the only main thoroughfare on the northern side of the mountains, but it goes nowhere near the library.

Talon makes his way back to his quarters. There are only two ways to get to the other side of the mountains. The first is by foot and means traversing the DragonTooth Pass. The pass is located northwest of Thorenn, about a half moonsign ride by horseback in the best of weather. The DragonTooth Pass bears its name because of the rough terrain, steep, sharp crevices throughout the eighteen-league span, and the rumor that dragon lords guard the holy mosques hidden in the mountains themselves. The other option is by sea. The only ships that head north to the barbarian lands are those controlled by the Pugs. If passage can be gained on a Pug ship, and for a price it certainly could, the entire trip can be made in two moonsigns.

As Talon realizes the only real option is to travel by sea, he falls back onto his bed and lets his breath out slowly as he contemplates his dilemma. The death of Katrivus may very well compromise his ability to transport the three visitors to the barbarian lands for the high priestess. It would take weeks for order to be restored and ships to leave the dock. The trip would have to be made over land, in the cold season, and without an official treaty with the dwarves of the Myth Mountains. Talon rubs his temples and yawns. He closes his eyes and ponders his next move.

Chapter 12

THE dreggans are not the greatest sailors but with the help of the human slaves are able to cross the Sea of Tears and land at the port of West Hollow on the far northwest tip of Arstevia. The trip takes almost a complete moonsign, though only one ship is lost to the treacherous waves and storms typical of the continental divide.

West Hollow is under the control of the orcs, and Kreel, the orcs' high battle lord, is sent to greet the visitors and escort Selentha to the Skeed Towers. Kreel is a high council member and has been faithful to Drak'thonn for the last half a century. Typical of orcs, Kreel stands a little over six feet tall with broad shoulders and tree-trunk thighs that ripple with muscle and are adorned with scars. His skin is a darker green, the top of his head is bald and his black hair is in a ponytail extending from his skull to the arch in his back.

He has two huge, sharp fangs that extend out of the top portion of his mouth and reach almost to his chin. He watches from the end of the docks as the frigates bearing the foreigners drop anchor and prepare to row to shore.

The War Stack with Selentha arrives first. They prepare for the introductions. They march in battle formation, with all weapons sheathed in a gesture of peace, and halt ten feet from the orc contingency. Kreel walks forward and faces the leader. He states in the common tongue while extending his hand, "I am called Kreel. I lead my people, the orcs, and we welcome you to West Hollow."

Selentha glances down at the hand and just stares, unaware of the custom. One of her human slaves whispers something to her in the language of the dreggans. She reaches toward the hand, takes it into hers awkwardly, and responds in the common tongue. "I am Selentha. I lead my people, the dreggans. We thank you for your warm welcome."

The two walk toward the city center with their respective guard surrounding them, and Kreel says, "Drak'thonn is eagerly awaiting your arrival.

He wishes us to leave at first light and march directly to the Dark Fortress."

"How long will it take to reach the fortress?"

"No more than three turns of the sun at a normal pace. We need less rest than most, and there are orcs who make it in two."

Selentha turns toward Kreel and looks down at him grinning, "Let's make sport of it. We will leave at early light tomorrow and see who arrives at the fortress first."

Kreel responds laughing, "Very well. I have two thousand making the trip with us as most of my force is already there. How many do you number?"

Selentha starts walking away from Kreel as she replies sharply, "Eighty thousand". She hears Kreel behind her try and whistle through his fangs as she smiles and walks toward the dreggan camp to retire.

The dreggans have no need for horses, as their strong legs can keep pace with the quickest of stallions. They have another advantage because they can run for as long as a week without stopping to camp. The orcs, of course, have no way of knowing this, and as they are preparing for the second day of travel, Selentha and her War Stack are approaching the fortress gates.

The fortress encompasses a huge territory in the northwest section of Arstevia, the landmark being the Skeed Towers, which can be seen from every direction. There are barracks for thousands of soldiers of all species; the followers of the Zagador, pens to hold countless slaves, and of course the Temple of the Dark Gods which lies on the western border overlooking the sea.

As Selentha and her War Stack approach the main gates, they open from the inside and eight men on horseback approach slowly in full battle regalia. They come to a stop ten feet in front of the dreggans and begin to part, with four going to each side forming a path leading to Selentha. A large black mount appears from the gates and trots with purpose between the parted soldiers. Atop the mount is a burning man, garbed in all black armor including a helm covering his entire face. He stops his horse in front of Selentha, dismounts, and walks toward her. Without a word they turn and start walking silently into the fortress followed by the War Stack.

"I have instructed my council to set up temporary barracks for your people right outside the fortress walls," says Drak'thonn as the two walk toward the Skeed Towers.

"That will be acceptable."

"When we get to the towers, your contingency will not be permitted inside," he says in reference to the War Stack following closely behind.

"That won't be a problem," replies Selentha as she turns around and issues an order in the language of the dreggans. Her War Stack hesitates and then turns and heads back toward the main gate. She turns to her companion. "They are joining the others outside the fortress."

Drak'thonn nods. The two continue the short walk in silence.

Selentha lets her eyes wander as she walks arm in arm with Drak'thonn. The buildings are all dark as night with pit fires scattered throughout the entire fortress. The grey cloud covering is shimmering with electricity, shooting lightning across the morning sky. Although the sun just broke over the horizon, the area inside the fortress remains dark as dusk. To their left, a few dozen paces away, she spies orcs whipping little people who are obviously slaves. As she slows her pace, glancing to her left, Drak'thonn utters, "Dwarves. They are similar to humans but smaller in stature.

They are strong and make good slaves." Selentha nods her head in approval and they continue to the Skeed Towers.

Drak'thonn leads Selentha to his private library where he pours each of them a small glass of smeeka – "a thick, dark liquor that Drak'thonn has become partial to over the years. They spend some time discussing the council. Drak'thonn explains the chain of command and the different representatives of the many cultures. After finishing a second glass of smeeka and telling Selentha of their meeting of the high council tomorrow, Drak'thonn refills their glasses, takes the seat beside Selentha and starts to remove his helm.

Selentha looks at the deformed face of Drak'thonn with no emotion whatsoever in her eyes. He says, "If you are to be my wife and my queen there are certain things you must come to understand. As my warrior wife, you must understand my pain. As my warrior queen you must understand my motive." Drak'thonn paces in front of Selentha and continues, "If you are to accept these terms you will be changed forever. Your mind will be consumed with the same vengeance I deal with daily. The pain you will endure will be beyond your comprehension."

Selentha faces Drak'thonn and replies, "The Zagador have ordered me to come to you and aid you in your quest. I will endure what I must. I have no choice. As your warrior wife I will understand your pain. As your warrior queen I will understand your motive."

"Very well," replies Drak'thonn as he gestures for Selentha to follow him. They descend a winding stone staircase leading down from the main floor to the recesses below. The two enter a circular room with a single candle burning on a dais in an otherwise empty room.

Drak'thonn leads Selentha directly in front of the candle and they sit down facing each other. Drak'thonn says, "I am going to put your hands in mine. Fear not: They will not burn. We will be entering a trancelike state where you are going to enter the deepest crevices of my mind and the Zagador will enlighten to you aspects of my life which will enable you to understand your role as warrior wife and warrior queen. Are you ready?"

Selentha extends her hands and places them in Drak'thonn's. She states, "I am ready." She closes her eyes. Within mere moments, she is already experiencing unbearable pain as she starts the journey into Drak'thonn's past.

Chapter 13

As Drak'thonn ran toward the forest outside of town, he glanced down at his bloody hands. His pace slowed as he reached the forest wall. He sat down cross-legged and started rubbing his hands together briskly. The feeling of exuberance he had felt while pummeling the helpless boy had changed completely the moment he'd realized he had just punched his brother in the face. Instead of dealing with the feelings, Drak'thonn had decided to escape from the situation and raced to the forest.

The person who had ripped him off his prey needed to be punished, and it was a blind right-hook that had landed on Ashcon's face and sent him tumbling to the ground. He'd felt a sense of euphoria as his fist connected with Ashcon's face. He could feel his twin brother's pain. It was the greatest feeling Drak'thonn had ever experienced.

It was as if many winters of pent-up rage from the jealousy he felt towards Ashcon was released in one vicious right hook.

Drak'thonn never apologized to his brother for hitting him and the incident was never brought up again. While Ashcon spent time studying books about honor and gods, Drak'thonn worked on honing his body. The rigorous training he put himself through would have killed a normal person of his age, but Drak'thonn had both the will power and the guidance to work through it.

It was soon after the snowball incident that Drak'thonn had his first encounter with the Zagador. They came to him in his dreams, always in different forms, but always with fire erupting from their bodies. They would show Drak'thonn visions of what could only be the future. They showed him pictures of his muscle-bound body with fire flying from his fingertips. These dreams occurred almost nightly from that day forward. It wasn't until Drak'thonn's fifteenth winter that the dreams changed his life forever.

Drak'thonn had constant visions of violence while he slept. He would see himself engulfed in flames, throwing balls of fire from his hands at helpless victims. He saw himself traversing a world of complete darkness and leaving fire in his path. He had dreams where the most beautiful women would throw themselves at him and he would have his way with them. But the true joy came after the sex when he would burn them alive using the fire from his hands as the instrument of death. The shocked expressions on the faces of bystanders watching the destruction thrilled Drak'thonn. The feeling he got while watching his brother's pathetic face look on in horror as Drak'thonn bathed himself in fire and brimstone was almost orgasmic. Right before rising from his slumber one fateful day, the Zagador entered his dreamlike state and took his hands into theirs. Drak'thonn started screaming from the pain until he woke himself. Covered in sweat, he looked down at his hands and with just a thought a flame arose from his right ring finger.

As he was approaching his sixteenth winter, Drak'thonn frequently left Seascape for days at a time to test out some of his newfound powers. One particular morning, when Drak'thonn was preparing for a short excursion to the forest, he noticed Ashcon following him. Drak'thonn killed a deer and then made a point to burn its head alive using only the fire from his hands to see his brother's reaction. While he sat back smiling, watching the rest of the carcass burn, he spied Ashcon, who was attempting to hide, holding his mouth to keep himself from throwing up. Drak'thonn spent the walk back to Seascape wondering how his twin brother could be so weak.

Over the winters, as Ashcon became the favorite of both his parents and the priest, Drak'thonn drifted farther and farther away. The jealousy he felt as a youngster festered in him until he ached with the desire to cause Ashcon pain for the many winters of living in his shadow. The right hook helped ease the pain a bit but created a powerful longing to do it again.

When Drak'thonn approached their house from the forest, he saw his brother talking to his father through the window and could tell from Ashcon's gestures that he was telling him about what he just witnessed. The younger brother could not fathom why his parents always favored the elder Ashcon, as he was so pathetic and weak. Ashcon exited the house and after glancing briefly in Drak'thonn's direction, made his way around to the stables. Drak'thonn walked into the house and stood in front of his father. Staring into his eyes, he asked, "Do you have anything to say, Father?"

His father paused before replying slowly, "No, Drak'thonn," and he lowered his eyes toward the floor.

Drak'thonn walked to his room, laughing mockingly along the way. As he approached his door, he took it by the handle and turned back toward his father. "You're a pathetic coward like your firstborn," he stated harshly as he entered his room and slammed the door behind him. From that moment on, Drak'thonn's dreams helped foster his feelings of jealousy toward his twin brother. The Zagador would impart to Drak'thonn visions of him destroying both his brother and Ashcon's beloved Star Gods with the power of fire.

The night before the boys' sixteenth birthday, Drak'thonn dreamt of a world of fire. There was fire on the ground, fire in the air, fireballs falling from the sky, and fire emanating from every pore in his being. Drak'thonn saw himself standing in front of a pool of flame with the Zagador surrounding it, all in forms of fire whelps. There were countless Zagador and baby dragons staring intently at Drak'thonn as his body, bathed in liquid fire, started to expand. His clothes burned off as his muscles bulged and he started growing, ten feet at a time. Within seconds, Drak'thonn was as tall as the largest skeem tree and the Zagador were all chanting the words, "chosen one." He glanced at the pool of fire in front of him and breathed in the power generated by the Zagador. The image of his brother suddenly appeared in the pool below and Drak'thonn roared with such force that the ground shook beneath him. There was a question posed in his mind by the Dark Gods, whispering, "Are you with us, chosen one?" In answer to the question, Drak'thonn raised his arms above his head and then launched balls of fire from his hands into the pool, obliterating the image of Ashcon. He rested his hands at his sides and started descending into the pool of fire to the raucous cheers of the Zagador.

The sight of Ashcon emerging from the Temple of the Stars repulsed Drak'thonn to no end. Ever since arriving on the temple grounds the day before, Drak'thonn had been fighting bouts of extreme nausea. Drak'thonn hugged his brother coldly, watched him head to the portal back to Seascape, and turned to face the temple.

Drak'thonn followed the high priestess over to the cistern to receive the goblet with the blood-red liquid to start the ceremony. He walked behind her as instructed and while sipping the nectar found himself heading downward into sand. His mind was completely at ease and his thoughts were on nothing but the power of fire as he noticed he was no longer in the sand but on a bed of liquid gold.

As the high priestess, hovering on top of Drak'thonn, reaching down with a leaf to place on Drak'thonn's tongue, he gazed up at her, wondering how his perception of power was so different from those like the priestess. The leaf dissolved on his tongue and visions of the skies appeared immediately before his eyes, with shooting stars bouncing in all directions, as if the vision was embedded on the inside of his eyelids. All Drak'thonn could think about was how much more powerful fire was. He imagined the scene in front of him with fireballs instead of stars.

He opened his eyes and found himself standing in front of the Pool of Shimmering Light with the high priestess floating in front of him. "It is time," Ka'alshene said, and floated backward making way for Drak'thonn to enter the pool. He stepped in and lay face up as instructed. He closed his eyes and his body submerged beneath the liquid.

Drak'thonn felt his mind being probed, and he fought off these feelings with all of his being. His body started lurching violently in the liquid which started to boil and turn black. As his entire body was in spasm, thrashing about, the temple began to descend into darkness. The picture of the sky covering the dome of the temple changed into balls of fire that started launching in all directions. Burning embers raining down from the roof destroyed the pillars surrounding the pool. Drak'thonn's body began to rise in its supine position, with his eyes still closed and fire dripping from him to the pool below.

Ka'alshene was praying fervently, hoping the Star Gods would intervene when Drak'thonn started to move into a standing position, hovering above the Pool of Shimmering Light. The high priestess stared, transfixed as his body started to become consumed by fire.

Drak'thonn opened his eyes to see the inside of the temple destroyed, with fire flying everywhere. He glanced down at his hands and saw that his entire body was consumed by flames. He flexed his hands and let out a scream of both pleasure and pain. He pointed his hand toward the cistern he had drunk from earlier and, with a slight grin, caused a stream of fire to erupt from his hand and consume the cistern, destroying it instantly.

With the temple burning, Drak'thonn made his way toward the exit, side-stepping the crying high priestess and emerging into the daylight transformed.

Drak'thonn awakens from his trance, opens his eyes, and sees Selentha rolled up in a ball on the ground in front of him. As he reaches for her, she looks up and he is stunned to see Selentha's skin is now the same burnt ash as his own. She has tears rolling down her cheeks as she reaches for Drak'thonn's face and slowly caresses his cheek. "I understand it all now, my love. We now share the pain and we share the burden."

Drak'thonn stands up proudly, reaching down for his future wife who is bravely dealing with the unbearable pain that will consume them both forever.

Chapter 14

"THIS Katrivus is slick, Talon," says Ashley as she pours herself a mug in the common room of the guild hall and prepares to give the thief her brief on the leader of the Pugs. She continues as she has a seat opposite Talon. "This morning he had four bodyguards and then after a quick meeting he's up to eight."

This makes Talon's eyes wrinkle as he contemplates the possibility of a spy in his house. "He's up before sunrise every day and leaves his home in the Loop to go to the guild house just as the businesses open up in the Emerald Center. He spends most of his morning alone in his library with two guards posted outside and the other six on shifts throughout the guild house. He takes his midday meal in the common room every day and sits alone. He has the leaders of each of his factions meet with him to discuss business. He retreats to his library for the rest of the afternoon. The only time he leaves again is closing time with his full guard contingency with him."

Talon sits in silence a moment before responding. "Tell me about his bodyguards."

"The four he started with have been with him since he started the Pugs. Two of them have a reputation of being consummate professionals and all of them are trained in hand-to-hand combat. It is believed there are no magic users amongst his guards; however, less is known of the four new ones. They have the look of mercenaries from the southern dessert."

This doesn't please Talon, as the nomads of the southern dessert are known to be merciless and absolutely faithful to those who pay them. He sighs audibly as he reclines in his chair, trying to figure out the best way to assassinate the young Katrivus. "Thank you, Ashley," he says dismissing her.

Talon is finishing off his first tankard of ale when Thorn walks in and takes the seat previously occupied by Ashley. The look on Thorn's face doesn't make Talon very happy as the spy dictates his latest findings.

"It's worse than we thought," starts Thorn. "Not only are the rumors true that the barbarians will only deal with Katrivus, but it's not a blood pact, Talon." Talon is at attention. "It's a death pact!"

Talon, speechless at this new bit of information, stares at Thorn. "You're kidding me," he replies.

"It's true," continues Thorn. "He has a working treaty with all three of the major barbarian villages on the coast and all three are part of the pact."

"That's quite a feat. I've never heard of barbarian tribes working together. Do you have the details of the pact?"

"I do," says Thorn as he fills a tankard. "Katrivus provided the high shamans of the three tribes a vial of his blood. They tested it true when he provided it and have kept it preserved over the winters. Each day, the high shamans test the blood of Katrivus. If the blood signature has changed in any way whatsoever, the barbarians will follow through with the death pact. They will immediately confiscate every ship in the Pugs fleet and any member of the Pugs unlucky enough to be on board will be killed."

"That seems to keep Katrivus safe from his fellow Pugs," replies Talon, "but how is that a deterrent to anyone on the outside?"

"The death pact also calls for a complete freeze on all trade routes from the barbarian lands for a period of two hundred winters," replies Thorn solemnly.

"He is smart," Talon replies. "Thank you, Thorn." He gets up and walks to his private quarters to digest this new information.

As Talon is lying on his bed staring at the ceiling, he has to decide on his next course of action. If he is to kill Katrivus, then the Guild of Slight is giving up on the trade routes with the barbarians. If what he has heard is the truth, the death of Katrivus will change his blood signature and the death pact will be implemented. If the blood of Katrivus even shows deception the death pact will be implemented. He smiles to himself thinking of just how smart this Katrivus is. He made sure that his own people can't kill him or they will die. He also had the barbarians agree to not deal with anyone else for two hundred winters upon his demise, making it impossible for anyone to take over his operation by force. Talon hops out of bed and walks purposefully toward Trey's private chambers.

After summarizing the information for Trey, Talon sits patiently as Trey paces back and forth, absorbing all he just heard. "So it comes down to this," starts Trey as he continues his aimless walking. "If we kill Katrivus we can destroy the Pugs, correct?"

"Absolutely," responds Talon. "With Katrivus gone it would be a matter of time before we completely obliterate them, and the barbarians will be doing some of the dirty work for us."

"Is it safe to assume that the barbarians will stick to the provisions of their death pact and halt all trade?" asks Trey.

"Without a doubt," replies Talon. "If they go through with any aspect of the death pact, they will go through with all of it. They are a spiritual society and the high shamans who made the pact will never allow any provisions of it to be broken. That would be a sign of weakness and since there are three tribes involved, none would dare break it."

"How much revenue are the Pugs taking in from the trade routes?"

Talon expected this question and put the startling figure to parchment before the meeting. He stands up and hands it to Trey. "This is a conservative estimate."

Trey looks down at the figure and with no expression at all, crumples the paper and tosses it into the fireplace. He stares at the fire for minutes on end without speaking before looking up at Talon and rising from his chair. "Walk with me. I have decided on a course of action." With that, Talon walks with Trey to the common room. Trey clears out the room, pours two mugs of ale, sits beside Talon, and quietly reveals his plans.

Chapter 15

"WE should reach Stagg by late evening," says Ashcon, riding at the front of the single file line of three. The days after leaving Crawkford were cold and wet and the ground had a constant thin white snow covering to it. It made it hard for them to cover their tracks, but on more than one occasion it kept them from running into others while on the road. Although they didn't have an overwhelming fear of being followed, years of being on the move through Arstevia led to prudence while travelling. They spent the days and nights in relative quiet with Skken usually scouting ahead for any trouble. Sapphyre's weapons training continued.

As Skken is teaching Sapphyre how to conceal her dagger properly, the trio approaches Stagg. The little village could have been mistaken for Crawkford, as it is laid out in a similar fashion, complete with the bridge leading to the northern part of the town. Upon closer inspection, Sapphyre sees that this was a town of herders, not farmers. There are young men tending to sheep and pigs, preparing them for the evening. The homes here have distinct large signs with the names of the homeowners on signs above the front doors. Sapphyre is reading one of the signs, thinking that Homespun is a strange name, when she finds herself outside the stable at the Slaughtered Boar.

The inside of the Slaughtered Boar is downright filthy. There are two people sleeping at the far table, empty glasses strewn about on the ground, and no other patrons about. A fat dwarf is behind the bar scrubbing some dirty mugs and eyeing the three strangers warily. Ashcon leads the three to the bar where seven empty stools sat facing the dwarf.

"Kendra first," says Horace as he walks to face off in front of Ashcon.

Ashcon reaches into his purse and drops a few coins onto the bar. "I hear the mead here is worth the travels," he says as the bartender snatches up the kendra and places three empty mugs on the bar.

"It is," replies the dwarf, looking at Ashcon awaiting his order.

Ashcon says slowly, "I have just journeyed from the far reaches of Glumby and can use a tankard."

Horace angles his head up toward Ashcon's face, starts pouring the mead from a ceramic pitcher, and acknowledges his remark with a slight nod. He glances from Ashcon to Skken and finally to Sapphyre and says, "I have a room for you if you so require. There's no food left tonight so after you drink you get some rest. Upon breaking the fast tomorrow you can tell me of the happenings in Glumby." He then walks to the end of the bar and reaches into a drawer and withdraws a key. He tosses it to Ashcon and says, "I retire shortly, which means you do too."

The three arise before first light the next morning and proceed to pack their belongings and meet Horace in the common room for breaking the fast. Sapphyre gasps as she enters a common room that is meticulously clean. There are white table cloths on all the tables and the filth from the evening before is nowhere to be found. As they walk into the common room, Horace greets them and walks them to a table in the corner.

"I take pride in my restaurant. Don't much care for the night life part of it," says Horace, in an attempt to explain the transformation between night and day. The three just nod in response. "So old Alwin sent you to visit, eh?"

Ashcon smiles and holds his hand out, "Name is Storn." Ashcon lies. "And as Alwin said, your mead is excellent." Horace takes his hand and shakes it with vigor. "Thank you, thank you. I do take pride in my mead as well as my restaurant. And a friend of Alwin's is a friend of mine." Horace takes a seat beside Sapphyre, across from Ashcon, and motions for a serving girl to bring food for the table.

Sapphyre has never seen a proprietor actually sit down and eat with patrons, so watching Horace devour eggs and bacon at the same table as hers throws her for a loop. He talks a lot and doesn't hesitate when he has a mouthful of food.

"So these Pugs are starting to really become a pain in the ass as of late," continues Horace, as the trio hopes they will learn some new information from him. They hear everything that Alwin imparted to them.

Ashcon decides to intervene, "So Horace, we've heard a lot about these Pugs but we need some real information." He then leans in so his face is inches from Horace's and continues whispering, "Alwin says you're connected and you know all there is to know with regards to the guild. Tell me something we don't know." Sapphyre notices that while Ashcon is whispering to Horace, a light red glow sparkles from the left side of Ashcon's chest. When Horace reclines in his chair, the rune fades. All of a sudden, Horace starts talking quickly and purposefully, revealing new information, some of which is pertinent, other bits and pieces of which are not. Sapphyre wonders whether it was the activation of his rune or Ashcon's plying of the man's vanity which led to this divulgence.

While Horace is rambling on about his own re-sponsibilities within the guild, Ashcon interrupts and turns the conversation toward the Pugs. "Are the Pugs and the Guild going to go to war?"

Horace starts laughing and after lighting up a smoke replies, "Not a chance. We'd never let that happen. There's only two choices regarding the Pugs and that's to kill Katrivus or kill them all. We can do either without a war. There was a meeting not too long ago to decide which option to take and no one outside the board knows how that meeting turned out."

Ashcon turns to Sapphyre, who has a solemn look on her face. Ashcon asks Horace, "If one wanted to meet with Katrivus to provide passage on a ship, where does one go?"

Horace looks at Ashcon and replies, "Down in Dock Bay there's a chap named Irok. He's your first point of contact, and if you're looking for passage you speak to him." He takes a long drag and continues, "You'll never get to see Katrivus. The guy doesn't talk to strangers. And you'll pay big for passage. Real big."

Ashcon stands up abruptly and his two companions do the same. He reaches for a handful of kendra and gives them to the greedy hand of Horace. "We must leave at once. Thank you for your hospitality and when I'm back in Crawkford I'll send your regards to Alwin," says Ashcon as the three hurry to the stable to get on their horses and continue their journey.

"I want to make Thorenn before all hell breaks loose between the Pugs and the Guild and it looks as if we're running short on time," Ashcon says in regard to their quick departure. Sapphyre is riding along in silence with her head down when Ashcon decides it is time to breach the subject.

"Sapphyre," says Ashcon softly as she turns toward him, "is there anything you wish to tell us?"

Sapphyre's eyes start to swell with tears as she looks back and forth from Ashcon to Skken. She then breaks down and starts crying as the three slow down the horses and prepare a small camp for a midday meal. Around the cooking fire, Sapphyre entrusts to Ashcon and Skken the truth of her younger days. She tells them both of how she spent many winters as a member of the Pugs and learned the tricks of the trade from Katrivus. Instead of telling them the truth about the woman and the feathers, she simply tells the duo that she felt it was time for change and she gathered her belongings and travelled west until she settled down in Tondor.

As they continue the journey eastward, Sapphyre continues to tell Ashcon and Skken about her life with Katrivus and the Pugs and the two gain a small amount of adoration for the ingenuity of the young man whom they have yet to meet. She even tells them of how she acquired Frostripper and realizes it's the first time she has revealed much of herself to anyone. "Would Katrivus agree to a meeting with you Sapphyre?" inquires Skken.

"I would think so," replies Sapphyre, "although it has been a few winters and its obvious things have changed. I can't see him refusing to see me."

"Then we go to this Irok fellow when we arrive in Thorenn and have him arrange a meeting," says Ashcon. Sapphyre nods to Ashcon and the three companions continue toward the capital.

Chapter 16

"Sit down," orders Talon to a stunned Katrivus as the leader of the Pugs enters his library sanctuary only to see a stranger aiming a short crossbow at his heart from less than three feet away. As Katrivus is assessing the situation, Talon continues, "If I wanted you dead you'd be dead already, Katrivus, so please have a seat. We need to talk."

Katrivus starts walking around his large oak desk toward his oversized chair when Talon stops him and directs him to one of the two simple chairs directly in front of the two thieves. Katrivus sits down warily and asks, "How did you get in here?"

"We'll get to that," replies Talon with the weapon still aimed at the center of Kat's chest, backing his chair away to a safe distance before taking a seat himself. "How long did you think you could go on doing what you're doing without the Guild of Slight taking action?" Talon asks rhetorically. "We've been in this business for quite a long time, as you know, and this is the first time that the action being taken isn't the total destruction of your organization and the death of you and everyone you care about." Talon pauses for a reaction, but getting none, continues. "That is a tribute to the business you've put together and, in particular, you."

He decides to push the situation a little bit and show Katrivus just how deep the Guild of Slight's influence goes. He rises for effect and, pacing in front of Katrivus, starts to relay some information. "As of today, Dockhelm Lumber has declared all contracts with you and the Pugs null and void. You will not be able to get your ships to expand to those routes to Sloan." This time Katrivus can't hide the surprise on his face and Talon chuckles a bit and continues. "I see I've finally gotten your attention. As we speak, the Imperial Navy is on its way to Cornice and Flotine to take control of the islands, arrest everyone they don't kill and confiscate anything they find. This will all transpire within the next twenty-four hours unless we come to an arrangement."

Talon sits down opposite Katrivus, looks him straight in the eye, and says, "Now I'll answer some of your questions, perhaps."

Katrivus is visibly shaken, contemplating this turn of events that could conceivably destroy all he has worked for. "How did you get in here?" he asks.

"That's what you want to know?" mocks Talon. "Out of all the questions you could be asking, I'm quite alarmed that's the one you asked first. Well, then again, I guess one's own safety and survival is an instinct that we all possess and since this is your fortress of solitude you want to know how it was breached. Sorry, but that one will have to wait. Why, instead, don't you ask me how we know every last detail about your death pact with the three largest tribes of the barbarians of the north?"

"You can't possibly –" says a truly surprised Katrivus before Talon rises out of his chair and interrupts him.

"You have no possible conception of what we can accomplish, Katrivus. The Guild of Slight has been around for centuries but you know that since you admire our ingenuity. At least you used to."

Katrivus puts his head in his hands and asks quietly, "Why am I still alive?"

"A much better question!" says Talon with enthusiasm. "You are alive because we like kendra, Katrivus, just like you. You were marked for assassination and I was the one assigned to take you out, but we decided instead to see if we might come to an accommodation."

"What type of accommodation?"

"One that you simply have no choice but to accept. It was quite ingenious the way you dealt with the barbarians in working out the details of your death pact. You protected yourself from your fellow Pugs by threatening them with death if anyone decided to try and take over the operation by taking you out. And to have the barbarians halt trade for two centuries was masterful."

"Thank you."

"You're welcome. But the one thing you didn't take into account was this. The Guild of Slight has been running operations and making tons of kendra for hundreds of winters without trading with the barbarians. We can kill you and continue making tons of kendra and not have to worry about some other organization gaining power and prestige through trade, as you have done.

Ironically, you've made that possible for us with your death pact."

"I see," replies Katrivus. "But you obviously have something else in mind or I would not be hearing any of this. I'd be dead."

"I knew you were a bright one, Katrivus," says Talon. "We've been monitoring your progress ever since the Steele Monthall heist. We even made sure that a ship would become available to you for a nice price so you could start your little trade experiment. Please, don't be surprised," Talon says in response to the look on Kat's face. "We have the largest spy ring on the continent so don't you think we infiltrated your organization?"

Talon pulled two long cigars from his shirt pocket and offers one to Katrivus, who declines. He lights the cigar, takes a few quick tokes, and continues. "We have tried unsuccessfully for many winters to work out a trade agreement with the barbarians of the north. For reasons unbeknownst to us they refused any offer we came up with. One day you'll have to tell me how you convinced them to do business with you."

As Katrivus is digesting this information, he realizes that one of two things will happen today. He will become a member of the Guild of Slight or he will end up dead. "What is your name?" asks Katrivus, buying time to assess his next move.

"Talon" he replies, watching Katrivus to see if his name elicits any reaction.

"I expected a man of your reputation to be a bit more – experienced," replies Katrivus.

"Let's cut to the chase, shall we?" Katrivus nods as Talon continues. "Trey would like to meet with you and I'm to escort you to see him immediately." He then rises and signals for Katrivus to do the same. "We're going to leave out the front door and you're going to tell your men to stay put. I have no more need for this, I assume," he continues as he slips the crossbow into his cloak.

As the two thieves are walking the streets of Dock Bay toward Skid Way, Katrivus has to constantly hold his hand up to ward off members of the Pugs who are curious as to why the leader of their group is without bodyguards in the company of a member of the Guild of Slight. Talon is slightly amused by this but at the same time is surprised by just how many people Katrivus has to signal. Talon also knows that there are at least six people following them and monitoring their movements; three are his people and he can only assume that the other three are Pugs. The streets narrow as they leave the area of Dock Bay, and Katrivus is surprised when they take a turn that leads away from the Slight's guild house. Talon notices the look on Kat's face and says, "Until we decide your fate we're going nowhere near the guild house. We haven't killed anyone on guild property in quite a while."

As the two round the latest corner and it dawns on Katrivus where the meeting is going to take place, he realizes he greatly underestimated the reach of the Guild of Slight. Talon can only guess as to what's going through Kat's mind as he steps up to the doors of the Black Pearl Tavern where they are opened from within. Talon steps inside, followed by Katrivus who glances at the proprietor. The man simply nods to him and disappears behind the bar. The inside is empty except for Trey, who is sitting by the fire with three empty tankards and a ceramic pitcher on the table.

"I thought this would be a suitable place for this meeting," the leader of the Guild of Slight says as the two approach. "Does it remind you of your younger days, Katrivus?"

"It certainly brings back memories," replies Katrivus, trying his best to hide his emotions.

"Please sit down," Trey says as he pours each of them a tankard of ale. "I know Talon has debriefed you on the current situation and now we must decide on the next course of action. You undoubtedly realize that you will either die here, where you first got started, or we will come to an accommodation."

Katrivus nods affirmatively.

"Good. We obviously feel you would be an asset to our organization or you would already be a corpse. You now know that we've been monitoring you from the beginning and we could have killed you at any time. You'll never know how many times you were close to being exterminated. We decided to kill you and make off with all the goods from the Steele Monthall heist, but once we saw you were attempting to get a ship to work out a trade deal with the barbarians, we decided to keep you around to see how you would do. If you were unsuccessful in your attempt to solidify a trade deal, you would have been killed as you would have been of no use to us."

Katrivus just listens intently, sipping his ale, wondering how much of his power and money he will have to give up in order to continue living.

"You will turn over all of your operations to the Guild and disband the Pugs immediately. You will continue serving as liaison to the Barbarians of the North, and we will work together to secure the routes to the west as you planned." Trey pauses as he sees Katrivus turning his head from side to side, indicating he would not be willing to do as he wishes.

"I would rather die than give up all I have worked for," says Katrivus.

"That could be arranged," Trey replies as he sneers at Katrivus.

"I'm sure we can come to some type of arrangement," Talon intervenes.

"Of course, we will make you a member of the Board of Slight and you will reap the profits that the position affords," continues Trey. "This will make you an even richer man, Katrivus. As a member of the board, you will get an equal percentage of the profits from all of the Guild's endeavors, and you will have a vote on the board."

Katrivus takes a sip of his ale, reclines in his chair, and carefully prepares his response. "I appreciate the generosity; however, the Pugs have a certain reputation I have solidified over the years and I'm not willing to give that all up. I propose a different type of relationship."

Trey shows no emotion as Katrivus continues. "Allow me to continue running the Pugs' operations, and we will share our profits with the Guild of Slight. We ask for nothing in return but that you allow us to continue our endeavors unimpeded. This will enable me to save face within my organization and you will gain significant income from the trade with the barbarians."

Talon looks at Trey and he nods to the young man. Talon immediately withdraws a dagger from his waist, slides behind Katrivus, whips his head back and positions the blade upon his neck for a killing strike. Trey stands up and moves directly in front of Katrivus. "I cannot allow the Pugs to exist after today and that is not up for debate. If that is out of the question then just tell me so we can slice off your head and end this now."

"I understand," replies Katrivus, and Trey signals to Talon who removes the knife from Kat's neck. Katrivus realizes that he will have to make many concessions, but he still holds a fair amount of bargaining leverage because of his death pact with the barbarians. "I have certain demands and

– kill me if you must – but I suggest you hear me out," says Katrivus boldly.

Trey nods to Katrivus and he continues. "There is one person whom I trust implicitly, and he will also gain a position on the board." Trey shows no emotion so Katrivus continues, "I know a bit about how your operation is set up. Talon here is the leader of the thieves. Thorn runs the spy ring. Nitios handles all of your political contacts. As a member of the board, I will be in charge of the trade for the Guild." Katrivus holds his breath awaiting a response from Trey.

Trey stares down the brazen Katrivus while deciding how to phrase his answer. It was his plan all along to have Kat continue as the liaison with the barbarians but if he can permit him to believe he won this concession, then all the better. "Fargo can have a position on the board," replies Trey, mentioning him by name to show Katrivus that nothing gets by him. "You will run the trade for the Guild; however, all decisions on expansion and changes will be voted on by the board. Furthermore, Talon will be giving up his role as leader of the thieves to work with you and the Barbarians. I know Fargo's reputation and he will take over the as the head of the thieves of the

Guild. It is more important to me to have Talon working with you to secure trade routes to the west and working on expanding the operation."

Katrivus nods in response.

Trey continues. "You will burn down your guild house in Dock Bay as a signal that the Pugs are no more. You may choose ten members of the Pugs to be absorbed as members of the Guild. All the others will become freelancers, whom we will pay handsomely to continue working with us. You will move into the guild house tonight, as will Fargo. Once we have fully integrated your operation into ours, you will make a trip to the north with Talon to make introductions to the barbarians and fill them in on the changes."

Trey stands up indicating that the meeting is over and Talon and Katrivus rise as well. Trey removes a dagger from his waist and, gripping it in his right hand, makes a small incision on his left palm beneath his middle finger drawing blood. Katrivus withdraws a dagger from its sheath and imitates the cut on his left palm. The two then clamp their left hands together, sealing the agreement in the tradition of thieves.

Chapter 17

Four days later, Ashcon, Skken, and Sapphyre enter the Emerald Center without incident through the lower west gates. It is rather close to midnight, so the three decide to find accommodations and tend to business first thing in the morning.

"I know many places we can spend the night," says Ashcon. Glancing at Sapphyre, he continues. "Is there a place we can go where you can gain some information before retiring?"

"There's a tavern in Skid Way and the proprietor there may be able to help," replies Sapphyre.

"Lead the way."

The Emerald Center is connected to Skid Way and the three head directly to the Black Pearl Tavern, with Skken making sure any thieves are not pursuing them. The fire is still roaring in the hearth as the trio enters the bar after taking care of the horses out back. The proprietor gives them a sideways glance and, to Sapphyre's dismay, there is no look of recognition on old Thomm's face. Ashcon leads them to a table by the fire, away from the other four patrons who pay them no heed.

Thomm walks over and states rather abruptly, "We have ale and mead. There is some leftover elk stew and the bread is only four days old. What will it be?"

"Three bowls of stew and three pints of ale," replies Ashcon as he hands six coins into the outstretched palm of Thomm.

"Do you know him?" asks Ashcon of Sapphyre.

"His name is Thomm and he owns the place. He obviously doesn't remember me, but then again my appearance has changed significantly since I saw him last. The Pugs started out in his basement and I lived here for a number of winters before we moved to Dock Bay. After we eat I'll talk to him," replies Sapphyre.

Thomm sets down the ale, and Ashcon and Skken reach for their mugs. Sapphyre asks Thomm, "Can you please bring one small loaf of bread with the stew, sir?"

Thomm grumbles, "Aye," in return and heads off to the kitchen.

The other four patrons all depart while the three enjoy their meal, giving Sapphyre the opportunity to approach Thomm.

"You don't remember me, Thomm," says Sapphyre as she sits on one of the bar stools. "It has been a number of winters."

Thomm leans over the bar and stares intently into Sapphyre's blue eyes. "I don't know you, girl. State your business or be gone."

"It's Sapphyre, Thomm," she says and lays her hand upon Thomm's on the bar. As he is scrutinizing her, she continues, "I know I look different, but it is me." She starts walking along the bar brushing her hand across the bronze rail, and then pointing says, "You used to let me read in the corner over there when no one else was around."

Sapphyre spins back toward Thomm and he walks around the bar to where she is standing and looking down says, "What's the name of the story you used to read to my granddaughter, Bess?"

"Hogun the Dragon," Sapphyre replies, meeting his eyes.

"Well by the Gods, come here, girl!" says Thomm as he puts Sapphyre in a friendly bear hug. He sits on the bar stool in front of her and says, "You've been gone a long time. Have the times been good to you?"

"They have, Thomm. I'm afraid this will be a short visit, a few days at most. My friends and I are just passing through and I was hoping you would have a room available for us."

"But of course, Sapphyre," says Thomm as he walks back around the bar to retrieve a room key.

"How is Bess?" asks Sapphyre.

"She is a good, spunky little girl. She's off to the south and it's too bad. I'm sure she would have enjoyed seeing you."

"Another time perhaps," says Sapphyre. "Have you heard from Katrivus?"

"He is alive for one, and that's a good thing considering," starts Thomm.

"Considering?"

"There was a lot of friction between the Pugs and the Slight." Thomm lowers his voice, and brings his face closer to Sapphyre's. "Trey, the leader of the Guild of Slight, met with Katrivus right here just the other night. I didn't hear anything but I did see them do the thieves embrace before they left."

"I'd like my friends to hear this if you don't mind" interrupts Sapphyre.

Thomm grabs Sapphyre by the shoulder. "You can tell them what you want but I'm not talking to anyone I don't know. No offense."

Sapphyre nods and Thomm continues, "Katrivus burned down the guild house in Dock Bay in broad daylight. He and Fargo moved into the Slight guild house. Business has been continuing without any major interruptions and it's been pretty peaceful."

Sapphyre'es mouth drops agape. She sits staring at Thomm in stunned silence for a long moment before blurting out rhetorically, "So Katrivus is now a member of the Guild of Slight?"

"The Pugs are no more," says Thomm with a hint of remorse in his voice.

Sapphyre gives Thomm a brief hug and returns to her table to give Ashcon and Skken a summary of her conversation.

"So if Katrivus is a member of the Guild of Slight, how does this change our plan to find out where Sorenthor resides?" asks Skken.

"I'm not sure it does," says Ashcon. "However, if he's not running the shipping routes it may be more difficult for us to obtain passage."

"It doesn't change our objectives, gentlemen," says Sapphyre with authority as she stands up. "I suggest we retire and get a good night's rest. In the morning I will get us an audience with Katrivus."

Ashcon glances sideways at Skken with his eyebrows lifted in mock surprise and says, "Apparently it's time to retire." The two men get out of their chairs and follow Sapphyre toward their room.

Chapter 18

"I DIDN'T know you could read, Sapphyre," says Ashcon as he's buttering up a biscuit at the breakfast table.

"I didn't know you were eavesdropping on my conversation, Ashcon," she replies.

"Hold on," interjects Skken, "I heard it as well, Sapphyre. You didn't lower your voices until you brought up Katrivus."

"Katrivus taught me to read and write."

"I'm very interested in meeting this young man," says Ashcon.

"I'm going to bid a good morning to Thomm and then we leave to see Horace's contact, Irok," says Sapphyre as she gets up off the bench.

"She is much more confident than when we first met her, eh, Skken?" asks Aschon.

"Aye," he replies.

Skken takes up his role as lookout and lead as the three head to Dock Bay. Sapphyre pauses briefly when passing the old guild house, which is just a pile of burnt rubble. As they approach the docks, they notice workers unloading goods from a recently arrived ship and others standing around hoping for work. They pause at the entrance to the docks and are still looking around when Skken approaches a worker and says simply, "Irok?"

The worker points to a husky dwarf with a long red beard sitting on a brown stool looking nowhere in particular, pipe in hand. Skken leads the way to the dwarf and is about to open his mouth when Sapphyre grabs his arm and steps in front of him to address their quarry.

"Irok, my name is Sapphyre, and Horace from Stagg thought you may be able to assist us."

Irok glances up from his chair at Sapphyre and then turns to the yellow-eyed stranger and his barbarian like companion. "I know no Horace," he says and returns his eyes to the pipe he is stuffing.

Ashcon steps forward and addresses the dwarf. "We require a meeting with Katrivus."

"Katrivus doesn't meet with strangers. State your business."

Sapphyre reaches forward and grabs Ashcon by the arm, pulling him back gently, moving forward to talk to Horace. "I am a friend of Katrivus, although I haven't seen him for many winters. Would there be any harm in passing a message along to him?" she asks as she reaches into her purse.

Horace looks greedily to her small hands and replies, "I suppose I could pass along a message if I happen to bump into him."

Sapphyre nods and drops a few coins into his dirty, outstretched hand. She then retrieves her dagger from her boot and shows it to Irok, whose eyes grow wide. "Describe this dagger to Katrivus. Tell him that Sapphyre needs to see him tonight. He will ask you to describe me and you will tell him I no longer look like the girl he knew. Tell him to meet me where and when we first met. That is all." She turns around and walks away and Ashcon and Skken follow.

"Nicely done," says Ashcon. "Where is it that we are meeting him?"

"I am going alone to meet with him initially. After I have spoken with him I will bring him to you."

"When?"

"Tonight at midnight," replies Sapphyre.

"Very well," says Ashcon. "There are some people I need to see. Why don't we –"

Sapphyre interrupts, "I have some things I would like to do as well. Why don't you take care of your business and we will meet up later?"

"We will meet back at the tavern for the evening meal then," says Ashcon.

Sapphyre is strolling through the Emerald Center as the shops are all opening for the morning rush, enjoying the sights and smells of the old city. She has a tiny grin on her face until she recognizes an old shopkeeper with a scar on his face dragging a bag into his store. Her smile fades as she reflects back on the morning Katrivus saved her from the clutches of Floren. As she is watching the old man lug the bundle into his shop, she comes to the realization that if not for this man and that incident, she would not be the person she is today. Joining the Pugs was in direct response to being saved by Kat and the boys with the clubs.

She walks into the shop and glances around the shelves at the various ceramic pitchers and trays. Floren looks up at her briefly and then goes about his business behind the small counter. Sapphyre feels a tinge of remorse for the scar on the man's face and reaches into her pocket, clutching three of the thickest coins, which is probably more kendra than Floren makes in a moonsign. While appearing to examine a rather large yellow vase, she slips the kendra behind it as she places it back upon the shelf. She then turns to Floren, flashes him a brief smile, and exits the store.

The Black Pearl Tavern is much busier during the evening meal and every table is occupied. Ashcon and Skken are sipping on mead as they await Sapphyre for supper and to discuss the evening plans. A few heads turn as Sapphyre waltzes into the tavern with her head held high and a small smile on her face. She takes a seat next to Skken just as Thomm skates over with a small glass filled with a chilled plum wine and places it in front of Sapphyre and says, "Your favorite."

"Thank you, Thomm," she replies as she brings the glass to her lips.

"If you're hungry I'll have the girl bring over some of the fresh stoop fish and bread."

"Please do," says Ashcon and Thomm nods politely and retreats behind the bar.

Sapphyre takes another sip of her wine, places the glass down, and says, "I will be meeting Katrivus tonight in the Emerald Center."

"Is it safe for you to go alone, Sapphyre?" asks Ashcon. "Skken can follow in the shadows and no one would know he's there."

"I need –" says Sapphyre as she turns to Ashcon and corrects herself. "No, we need Katrivus to trust us. Plus he has no reason to harm me." She looks from Ashcon to Skken and continues. "I'll talk to him and I will get him to come back to the tavern."

"What if he refuses to come?" inquires Skken.

"He won't. I expect we should return here before two strokes after midnight," says Sapphyre as she clears the spot in front of her for the food being delivered.

In between bites of the grilled fish, Sapphyre looks across at Ashcon and says, "I'll speak with Thomm and make sure we're the only ones here when I return with Kat."

They both nod affirmatively in response.

Sapphyre excuses herself from the table and, turning to retreat to the room says, "I'll be taking a bath, gentlemen, so please occupy yourselves elsewhere."

Chapter 19

SAPPHYRE is looking in the mirror, deciding between the black scarf with the eagles that matches the tight black knit pants or the beige scarf that has the same design as the button-down blouse. She makes sure Frostripper is secure in its sheath within her boot, takes one last glance in the mirror, wraps the black scarf around her long blonde hair, and exits the room.

"I'll see you two shortly," says Sapphyre, gesturing toward Ashcon and Skken at the bar. "Don't follow," she continues, waving to the men and leaving through the front doors.

Sapphyre, planning on being early, takes the route she used to take when she was a much younger girl. She picks up her step as she approaches her sanctuary from so many winters ago. Sapphyre hesitates briefly as her left foot steps up onto the ladder she has braved so many times before. As her head peeks over the railing, she pauses while surveying the top of the building. Seeing no one, she steps on and turns in a circle taking in the view of the city before resting her eyes on the Imperial Palace. She is admiring the beauty as she has so many times in her young life when a voice interrupts her.

"Turn around slowly," says a man from behind her.

Sapphyre holds her hands by her sides, palms outward, and turns toward the voice. She sees the shadow of a man standing at least ten feet away, wearing a hooded cape making it impossible to identify him. "Is that you, Katrivus?" asks Sapphyre.

Without responding, the young man walks toward Sapphyre and stops two feet in front of her. He pulls his hood back, revealing long black hair and a distinctive scar beneath his left eye. Sapphyre smiles in recognition and tears well up in her eyes as she says, "It is you."

"You look different," Katrivus says as he cocks his head, looking at Sapphyre who is nodding in agreement. "Yet I knew it was you as soon as you turned around," he says as he steps toward her and the two embrace as her scarf falls away.

With her head resting on his shoulders and tears streaming down her face, she says through shallow breaths, "I'm sorry I left without saying goodbye."

Katrivus rubs his hand through Sapphyre's hair and replies, "I am sure you had your reasons." He then takes her hand and leads her to the east side of the roof and they sit facing the city. "You obviously have a story to tell," continues Katrivus while outlining the blue streak in her hair with his hand.

"The day I left I had a vision and my appearance changed," starts Sapphyre, sitting cross legged with her head bowed slightly toward her chest. "Through this vision I knew I had to leave and head west. You had just left on the new ship, and I couldn't wait weeks for you to return."

"I know Sapphyre," replies Katrivus. He reaches to Sapphyre's chin and lifts it gently with his first finger. He twists her to face him and says, "You explained as much in your letter and I hold no remorse. Tell me what has happened since you left on your journey west and why you're back here now."

Sapphyre then proceeds to tell Katrivus almost everything that has transpired over the last few winters. She explains to him how she was able to get onto a military caravan on tax patrol heading west and settled down in Tondor. She left nothing out except for a few things about her current companions and their quest. She trusts Katrivus but saw no reason to test his faith with regard to runestars.

As she's finishing up her story, she leans in to Katrivus and says, "So will you meet my friends and see if you can help us locate this person?"

Katrivus stretches his arms and starts to stand up and says, "It sounds like they are trustworthy from what you have said of them, so I don't see why not."

Sapphyre jumps to her feet and walking to the ladder says, "Thank you, Kat. They are waiting for us now at the Black Pearl."

Katrivus chuckles and then follows Sapphyre down the ladder and the two walk side by side in relative silence back to the Black Pearl Tavern. They enter to see Thomm behind the bar and Ashcon and Skken seated at their new favorite table by the fire. Katrivus nods to Thomm who waves in response and Sapphyre leads them over to the table.

Ashcon and Skken both stand up as the two approach and Sapphyre handles the introductions. "Ashcon, Skken, this is Katrivus," and she stays back while Kat moves forward to greet the two men. They nod politely to each other and Katrivus sits down beside Sapphyre across from the two strangers.

"Sapphyre speaks very highly of you," says Ashcon.

"And of both of you," replies Katrivus who moves slightly to the right to allow Thomm to put a pitcher of ale on the table.

"You're alone," Thomm tells them as he distributes four mugs. "I'm off to bed so if you want more, you're gonna have to help yourselves."

"You look like you're of the Hanta or maybe Shinto, Skken. Am I right?" asks Katrivus as he sips his ale.

"The Hanta. A long time ago, yes," replies Skken. "You have a good eye."

"When I started my business up north I made it a priority to learn of the different peoples and tribes. If I remember correctly this means you're from the region in the far northeast, beyond Starrk."

"And a good memory as well, it appears," replies Skken.

"As I'm sure Sapphyre told you," says Ashcon sitting upright, "we are going to need passage on one of your ships to the northern lands. We will pay of course."

"She mentioned you weren't exactly sure of where you needed to go as of yet, and you were searching for a particular person," replies Katrivus.

"This is true. We are searching for a man named Sorenthor who resides somewhere north of the Myth Mountains. We know that he travels to Thorenn at least twice every eight moonsigns for supplies but we don't know how he gets here. We thought maybe he would show up on your passenger manifests. And if you can ask members of your guild who may be able to find out some information."

"That can be done," says Katrivus placing his mug on the table and leaning back in his chair. "Is there anything else you can tell me about this Sorenthor?"

"Only that sometimes he is known as the Lost Seeker or the Lonely Hermit."

"Very well, it's getting late and I'm going to retire," says Katrivus standing up and finishing off the last of his ale. "Why don't we plan on meeting for the midday meal and I will have some information for you?" Ashcon and Skken both get up and nod to Katrivus and he turns to leave with Sapphyre following.

"Is the Flaming Hearth still open over in the Loop?" asks Sapphyre.

"Yes it is. I will see you there tomorrow," says Katrivus as he leans in and hugs Sapphyre good-night.

Chapter 20

KATRIVUS slept restfully, which had become a commonplace incident since moving into his new residence only days ago. Rising from his bed, his mind is wandering to only a few weeks back when he was the leader of the prospering Pugs. His thoughts were focused entirely on dominating trade with western Arstevia and expanding Pug operations abroad. Now he's a member of the Guild of Slight and although he will make more kendra through the various businesses, his dreams of an empire of his own have practically vanished. As he's washing his face in the cold water, he promises himself that he will not let remorse dictate his thoughts but instead will make bold new plans for the future. After attaching his daggers to his waist, he leaves his room and walks toward the guild hall to break the fast and make some inquiries.

Katrivus makes his way to a table occupied by Talon and a younger member who is not familiar to him. As Katrivus takes the seat opposite Talon, Talon leans toward the stranger and says, "Excuse us." He turns toward Katrivus as the two are now alone at the table.

"Good morning, Talon."

"And to you, Katrivus."

"I ran into some old friends last night who were looking for some information," says Katrivus, reaching for a roll from the basket on the table.

Katrivus continues since Talon does not reply. "One was a girl who's a former member of the Pugs whom I trust implicitly. She's travelling with two companions –"a barbarian and a strange man with yellow eyes, whom I could not place."

Talon looks up and replies, "What type of information do they seek?"

"They are looking for a man who they believe resides north of the Myth Mountains," says Katrivus as he reaches for the butter, missing the surprised expression on Talon's face.

"Does this man have a name?"

"Sorenthor. Most know him as the Lonely Hermit. Does this mean anything to you?" asks Katrivus.

"No," Talon quickly lies. "I will make some inquiries. When do you need the information?"

"I plan on meeting them for the noon meal," says Katrivus as Talon rises to excuse himself from the table.

Talon slides around the table and says, "I'll see what I can find out." He heads to the front door of the guild house.

Talon makes his way around the guild house to his hidden entrance to his room and crawls inside. He opens his door, glances both ways, and turns left and knocks on the third door on the right. He closes the door behind him as he walks in.

"Whom did Katrivus meet with last night?" asks Talon to the man on the edge of the bed.

"Sapphyre, a gal from the old days and two of her friends."

"Tell me about Sapphyre."

The man leans one shoulder back on the bed, wipes his nose on his sleeve, and coughs twice before starting. "Katrivus recruited her when she was only about five or six winters. She became his favorite little thief and he even taught her how to read and write. She was pretty good with a dagger, and no, before you ask, they were never together."

"Why is she here?"

"I'm not yet privy to that information. I have yet to talk to Katrivus to find out what they were meeting about." He sits up on the bed, and places his chin in his hand and continues. "She left rather abruptly a few winters ago. Katrivus was gone to sea and she left him a note and disappeared."

Talon starts toward the door, grabs the knob, and turns to Fargo. "Stay close to Katrivus this morning and find out what you can. He's having his morning meal as we speak. Make sure that he's in the guild house one hour before noon as I will need to speak with him then."

"It will be as you say," replies Fargo as he puts on his shoes and prepares to go meet Katrivus.

After spending the next few hours locked in his room, preparing for the upcoming meeting with Katrivus, Talon washes his face in cold water and slides his daggers into place before exiting through the secret passage to the streets. He makes sure a few members of the guild see him as he makes his way to the front entrance and opens the double doors to the guild hall. He helps himself to a pint of ale and walks the length of the room searching for Katrivus. Just as he is about to broaden his search he spies Katrivus walking in from the hallway with Fargo in tow and approaches the two of them.

Talon gestures to a table and the two follow him over. As he sits down he turns to Fargo and says, "I will speak with Katrivus alone."

Fargo glances at Katrivus, who nods slightly and Fargo takes his leave. "You can trust him," says Katrivus to Talon.

"I trust no one Katrivus," replies Talon smiling inwardly. "I do have some information for your friend," he says as Katrivus leans forward.

"You know who Sorenthor is?" asks Katrivus.

"I know quite a bit more than that, actually," replies Talon leaning back in his chair. "I would like to meet your friend and her companions and then I'll decide as to whether I will share this information."

"If it's about kendra, Talon –" starts Katrivus.

"It's not kendra!" Talon replies as he places both hands on the table. "Kendra is nothing when compared with information. Information is the most valuable commodity you can have." He leans back again and continues, "I don't share my information with just anyone. I will meet your friends and then decide how to proceed. Agreed?"

"I'm not comfortable with this Talon," Katrivus replies as he sits up with his arm crossed on his chest.

Talon sighs, leans in, and says, "I know who Sorenthor is and I also know where he resides. Whether I share that information with your friends is something that has yet to be decided. Take me with you to meet them and, as long as things work out, I will tell them what they need to know."

"Very well," says Katrivus standing up from the table.

The two walk side by side toward Granite Loop to reunite with the trio at the Flaming Hearth. The restaurant was always a favorite of both Katrivus and Sapphyre from many winters before. Like all of the eateries in the Loop, the restaurant was not under the control of the Guild of Slight, nor any organization. It was an unwritten rule of the underground society that Granite Loop was off limits. There was no future in an organization that is willing to take advantage of the common citizens in their homes. Any business ran in the Loop that benefitted only the family of the proprietor fell under this umbrella. The people in the Loop were happy with this arrangement, and as long as they didn't try and expand their business outside the Loop, they were able to operate in relative safety.

Sapphyre, Ashcon, and Skken are already seated in the back table by the extra-large hearth lending the establishment its name, when Katrivus and Talon enter through the front door. Sapphyre gets out of her chair and goes to greet Katrivus, immediately taken aback by the stranger at his side. She almost stumbles over herself walking toward the door. Talon is also struck by a thunderbolt that leaves him dead in his tracks when he sees Sapphyre for the first time.

Sapphyre gets control of her emotions and gives Katrivus a brief hug. She asks, "Who is your friend?"

"Let's get seated. My friend has some information but requires some as well," says Katrivus as the three walk toward Ashcon and Skken.

The four men all acknowledge each other with nods and take a seat around the table.

Katrivus starts the conversation. "This is an associate of mine who specializes in acquiring information and I believe he has some that may be of interest to you." He glances to each face and continues, "This is Sapphyre, Ashcon, and Skken. My associate is Talon."

Talon nods his head toward each man, trying desperately to keep his eyes from wandering to Sapphyre. "I understand you are searching for Sorenthor." Getting no reaction he continues, "Tell me why."

Ashcon replies, "Our business is our own. We seek out Sorenthor for reasons that need not be imparted to you."

Talon starts to rise from the table when Katrivus grabs his shoulder to keep him from leaving and Sapphyre interjects, "Please don't go, Talon. We really need your help."

Talon eyes Sapphyre before sitting back down in his chair and speaks. "I am interested in learning your motive rather than your direct intentions. As you know, Sorenthor comes here sporadically for supplies and his business is very profitable for our organization. He needs extremely rare items that we can procure. If your reason to find Sorenthor is to neutralize him then your motive is in direct opposition to ours: profit."

Ashcon leans into the table. "We have no ill intentions toward Sorenthor and you have my word that our goal is to simply acquire information. No physical harm will come to him as a result of you imparting your knowledge."

Talon looks to Katrivus for a reaction and gets an affirmative nod in response. "Katrivus trusts Sapphyre with his life and it is apparent that she holds you two in the same regard." He leans back before continuing carefully. "I know where Sorenthor resides."

Hearing this, Sapphyre leans forward and turns her head toward Talon while Ashcon and Skken show no reaction. "Will you tell us?" asks Sapphyre.

Talon reaches into his pocket for his pipe and starts stuffing it and then replies. "If we can come to an accommodation I can share the information with you."

"What type of accommodation?" asks Skken, opening his mouth for the first time.

"It won't be cheap. We're talking about passage northbound on one of our ships in the heart of the cold season. It is a long journey."

"How much?" asks Ashcon.

"We'll see," says Talon as he lights his pipe and takes a few puffs. "Besides the trip being long and treacherous, there are a few other consider-ations. The barbarians of the north will have to agree to allow passage for you across their lands. Sorenthor resides far west of the coast, and you will need a guide."

"We need no such thing," says Skken as he grips the table with both hands.

"You do," says Talon, "and Katrivus and I will provide that guidance." This statement brings a startled glance from Katrivus and before any interruptions take place, Talon continues. "Katrivus has a long-standing relationship with the barbarians and he will be able to negotiate safe passage. I am the only one who knows how to get to Sorenthor's Library. Plus, you need us to provide passage on our ship – unless you plan on traversing the DragonTooth Pass in the dead of the cold season."

Ashcon glances at Skken and then at Sapphyre who is nodding her head vigorously. "If we agree to your conditions, when can we depart?"

Katrivus replies, "The Sweeping Swallow, our fastest ship, is due in to dock within three days. If we turn it around immediately, we can cast off in five days."

Ashcon sits up straight staring into Talon's eyes, "We are in charge of this expedition, period. Any decisions made along this journey are ours to make. You provide passage and lead us to our destination. Whether we join you on the way back will be decided after our visit with Sorenthor."

Talon stands up and says, "Agreed. The fee will be negotiated before we cast off. In our society, we seal our deals with a certain type of handshake."

Ashcon stands up and knowing the ritual withdraws his dagger from its sheath and makes a small incision under the middle finger of his left hand. Talon does the same and the two shake their hands, sealing their agreement.

Chapter 21

Zidi has just finished his morning briefing with Drak'thonn and starts to return to his residence beneath the Temple of the Dark Gods. Before he exits the Skeed Towers, he grasps his staff, closes his eyes, and silently summons his apprentice to meet him at the temple. As he steps out into the darkness, he is taking in all he has just learned. Selentha, leader of the dreggans of the northern continent, is now equal in power to Drak'thonn and will become his bride. Zidi cringes at the thought of imparting this information to the council, as Drak'thonn made it his charge to do so. He rides up to the entrance to the temple and starts mentally planning the rest of the day as he hands his horse to the stable boy and goes to meet his apprentice.

Zidi enters the library, the first room at the bottom of the stairs beneath the temple, to see his charge sitting in a chair with his feet resting on the table. "Make yourself comfortable, Sleeth."

Surprised, Sleeth jumps up, stands with his usual lean to the left, and says, "You summoned?"

Zidi sighs and walks to his chair at the table. He rests his hand on the back with the other on his staff and scans his apprentice. Sleeth, like most warlocks, is thin and pale, yet he is much shorter in stature, standing an inch above five feet. His eyes, though hollow, are bright blue as opposed to the usual jet black. He shows an exorbitant amount of promise and is a brilliant practitioner of the black arts even at a young thirty-two winters. Although he has a propensity toward violence and he too often lets his emotions take the better of him, Zidi admits to himself he is very happy with his choice of successor.

"We will have a meeting of the high council tonight immediately after the evening meal. See to it that everyone attends. It is imperative," says Zidi as he takes his seat.

"I will," replies Sleeth. "May I inquire as to the agenda for the meeting?"

"You have met Selentha, I assume?"

"I have," says Sleeth as he inches up toward the table.

"Drak'thonn is going to take her as his bride," starts Zidi looking at the startled expression on Sleeth's face. "Apparently it has been ordered by the Zagador who spoke to both of them. She will be equal in power to Drak'thonn, which means any order she gives is to be adhered to as if given directly from Drak'thonn."

"He is mad," starts Sleeth before Zidi cuts him off.

"Who are you to question the Zagador? If this is the wish of the Dark Gods, then it is to be." He stands up and starts pacing around the room slowly and continues. "We will not need to wonder if it is or is not the wish of the Dark Gods."

"What do you mean?" asks Sleeth.

"I have been charged with telling the council tonight all I have imparted to you – plus this: Tomorrow the wedding of Drak'thonn and Selentha that will take place here, at the temple. Drak'thonn assures us that at the reception following, in the Obsidian Sepulcher, all will understand the wishes of the Zagador."

With nothing left to say, Sleeth rises from his chair and says, "I will summon the council members, high warlock."

"Thank you, Sleeth," Zidi replies as he stares upwards and then walks back to his quarters to prepare for the meeting and the pending nuptials.

One would believe that the wedding of Drak'thonn to Selentha would be an historic affair that would be attended by the masses, and they would be half right. The wedding itself is a solemn affair while what is to follow in the Obsidian Sepulcher will be momentous.

Drak'thonn and Selentha are both completely nude in front of Zidi, who is presiding over the union of the two in the Temple of the Dark Gods. Selentha's War Stack is behind her, in full battle regalia minus their weapons, kneeling on one knee. Sleeth stands behind Drak'thonn, followed by the remainder of the high council. The temple is empty of any other guests as Zidi grasps the DarkFlame Staff and starts the short ceremony.

Holding the staff above his head and rotating it from right to left, Zidi starts to chant in the language of the warlock. Fire emerges from the tip of his staff and forms the shape of a large crown. The crown starts to move toward the royal couple. As it descends toward them, Drak'thonn and Selentha each take to a knee, and the crown situates itself above both of them.

The words which emerge from Zidi's mouth belong to none other than the Zagador. "Behold your Gods, chosen ones," starts the voice and the audience drop to their knees. The voice continues, as Zidi sets his gaze upon the couple. "Drak'thonn and Selentha, we bless your most holy of unions. Rise before your Gods."

Drak'thonn and Selentha stand up, hand in hand, while the rest of the crowd remains kneeling. "Drak'thonn, will you take Selentha, in the name of the Zagador, and make her your equal?"

This declaration by the Zagador brings gasps from the crowd, but Drak'thonn, unfazed, answers, "I will take her as my equal in the presence of the Zagador."

Zidi turns toward Selentha, "Selentha, will you take Drak'thonn, in the name of the Zagador, and make him your equal?"

"I will take him as my equal in the presence of the Zagador," replies Selentha.

Zidi holds up both of his hands and the Zagador declares, "You will bathe in the holy fire," upon which their bodies are both immediately consumed in flames that reach the top of the temple. "Emerge the chosen King and Queen of the

Dark Horde. All followers of the Zagador will bow before you and the world will be yours to rule."

Zidi then lowers his arms and as the fire consuming the king and queen extinguishes, he drops to his knees, out of breath from the rigors of the ceremony. Sleeth tends to Zidi as Drak'thonn and Selentha exit the temple, officially king and queen.

The Obsidian Sepulcher is the largest tomb on the continent of Arstevia. It is said to have at one time contained the entirety of the Zagador when they were flesh and bones, before ascending to deity. Only the most holy of ceremonies takes place on this sacred ground and there has been no such observance for over a millennia. The tomb itself is over two hundred yards long and one hundred yards wide. As the two leaders are making their way to the Sepulcher, the crowds converge at the center where there is a circular riser set up. Zidi approaches the stage first and raises the DarkFlame Staff blasting fire in all directions from the tip, to the raucous cheering of the crowd. He then waves his arms in a circular motion and a whirlpool of silver light blasts out from the eyes on the hilt of his staff in all directions, the spell allowing everyone to see the stage and hear the proceedings regardless of where they are situated.

Zidi walks off the stage and positions himself next to Sleeth while the remainder of the high council surrounds the huge circle. A group of warlocks from behind the stage start chanting and waving their staves and the sound of bass drums fills the air, the beat starting measured and deliberate, with complete silence in between the echoing booms. Lightning flashes across the sky in all directions, the clouds themselves alive with dark electricity. The pounding is getting faster and the crescendo is building while the clouds start to explode and red, amber, black, and grey balls of lava launch in all directions. The crowd is staring up at the sky in awe, not in danger of the fire that is dissipating right before impact.

Without warning, the sky returns to darkness and the drums stop beating. The entire Fortress of Darkness is in complete silence. Zidi stands in front of the stage and opens his arms to the sky and with a booming voice declares so all can hear, "Behold your king and queen, chosen by the Zagador to rule until the end of days. Kneel now before King Drak'thonn and Queen Selentha."

Above the stage, an orb of fire descends slowly, and as the crowd sees the king and queen atop this hovering ball of flame, they immediately take to their knees in front of them. The king and queen are dressed in full battle regalia, with the exception of their heads, which upon each rests a crown of flame. Their black plate armor has the symbol of the Zagador burning with living fire in the center of the chest. Even though the armor covers most of their bodies you can still see the burning flesh of both the king and the queen. As they are levitating on the ball of fire in the center of the Sepulcher, they both take to their knees and look at the sky above.

The crowd follows suit and all eyes are on the clouds which start bubbling with fire and lightning. The cloud directly above the king and queen is expanding with pulsating energy, but no one can take their eyes off the phenomenon. The cloud explodes into thousands of pieces leaving a black hole sparkling with streaks of light. The streaks start to form a shape above the clouds and those mesmerized in the crowd all close their eyes in unison and behold a vision from the Zagador.

To Zidi, the Zagador appear in the form of a much older warlock, one who resembles his grandfather. That has always been as he pictured the Dark Gods. Drak'thonn sees the vision of the Zagador as he did when they came to him in the form of a dreggan. What comes to the mind of Selentha is that of an eternal ball of flame. Even though each member of the crowd sees their own personal vision of the Zagador, the message passed on to all is the same.

King Drak'thonn and Queen Selentha have been chosen by the Dark Gods to lead the people. After witnessing such an unprecedented event, every one of the followers of the Dark Gods would willingly give their lives for the new king and queen. The followers of the Zagador are united as one under the rule of the chosen ones, and they will not be denied.

Chapter 22

Ashcon and Skken are sipping on warm cider in front of the fire in the Black Pearl Tavern when Talon and Katrivus stroll in and take a seat opposite them. They acknowledge each other with nods when Talon says, "We leave on the morrow and have yet to discuss the fee."

Ashcon leans forward and places his mug atop the table before replying, "In addition to other things." This causes both Talon and Katrivus to cringe and Ashcon continues. "First off, we need to know our exact destination before we depart. Second, once we are off to sea, we want a copy of the map with assurances that we will only open it if you become incapacitated. Third, discretion is of the utmost importance to us. I'd like to know what safeguards you have taken to insure discretion."

Katrivus is about to respond when Talon cuts him off and speaks. "Our destination is the north port of call, Thull. Katrivus will fill you in on security measures, but in response to your second request, the answer is no. Under no circumstances will I put the map to parchment. It is a deal breaker gentlemen, so objecting will fall on deaf ears." He looks to Ashcon and then to Skken and asks, "Will that be a problem?"

Instead of answering, Ashcon turns toward Katrivus and says, "Tell me about the security measures."

Katrivus puts both hands on the table and says, "We will be travelling on our long ship, The Sweeping Swallow, which can hold up to fifty-five people. On our departure from port we will be leaving with a full contingency, as is always the case, and therefore will not attract unwanted attention. There will be ten officer crewmen, forty laborers, and two wizards."

"Wizards?" interjects Skken.

"We have wizards on board all of our ships to forecast weather, help with navigation, but most importantly for defense in case of attack. Incidents with pirates are becoming less frequent as we hire the majority of them to work with us.

There are occasional raids from organized bandits upon our return south with valuables although they rarely bother us as we head north. There are different creatures of the sea that sometimes give us trouble and it has proven cost effective to have wizards aboard."

"With a full crew, how do you expect our passage to remain a secret?" inquires Ashcon.

Talon responds, "As far as the crew goes, they all work for us or are members of the House. We pay them for their discretion and we pay them handsomely. All they will know is that you are passengers on a trip to the north. That is not uncommon."

Katrivus intervenes. "Once we depart from Dock Bay, our destination will be the island of Flotine, which is under Guild control. As an added security measure we will be swapping out our crew in Flotine." Katrivus reaches into his shirt for a pipe and starts to fill it as he continues. "When I started the trade route I wanted to make sure it was departmentalized so I would be in complete control. So, each crew we have works only with each other, and only travels between two distinct ports of call. Only my captain, who takes us from here to Flotine, knows that route. He is unaware how to navigate the seas to reach the barbarian lands. And such is true with the crews who travel to the barbarian lands. They only travel between either Cornice or Flotine to one of the three ports of call." He sits back, lights his pipe and says, "As you can see we, we have it under control."

"Four thousand kendra," says Talon leaning back in his chair.

Ashcon stares at Talon and replies in a husky voice, "One thousand."

"Don't waste my time, Ashcon. You're asking for passage on our ship, permission from the barbarians to traverse their lands, and escort to the Lonely Hermit's lair. We get one thousand for simple passage," replies Talon.

"One thousand now and one thousand when we arrive at Sorenthor's," counteroffers Ashcon.

Talon turns his head to look at Katrivus, who looks back, expressionless. Just as he is turning back to Ashcon, he spies Sapphyre approaching their table from her quarters. His eyes linger a bit longer than he wishes, and he rises to greet her. He takes her hand in his and with a gentle kiss upon the back side of her palm says, "Good evening Sapphyre."

Sapphyre withdraws her hand, and replies with a blush, "Good evening to you, Talon." She grabs a chair from the table beside theirs and pulls it up to the side, situating herself between the two sets of companions.

Talon then looks at Ashcon, stands up, and exclaims, "Done!" to the surprise of all three men. "Katrivus, please collect the funds and complete our business with Ashcon and Skken." He then turns toward Sapphyre, holds out his hand, and says, "If it pleases m'lady, may I have the honor of your companionship for dinner this evening?" Sapphyre glances up at Talon and he continues, "There is a new eatery open in the Loop and I have reserved their prized table."

Sapphyre rises and says, "I would be honored." She turns to the three men at the table and says, "Gentlemen" as Talon takes her arm in his and leads them to the exit.

"So business has gone well between you and Ashcon?" inquires Sapphyre as they walk side by side toward the Granite Loop.

"As well as can be expected, I suppose," replies Talon. "What puzzles me about this whole arrangement is how you fit in to all of this. Why do you want to go to the hermit's lair?"

Sapphyre releases her arm from his, but continues in stride replying, "Let's not discuss business tonight." She skips in front of Talon, swirls around toward him and says excitedly, "So tell me about this new eatery we're heading to."

Talon stops briefly, smiles up at Sapphyre and grabs her hand and turns her back around and he leads them up the hill to the eastern gates of the Loop. Through the gates they take a quick right in the direction of the Bay of Thorenn. The sky is filled with stars illuminating the night and reflecting off the water as the two are escorted to their bayside table at the Seafarer.

"Wasn't this the Whale's Tail Inn?" inquires Sapphyre.

"Yes it was. The old Tail fell to a wave from a sea storm a few winters back. The owners have switched hands and this just opened within the moonsign."

Sapphyre glances around noticing that the tables are all full and they indeed were seated at the prized table. The patrons were mostly nobility by the look of their clothes and the servants in the stables attached. The proprietor is human while the servers are dwarves, which is unheard of in the Loop. "How is it that there are dwarves serving?" Sapphyre asks Talon. "I was under the assumption that only family may work eateries."

"You have an inquisitive mind, don't you Sapphyre?" starts Talon. "You are correct although there are some exceptions to every rule. In this case, the former owner was a dwarf and when he sold it to Paulder after the storm, his kin were permitted to continue working here. The former owner, on the other hand, is not permitted to open any establishment in the Loop in return. He was on the verge of retiring anyway so it worked out well for everyone." Talon smiles to Sapphyre and gestures for a serving girl, who approaches with a slight limp. "Plum wine for the lady and mead for myself," Talon orders.

Throughout dinner, Sapphyre learns a bit about the young thief, but the predominant truth she discovers is that he is still hiding a lot. That is part of what attracted Sapphyre to Talon since she shares the same character trait. As she's pushing her chair in to depart the eatery, her lips curve to form a slight smile as she thinks maybe it's a character flaw.

Walking hand in hand through the streets of Skid Way in the direction of the Black Pearl, fearless with Talon by her side, Sapphyre stops in her tracks and turns toward Talon. She moves closer, pulls his head down to her with her right hand, and locks her lips to his. He puts both his hands on her cheeks pulling her closer, breathing in her scent. Sapphyre lingers a bit longer and then pulls back with a smile on her face.

"I wanted to share a kiss before our departure in the morning," says Sapphyre gazing up at Talon. He starts to speak, but Sapphyre cuts him off by placing her finger on his lips. "I just wanted a taste, Talon. Once we depart it is all business until we return."

Talon pulls her closer and replies, "Then let's spend the night together, Sapphyre. Let us share that memory that we may call upon while we travel."

Sapphyre leans in and kisses Talon on the cheek and with a smile replies, "No, Talon, it will be a due reward upon our successful return." She brushes her hand upon his right cheek, turns around and waving while walking backwards says, "Thank you for a lovely night."

Talon responds by blowing a kiss followed by an extravagant bow.

Chapter 23

SORENTHOR leans back in his tanned leather chair and looks up at the sky above through the glass ceiling at the top floor of his library, the tome beside him finally closed after continuous days of studying and interpreting. He waves his arm in a small arc in front of his face and the ceiling turns from glass to the image of the mouth of a cave surrounded by birds of every color of the rainbow. Although snow covers the terrain, it doesn't seem to bother the birds in the image. Sorenthor studies the image and then closes his eyes and burns the image into his mind. Sitting up he reaches down with his right hand to grab the book as the ceiling returns to its glass state. With book in hand he heads toward the spiral staircase leading to the thirteen floors below. The stairs are mainly for show and the infrequent visitor as Sorenthor can easily teleport himself to any area within his domain. Since he is only descending one floor to put away the ancient tome, the stairs are the quickest route.

The library is built pyramid style with the largest floor at the bottom. Library is a bit of a misnomer, as the entire dwelling is considered his library, including living quarters, dining quarters, the study, and the lab, even the outside farm where he grows his valuable herbs. The cylindrical staircase starts immediately upon entering the dwelling on the right before you enter the first floor proper. There are fourteen floors in all, thirteen of which contain books of every type. Sorenthor is putting away this ancient tome of prophecy on the thirteenth floor, which holds only three hundred sixty one total books. As one climbs the tower, the number of books on each floor drops from eight thousand on the second floor to only one at the apex.

Sorenthor has read them all and knows where each one is located. His classification system is his alone and there is no one alive who would be able to find a book in his library without his permission. Every book is in constant motion, invisible to the naked eye, yet they remain in order. Whenever Sorenthor wants a book, he simply stops the motion and inspects a book. Based upon that book, he can find the location in his library of the volume he wishes to withdraw.

It took Sorenthor over a hundred winters to perfect the system and it is one he is very proud of. Over the winters there have been people willing to brave the famed lost seeker and attempt to steal his books. It has never been done successfully and over time more and more safeguards have been put into place as his powers have increased.

He puts away the volume and transports himself to the main study, where he pours himself a glass of smeeka. Reading prophecy has always intrigued Sorenthor as he has read about himself on more than one occasion. He has seen himself noted by name as Sorenthor, the Lonely Hermit, the Lost Seeker, and the Fallen Star, among others. This latest tome, delivered by the high priestess, in itself not a rare occurrence, has kept him up for a straight half moonsign. The high priestess has given him hundreds of books over the winters to keep safeguarded in his library, but this one came with a note.

Read this before your visitors arrive.
Ka'alshene

Over the winters, Sorenthor and Ka'alshene have formed a mutual respect and then a friendship, which many would have thought impossible at one time. After all, Sorenthor is the Lost Seeker who cursed the Star Gods for what they did to Kentin. It wasn't until two hundred winters after Sorenthor left the Temple of the Stars that Ka'alshene came to visit and forged the beginning of that friendship. Sipping his smeeka, he lets his mind drift back to that day.

"I'm surprised to see you, Ka'alshene," says Sorenthor, sitting in his study, biting on the edge of a cigar.

"I wish to discuss with you what transpired on Kentin's Ascension Day," replies Ka'alshene.

"There is nothing to discuss. Kentin did not wish to ascend to deity and leave Nestair behind. He wanted to live until she passed on and then he would ascend. He would never say anything, so it fell on me to refuse."

"That is not the way it is done, Sorenthor." She sits down beside him with a small round table between them and faces him. "Kentin was a runestar and you were his seeker. You were fully trained and you were the most brilliant seeker the world has ever seen." She takes his hand and puts it into hers and continues. "You refusing to become a runestar would never have stopped Kentin from ascending from runestar to Star God, and you know that."

Sorenthor glances up at Ka'alshene and says quietly, "It was my duty since Kentin was too devout to share his true feelings. I felt it was the only possible recourse."

"I knew, as the Gods did as well, that you were only acting out of love for your runestar." She takes his face in her right hand and shifts it toward hers. "The Star Gods will not make you a runestar now or ever, Sorenthor."

Sorenthor pulls back his hands, and laughing replies, "A runestar? I have no desire to become a runestar any more, Ka'alshene. I will become just as powerful and not have to answer to anyone but myself." He stands up and stretches and looks to Ka'alshene. "Trust me when I tell you I have no hard feelings toward you or the Star Gods. Over the last two hundred winters, I've amassed quite a library. I have powers beyond most runestars' comprehension. My only thirst is for knowledge, not power. I am a threat to no one, nor am I an ally to any. I am as neutral as the Oracle of Anon."

Ka'alshene stands up and smiles at Sorenthor, holding her arms to her side. He smiles in return and takes her left arm in his right and walks toward his lair. "You are welcome any time, Ka'alshene, and if you have any books to contribute to my library – ."

She smiles and pats his hand. "I'm glad we had this time to talk, Sorenthor. I am certain there are many books I would like to read, so I may have to visit from time to time. And if I send you any books, they are only on loan- I may want them back at some point." She turns toward Sorenthor.

"Of course," he replies and places both his hands in hers. "Take care of yourself, high priestess."

"You as well, Lost Seeker."

As Sorenthor is about to take notes from the latest reading of the tome, he realizes it has been a little over one hundred winters since that first meeting with Ka'alshene. Over time she has visited countless times and has contributed well over five hundred items. This is the first time one came with a note.

Chapter 24

AFTER two days at sea, Sapphyre's seasickness subsides and she is contemplating exiting her quarters and venturing above decks. The constant sound of pattering feet and the dim shouts of the sailors confirms that it is daylight and Sapphyre sits up warily. As her socks hit the wood and she starts to rise, the ship swerves violently, knocking her to the floor leaving her scurrying to get up. The shouts of the men are louder now, and Sapphyre reaches for her dagger and sheaths it in her belt before bolting out the door and up the stairs to the deck.

As Sapphyre's eyes adjust to the light, she turns her head to the right, and coming into focus she sees sailors with their weapons drawn. They are running past her to the back of the ship in some type of battle formation. Sapphyre turns the corner and stops dead in her tracks at the vision in front of her. There are at least twenty sailors with weapons drawn and ten archers situated behind them, all raining arrows down on a beast of the sea. Both wizards are hovering above the water flanking the seventy-foot, worm-like animal as it was oozing its way onto the deck. With a horrifying cry the beast opens its jaw and devours one of the sailors whole, the entire time whipping its head around knocking the attackers back. The wizards are surrounded by a green aura, eyes closed, chanting and preparing to unleash a spell. The beast's weight is starting to bear on the back of the ship and the bow is raised above the waves. As the monster opens its mouth preparing to feast on another crew member, the wizards simultaneously unleash four bolts of electricity, two from each of their outstretched arms. As the bolts hit the target, the beast writhes and screams in agony and . The crew sheathe their weapons and back away from the spectacle, knowing what is to come next. The wizards, using the electricity as a net, slowly lift the monster from the deck and direct it over the sea. Once the beast is a safe distance away, the wizards unleash the full power of the spell and the bolts release from their fingers and disintegrate the beast above the ocean.

Sapphyre stares with her mouth agape as the crew starts to gather rags nonchalantly and scrub the deck. The wizards, still levitating above the sea, silently make their way back to the main deck, conversing between themselves. There is a bustle of activity as many of the sailors return to their regular assignments, leaving some to get rid of the remnants of the short battle. Sapphyre walks over to the railing and grips it until her knuckles are white, staring out over the vast ocean, a little disturbed that she can't see land in any direction. After what seems like an eternity, she feels a hand on her shoulder and turns to see Katrivus smiling down at her.

"So, I see you've finally ventured out of your room," starts Katrivus. Sapphyre blushes and smiles slightly as Katrivus continues, "That creature was a lushwyrm. They are a constant burden to our business, but as you can see, we have a means to destroy them."

"You lost a few crewmen in the battle," replies Sapphyre.

Katrivus closes his eyes, and with a sigh, replies. "Sad but true. The wizards can easily dispose of the lushwyrm; however, if it isn't spotted until it attacks, as was the case today, our crew's responsibility is to stall it until the wizards' spell is ready to cast. Unfortunately, when this happens it is not uncommon to lose a crew member or two." Katrivus turns toward the front of the ship and beckons Sapphyre to follow. "Lushwyrms travel in packs, like wolves, but they never attack together. It is quite the puzzle." Katrivus points to the wizards who have now flanked the ship, levitating approximately fifteen yards out. "We won't be surprised again. They will take care of any lushwyrms that may be in the area."

The two reach the bow of the ship and Sapphyre asks, "How long will it take to reach Flotine?"

"If the weather holds and the wind is favorable, we should make it in eight or nine days."

"How long from Flotine to our destination?"

"We will spend one or two nights in Flotine. It all depends on the state of the ship and crew taking us north. If the gods favor us we will reach the barbarian lands eight days after departing."

The two are gazing north while the sun is rising to the east when Ashcon and Skken approach from behind and Skken says loudly, "I see you made it out of bed, Sapphyre."

The three men share a laugh and Sapphyre turns to them and retorts, "And where were the three of you when we were attacked by the lushwyrm? Under the covers keeping each other warm?"

The laughter stops abruptly and Katrivus breaks the sudden silence by leaning forward and saying in hushed whisper, "I told the men before we departed that under no circumstances are they to get involved in any altercation on the ship. The wizards and the crew are equipped to handle any situation. The crew expects the passengers to stay out of the way and that is what must be done. No exceptions."

Sapphyre glances down, embarrassed by her sudden outburst, and then replies quietly, "I understand. Please excuse me, I feel a little queasy." She bows to the men as a group and starts toward her quarters below deck.

Ashcon says, "Excuse me," and follows after Sapphyre. As she arrives at the entrance to the quarters below, Ashcon gets hold of her shoulder and says, "May I have a moment please?"

Sapphyre nods her head and walks side by side with Ashcon toward a spot on the deck out of eye and earshot from anyone. He turns to her, "If I am to use my powers to help in the protection of the ship, the wizards would immediately sense my magic. They cannot see my runes when I activate them, as you can, but they can sense them."

"I understand, Ashcon," replies Sapphyre. "When the wizards were channeling their spell I saw a green aura around them. If you were to activate your runes, I suspect they would see something to alert them of your ability." He nods in affirmation. "I'm sorry for my outburst earlier. I certainly didn't mean to brand you as cowards. I'm embarrassed and I apologize."

"Apology accepted," says Ashcon and he mockingly salutes Sapphyre. "Shall we break the fast?"

"Lead the way," replies Sapphyre.

Chapter 25

SAPPHYRE fights bouts of nausea over the next eight nights on the voyage to Flotine, but there are no lushwyrms, pirates, or any other hostile obstacles impeding their passage. The weather turns sour the evening of the battle and snow falling like sheets of ice pounds the Sweeping Swallow relentlessly day in and day out. Although the sailors can't see three feet in front of them on some occasions, Katrivus assures Sapphyre and the others that thanks to the wizards, they know they are on course. Sapphyre finally catches some sleep when the weather breaks on the night before they arrive at Flotine.

Sapphyre awakes to the sound of jubilant cheers from the crew above and quickly rises from her slumber to see what is afoot. She exits her cabin and instead of heading directly upstairs turns left and goes down the hallway to see if

Ashcon and Skken are awake. The torches in the hallway aren't lit as the sun is making its way over the horizon. Sapphyre pauses before turning the corner as she hears whispers from around the bend. She strains to hear but the voices are muffled gibberish to her at this distance. Sapphyre crouches down, closes her eyes, and concentrates deeply on the voices coming from around the bend. Suddenly, the voices are crystal clear inside her head, and she can hear the conversation as if she is a part of it. The crewmen are talking about the whorehouse that is waiting for them in Flotine and betting on whether the blonde, blue-haired beauty on board is going to be one of the new girls. Sapphyre is about to charge at them from around the corner and give them a piece of her mind when the door to Ashcon's cabin bursts open and he and Skken rush out, almost knocking down the two crewmen as the duo head directly toward Sapphyre.

"Sapphyre!" yells Ashcon. Sapphyre immediately glances up at a furious looking Ashcon, who grabs her by the arm and drags her back to her cabin.

"What do you think you're doing?" exclaims Sapphyre as she rips her arm out of Ashcon's grasp.

Ashcon closes the door behind the three of them and turns to Sapphyre and replies, "I'm sorry, Sapphyre, but you took me by surprise."

"What are you talking about?"

"You activated some type of magic within you that can be sensed by the wizards. What were you doing and why?"

"How did you –" starts Sapphyre.

Ashcon interrupts her. "I can sense magic, just like you can, but more importantly at the moment so could the wizards. So I ask you again, what did you do?"

Sapphyre's eyebrows turn downward as she thinks about the question before replying. "All I was doing was trying to listen to a conversation. I started concentrating deeply and then the voices were in my head as if I was right next to them."

Ashcon sits on the cot and gestures for Sapphyre to sit beside him, which she does. "We can't speak of this in depth at the moment, but you are probably going to have more of these occurrences as we continue our journey together. There is definitely a powerful magic ingrained in your being that you have yet to master. All we ask is that you control your innate desire to bring these powers to the surface until after we have met with Sorenthor."

"But I didn't even know what I was doing. I was just straining to hear what the men were whispering about and the next thing I knew I could hear them loud and clear. I didn't do it on purpose."

"I understand, Sapphyre. Truly, I do. The wizards probably sensed your magic as I did, but there was no threatening tone to it. I will talk to Katrivus immediately and have him put the wizards at ease. You just need to control your emotions and not do anything out of the ordinary."

"What will you tell Kat?"

Ashcon glances briefly at Skken and replies, "You no doubt realize that Skken hails from the lands we are travelling to. I will have Katrivus tell the wizards that Skken is a barbarian shaman in training, and we are escorting him back to his tribe. It's not uncommon for a young shaman to learn the ways of the southern peoples before coming into his own. That should appease them as long as there is no further activity."

"Shamans do not have the power to hear from a distance, Ashcon," says Skken.

"The wizards sensed a magic, but they won't be able to figure out exactly what type of magic it was. The tone, as I mentioned before, was not threatening, and that serves us well. We will have Katrivus tell them you were reaching out to your tribe to tell them of your pending return. That should satisfy them."

Skken nods at Ashcon, but Sapphyre turns to Ashcon with a twinkle in her eye and says, "But you knew it was me."

"This is true. And it makes our trip to see Sorenthor all the more urgent." Before Sapphyre can reply, Ashcon rises from the cot and says, "Why don't you two venture above deck and see how close we are to Flotine. I'm going to take care of this business with Katrivus before the wizards take the matter into their own hands." With that, Ashcon exits quickly leaving Sapphyre and Skken behind.

As Skken turns to the door, Sapphyre grabs him by the arm. "What's going on, Skken?"

"I promise you that we will all find out in due time," he replies. "But we mustn't speak further of it now. Come, let us go above." Before Sapphyre has a chance to respond, Skken is three feet out the door and heading to the steps.

Katrivus and Talon are conversing in hushed tones in Kat's cabin when Ashcon interrupts them. "I need a word."

Katrivus points to the only open chair and Ashcon takes a seat. He looks back and forth between the two of them and starts carefully. "We have an issue, but I believe we can take care of it rather quickly."

"What type of issue?" interrupts Talon.

Ashcon glares at Talon and continues looking at Katrivus. "Skken is an aspiring shaman," Ashcon lies, "and as such he is not aware of certain abilities other magic users have. Unfortunately, he decided on his own to contact his tribe via magic and inform them of his pending return."

"The wizards!" exclaims Katrivus as he jumps to attention. As he turns to exit the cabin, Ashcon jumps in front of him and holds out his hand, causing Kat to stop cold in his tracks.

"I know a bit about magic, and you can rest assured that the wizards are aware magic was used; however, they can also sense the tone of the magic, and they will no doubt be aware it was not of malicious intent. Go to them and tell them the

216

truth. They should not feel threatened.Guarantee them it will not happen again."

Katrivus's face turns a dark red and he takes a few deep breaths before forming his response. "The Wizards Consortium agreed to work with us and they have one condition and one condition only. Any magic users who obtain passage on the ship have to be vetted by the wizards ahead of time. You've put me in quite a bind, Ashcon. Since we will be reaching Flotine today, I don't anticipate a major problem; however, I will have to compensate them for the transgression, and you can bet your ass it's coming out of your purse."

As Katrivus readies to storm out of the room he pauses briefly, eyes both Skken and Ashcon, and says with a fierce determination in his voice, "I've been to the barbarian lands, and I've met with their shaman as you know. Skken is as much a shaman in training as I am. Since we have met, I have let my relationship with Sapphyre and her trust in you impede my judgment. That ends now. We don't leave Flotine for the barbarian lands until I am satisfied I have heard the truth." He then exits the cabin slamming the door behind him leaving Ashcon with a solemn look on his face.

Chapter 26

THE stronghold at Flotine is nothing Sapphyre could have imagined. There are twenty-foot-high walls of limestone surrounding the entire island fortress and both humans and barbarians in full battle garb guard the only pier. There are ballistas on each of the four docks and sentries every one hundred meters perched atop the wall. When the Sweeping Swallow berth, two humans and two dwarves who are obviously in charge meet them.

"Hail, Katrivus, and welcome back to Flotine," greets the taller of the two humans.

"Well met, Tilton." Katrivus gestures toward his companions and introduces them one at a time. "Please see to it that my friends are put up in the main house. We are here briefly before departing northbound. How long until the crew for Starkk arrives?"

"There was a storm and they had to divert to Cornice for repairs, so they should depart on the morrow. Another three nights from there so we can set you assail within five days' time," replies Tilton.

"Good. I have business to attend to here and five days should be ample time. After the evening meal, please gather the hierarchy. We will meet in the council room. We have urgent business to discuss." Katrivus then dismisses Tilton and walks briskly to the main house with his companions in tow.

The main house resembles the old Pug guild house in Dock Bay – complete with the library that was Kat's sanctuary. There is a large common area at the entrace with a huge stone fireplace and a kitchen larger than any Sapphyre has seen before. There are servants cleaning the common area and preparing a table for an exorbitant feast. Katrivus directs his companions to their respective quarters and suggests a hot bath to take the smell of the sea off their bodies, to which the group enthusiastically agrees. As Sapphyre, Talon, Skken, and Ashcon turn toward their rooms, Katrivus grabs Ashcon by the shoulder and signals with his head for him to follow.

Dark brown shelves line the walls of the circular chamber and a black onyx table with elaborate carvings of exotic creatures rests in the middle. The table is cold to the touch, with a feel of wood, and Ashcon can sense magic innate within the surface.

Just as Ashcon is about to inquire, Katrivus speaks as he sits down in the matching chair. "It's a one-of-a-kind item and no one is sure of its origins. The high shaman of a tribe on the outskirts of Prospekt gave it to me as a gift for finding his daughter many winters ago."

"Quite a gift," replies Ashcon as he takes the only other chair in the room.

"Yes," agrees Katrivus as he opens a drawer on the desk and retrieves a bottle and two goblets. He continues as he pours the dark red wine. "First off, you owe me six hundred kendra for the wizards."

Ashcon says nothing as he reaches into his pocket,counts off the coins and places them on the desk.

"Now, if you plan on continuing this journey, you will answer some questions." Katrivus takes a sip of the wine, and places the glass down on the table. Getting no response at all from Ashcon, he continues. "I want to know if it was you or Sapphyre who utilized magic and alerted the wizards."

A quick flicker of Ashcon's left eye gives away his surprise. "It was Sapphyre," admits Ashcon.

"What was she doing?"

Ashcon looks at Katrivus and rises from his chairwine in hand. He walks toward the bookshelves near the door. Katrivus waits patiently for an answer as Ashcon runs his right hand along the bindings of some tomes before finally responding. "How did you know that I have magical capabilities?"

Katrivus stands up and, leaving his wine on the table, joins Ashcon and turns toward him. He gestures to all the shelves and replies, "I have read every single one of these tomes and scrolls. There are over seven hundred volumes here and I can proudly say it is one of the greatest collections outside of Sorenthor's Library."

"How do you know of the library?"

"Knowledge is power and the power to read and decipher old tomes and prophecies is my true passion. I have come across Sorenthor's name and references to his library quite a few times. According to what I've read, his library houses over thirty thousand one-of-a-kind items. I am quite excited to see it."

Katrivus returns to the desk and reaches for his wine glass. He sits. "In response to your question about how I knew you were a magic user, I wasn't one hundred percent sure until just now."

Ashcon laughs quietly and takes his seat opposite Kat. "So tell me what you know about Sorenthor from your reading."

Katrivus leans back in his chair and takes a deep breath and replies. "Well, he's been referenced as both the Lonely Hermit and the Lost Seeker in some prophecies. Word is that he was a Seeker a few hundred winters ago – one of the most powerful. He was so in tune with the teachings of his runestar." Katrivus closes his eyes as he tries to remember the name of the runestar.

Ashcon interrupts, "Kentin." Katrivus looks up at Ashcon in surprise. "His runestar's name was Kentin."

"That is correct, Kentin. The legend states that upon Kentin's Ascension Day, Sorenthor refused to become a runestar and was banished from the Temple of the Stars."

Ashcon leans forward and asks Katrivus, "Do you know why he refused to become a runestar?"

"The tomes are not clear on that point. It's something I have often pondered when I would come across his name."

Ashcon stands up and says, "Sorenthor was the most proficient Seeker the world has known and would have made a powerful runestar. Kentin was quite young when he was called for his ascension to deity. If I remember correctly, he was only four hundred winters old, which is the youngest ascension I've heard of." Ashcon takes a sip of wine and continues. "Kentin fell in love with a mortal woman named Nestair. When he got his summons for ascension, he was saddened to say the least."

"Why was he summoned so young?" asks Katrivus.

"Actually that is probably due to the fact that Sorenthor was such a quick study. Once a runestar fully trains his Seeker, he will become a Star God and the Seeker will become a runestar." Katrivus nods in acknowledgment. "Since Kentin found his Seeker while he was still young, and because Sorenthor's training did not take very long, he was summoned at a young age."

Ashcon returns to his seat, places his empty glass on the table, and continues as Kat pours him more wine. "Under normal circumstances, Kentin should have been able to live with Nestair for many winters before she died a mortal death. This was not the case because of the early summons. Kentin was extremely devout and even though it broke his heart to leave Nestair, he would never question the Star Gods. So Sorenthor took it upon himself and breached the ritual with the Star Gods."

"How does one do such a thing?"

"On Kentin's Ascension Day, two things are supposed to happen. The first is Sorenthor becoming a runestar and the second is Kentin's ascension to deity. Sorenthor actually refused to become a runestar in the hopes that by doing so, the Star Gods would delay Kentin's ascension until Nestair passed on."

"But Kentin became a God," interjects Katrivus.

"Of course he did. The route Sorenthor took was a foolish one that could not possibly work. However, he must have felt it was the only thing he could try, as he loved Kentin like a father and wanted to see him happy. So the Star Gods banished him from the temple and he has been locked away in his library for the last three hundred winters."

"That's an interesting tale, Ashcon, but you still never answered my question," says Katrivus as he sips from his full glass of wine.

"Indulge me, please. All will be clear, I promise you," replies Ashcon, leaning back in his chair.

"Very well."

"Tell me what you know about the history of runestars. I mean before seekers," says Ashcon.

"Well," starts Katrivus slowly, "the story goes something like this:long ago there were runes carved into stone and they bestowed magical powers to the wielder. They were used primarily in warfare and for survival. For example, someone would carry a tablet with a Fire Rune and in harsh weather conditions it could be used to light a fire for cooking."

"Continue," says Ashcon, watching Katrivus closely.

"Well, after the second War of the Sanctum, a few thousand winters ago, the Star Gods wanted to make sure peace reigned and decided they needed representatives of the Star Gods to enforce their covenants. They chose to take the power of the rune and instead of carving into stone, they would impart the powers to certain individuals: runestars. So these runestars would have intricate designs all over their bodies, each with a magical ability."

Ashcon rises and says, "Very good. Please, allow me." Katrivus nods and Ashcon continues. "The Star Gods decided to impart these powers to individuals whose role in life was to keep the peace and do the Star Gods bidding. Two thousand winters ago there were many runestars and it looked like the Star Gods plans were working. Then about seven hundred winters ago that all changed."

"That's when Seekers were introduced," interjects Katrivus.

"Actually, Seekers were introduced about one hundred winters or so later. Do you know why this happened?" asks Ashcon.

"I have not come across any information relating to that, but then again, I have not really looked for any."

"Eight hundred winters ago a young man went to the Temple of the Stars to be ordained a runestar. Potential runestars were born with the Sign of the Sun behind their left ear. If this mark was found, they were to present themselves at the Temple of the Stars on the first day of their sixteenth winter. They would then go through a ceremony where they would either leave a runestar or leave a mere mortal."

"Go on."

"On this particular day, the boy did not become a runestar. He was apparently a vessel for the Zagador. He burned down the temple and fled north where he resides to this day and still vows revenge on the Star Gods."

"I have heard this tale before, but I have always thought it legend," says Katrivus.

Ignoring this remark Ashcon continues. "For the next two hundred winters, this pawn of the Zagador went all over the land killing every runestar he could find. As the systematic butchering of runestars continued, the Star Gods felt that something must be done."

Ashcon finishes the wine in his glass and pours another, then stands up and continues. "The Star Gods decided that runestars were no longer to be born into existence. You see, the minions of death from the north were killing children born with the Sign of the Sun. They weren't even waiting until they were ordained runestar. So the Star Gods decided they would limit the number of runestars as well as give them more power." He pauses in thought and continues. "A power necessary to fight the evil in the north. No one knows how many runestars are in existence today, and that is exactly how the Star Gods want it."

"So where do Seekers come into play?" asks Kat.

"The Star Gods needed to keep the runestars hidden from the minions of the Dark Gods. The intricate runes on the runestar's body, once visible to the naked eye, are now hidden." Ashcon continues pacing as he speaks. "The Gods were faced with another dilemma as well. Their own numbers were decreasing and with that, their power. They therefore decided that runestars would eventually ascend to deity to replenish their ranks. Someone would have to take over for the runestar, and that led to the creation of the Seeker."

"So when does the runestar start training his Seeker?" asks Katrivus completely captivated by the tale.

"It's not that simple," replies Ashcon as he takes his seat. "Seekers are born with the innate ability to see runes on their particular runestar." He explains further. "So if Sorenthor were to meet another runestar, he would be unable to see his runes. Are you following?"

"Yes," replies Kat as he takes another small sip of wine.

"The problem lies in the fact that seekers do not know what they are until they meet their runestar. And runestars are not aware of their seeker's identity until they meet."

"So you're saying that they may never meet?" asks Kat.

"I've wondered that myself and have posed that question to the high priestess. She said every runestar is predestined to meet their seeker and vice versa. Basically, you must have faith, and when the Gods decide it is time for you to meet, that's when it will happen."

"That is an interesting story, Ashcon. Please tell me my permitting your embellishment was not to listen to fairy tales."

In response, Ashcon stands up and looks down at Katrivus. "The man who destroyed the temple seven hundred winters ago and is a vessel for the Zagador is known by the name Drak'thonn. He was my brother. We are travelling to Sorenthor's Library because I am a runestar, and Sapphyre can see my runes when I activate them. We need to find out if Sapphyre is my seeker."

He then finishes his wine in one swallow, places his goblet on the table, sits down, and says to a stunned Katrivus, "May I have a refill, please?"

Chapter 27

Without waking his queen, Drak'thonn slips out of his Bed of Perpetual Ice and walks over to the window overlooking the expanse of his army. He breathes deeply as he gazes over the thousands who have answered the call to fulfill the destiny chosen for him by the Zagador. He turns to look at his sleeping wife and notices a large tome on the only cabinet in the room.

Selentha opens her eyes and, noticing her husband's stare, follows his eyes to the tome on the table She silently walks over beside him and they both look at the large book. It is the largest either has ever seen and is adorned in solid gold. There are symbols on the cover of the tome that neither Drak'thonn nor Selentha can interpret. When Drak'thonn tries to open it, he cannot. His wife tries but cannot open it either.

"It must be from the Zagador," says Drak'thonn, to which his wife simply nods. "We dress, break the fast, and bring this tome to Zidi," Drak'thonn says matter-of-factly.

The two enter the Temple of the Dark Gods with the tome, surprising Zidi, who is instructing some young warlocks.

"Leave us," commands Drak'thonn. The class immediately takes their leave. Drak'thonn and Selentha walk to the back of the temple with Zidi following and proceed down the steps and into the library. Once inside, they place the tome on the large oak table and Zidi leans forward to look.

"This was in our chamber when we woke," Dark'thonn explains. "The symbols are nothing I have seen before and it will not open."

Zidi runs his fingers along the cover of the ancient book, studying the symbols, and says, "I believe these are symbols from a lost age when warlocks reigned supreme. I cannot interpret them yet, but let me retrieve the DarkFlame Staff and see if it will shed light on this."

Zidi excuses himself to get the staff from beside the altar and returns with the ancient relic in hand. He places the staff above the tome but there is no reaction whatsoever.

"I will need time to study this," says Zidi.

"Time we do not have," replies Selentha to which Zidi nods.

As Drak'thonn is about to interject, Sleeth comes running down the steps and into the library. Surprised to find the three in the room, he immediately stops short and apologizes for the interruption.

"How dare you intrude!" exclaims Zidi.

As Drak'thonn is about to admonish the warlock himself he notices Sleeth staring at the tome on the table. Without a word, the young warlock glides over to the tome and places his hand on the cover. As Zidi is about to further berate his protégé, he is stopped by a gesture from Drak'thonn.

Sleeth, ignoring the other three in the room, takes a seat and to everyone's surprise, easily opens the tome and starts thumbing through the pages.

"How did you do that?" inquires Drak'thonn.

"Do what?"

"Open the tome," replies Drak'thonn to a puzzled Sleeth.

"I don't understand. I just opened it."

Zidi takes a seat with a distressed look on his face and says to no one in particular, "So the time has finally come."

The three turn toward Zidi and without asking a question, the old warlock continues. "There is a passage in an old prophecy that discusses what is transpiring here today. I didn't realize until Sleeth was able to open the tome." He turns toward Sleeth and asks, "You cannot read it, can you Sleeth?"

"No, I cannot," replies the young warlock.

"You will be able to tomorrow, with the Dark-Flame Staff in hand," says a defeated Zidi.

"Explain yourself, Zidi," demands Dark'thonn.

"The prophecy I'm referring to says that there will come a day when a holy tome will come to the temple, one which can only be interpreted by the reigning high warlock with the DarkFlame Staff in hand. This tome will also signify the culmination of the chosen one's destiny."

"So the time of Prophecy is truly upon us," exclaims Drak'thonn triumphantly.

"Yes," replies Zidi. "I just wish I could be around to see it." He turns to Sleeth and says, "Your time has come my young protegé. The ceremony will take place on the morrow." He turns to Drak'thonn and states, "It has been my honor to serve you, Chosen One. I only hope the Zagador grant me the ability to see your glory from behind the veil of death."

Drak'thonn, not partial to sentimentality, simply nods to Zidi and turns to Sleeth. "Once the ceremony is finished, you will spend all your time interpreting this tome. Is that understood?"

"Yes, Chosen One," replies Sleeth.

"The ceremony will take place at first light," says Drak'thonn as he and Selentha exit the temple, leaving Zidi and Sleeth in the library.

Zidi rises from his chair and stands behind Sleeth who is still hovering over the tome. "I am going to my chambers to prepare for tomorrow," says Zidi solemnly.

The morning arrives with the onset of a tremendous storm; winds gusting and rain falling sideways. A barrage of lightning sets the skies afire. As Drak'thonn and Selentha enter the temple, they are greeted by all of the aspiring warlocks standing shoulder to shoulder in their black robes lining the walls. Zidi has yet to enter the temple proper as Drak'thonn and Selentha take their seats in front of the altar.

Once all have settled in place, the warlocks begin chanting and the temple grows as dark as night, with the only light coming off the flames of both Drak'thonn and Selentha. Zidi then appears behind the altar with the DarkFlame Staff in hand and raises it to the skies and the chanting ceases and the light returns to the temple.

"The time has come for me to pass on to the realm of the Zagador, and for that I am truly blessed," starts Zidi. "Sleeth, come forward."

One of the black-clad warlocks along the wall steps forward and removes his hood, revealing Sleeth's slanted blue eyes and black lips. He approaches the altar and bows in front of it.

Zidi stands atop the altar with the DarkFlame Staff in hand and proclaims, "The Zagador have chosen you, Sleeth, to wield the DarkFlame Staff and to do the Chosen One's bidding. Do you accept this responsibility until the Zagador see fit to release you from it?"

"I do."

Without another word, Zidi steps down from the altar and approaches Drak'thonn and Selentha. "Chosen Ones, I hereby offer you Sleeth. His ways are that of the Zagador, as they have chosen him to continue my work. Do you accept?"

"We do," reply Drak'thonn and Selentha in unison.

Zidi nods, turns back to the altar, and places the DarkFlame Staff lovingly into its resting place. He then glances at Sleeth, removes his robe, and lies naked upon the altar with his eyes facing the ceiling of the temple.

The warlocks around the room begin chanting as Sleeth makes his way to the altar and situates himself behind the supine Zidi, facing the king and queen. As the chanting gets louder, flames start to rise around the altar surrounding Zidi. The DarkFlame Staff glows a burning amber in recognition of the ceremony as Sleeth removes his robe and lets it fall to the ground.

Sleeth approaches the DarkFlame Staff and removes the dagger embedded in its handle. The dagger is alive in his hand, the power coursing through it almost blinding the young warlock. As he grips the dagger, the flames around Zidi start to dance igniting the priest and burning him alive. Sleeth then recites a passage in the language of his ancient forefathers and the chanting subsides.

The ceiling of the temple becomes a glowing sphere as the Zagador look down from above. With the eyes of the Dark Gods upon him, Sleeth strikes the dagger down onto the chest of the burning Zidi, the blade easily breaking the chest plate. He then reaches down into his chest and removes Zidi's still-beating black heart. He holds up the heart for all to see, and the chanting begins once again. Sleeth then looks down onto the burning body of Zidi and slowly starts to eat his heart. With each bite a scream of agony escapes from the burning Zidi's lips, and the power grows inside Sleeth. As he consumes the last of his mentor's still-beating heart, the fire completely consumes Zidi's body, and as soon as Sleeth swallows the last of it, Zidi's remains shoot up into the realm of the Dark Gods, gone forever.

Sleeth turns toward the DarkFlame Staff and places the dagger back into the hilt. He then wields it for the first time and is transfixed by the power within. He turns toward Drak'thonn and Selentha and takes to a knee, signaling the ceremony has come to an end.

Sleeth is pondering this latest turn of events that evening as he finishes moving his belongings into his new quarters. He puts the last of his meager items away and heads to the library with the DarkFlame Staff to get started on interpreting the tome.

Holding the staff he rests his hand upon the tome and a sudden realization takes place. Although he can't read the symbols or the text within, he has a clear understanding of what is written. The meaning comes to him in visions, not words, and these visions are extraordinary. He knows without a doubt that this tome holds the answers to the prophecies that are coming into play. His job is to interpret the tome for Drak'thonn and impart to him the knowledge within.

But Sleeth does not hold Drak'thonn and Selentha in the same light as his predecessor. He is fully devoted to the Zagador and would do the Dark Gods' bidding without question, but as far as he is concerned, the Zagador chose him to receive the tome. He will decide what information to pass on to the Chosen Ones and what information he will keep from them. After all, he is the representative of the Dark Gods, the wielder of the DarkFlame Staff, and the high warlock to the Zagador.

Chapter 28

KATRIVUS shakes his head from side to side and, gaining his composure, fills Ashcon's wine goblet and then his own. Leaning back in his chair, goblet in hand, he finishes the wine in one long gulp, never taking his eyes off of Ashcon.

"Sapphyre a seeker?" says Katrivus out loud.

"Possibly," replies Ashcon as he rises from his chair. "There have been others who can see my runes, and this is why we travel to Sorenthor."

"But you said only your seeker can see your runes. I don't understand."

"It is true that only my seeker can see my runes, but let me explain further. If you put three seekers in a room with me, only my true seeker can see my runes when I activate them. There are other magic users who may be able to see my runes – magic users rather than seekers."

Katrivus's crumpled brow let Ashcon know that further explanation is needed so he continues. "There are many magic users in Arstevia." Katrivus nods. "Sorcerers, wizards, witches, shamans, mages, warlocks, etc. Each of these magic users depends on a different school of magic to perform their powers. Wizards use the elements to their advantage while witches need potions or solvents in order to procure their power. Warlocks use shadow magic and in the past summoned demons to do their bidding."

Ashcon rises from his chair and starts pacing, wine goblet in hand. "If a magic user is proficient enough, he can detect other magic users just like your wizards did upon the ship. If they are extremely powerful, they may be able to see a runestar's runes when they are activated."

"So how do you know that they aren't seekers – just because they may be a wizard or a sorcerer?" asks Katrivus.

"You simply can't be both," replies Ashcon. "Runestars' and seekers' powers come directly from the Star Gods. That's where the power is generated. Sorcerers and wizards derive their power from elsewhere. That's what makes the case of Sapphyre so interesting. She is not a sorcerer or a wizard and I sense that she gains her powers from the Star Gods."

Katrivus stands up and says, "I've known that Sapphyre has the ability to detect magical auras and such, but the power you are alluding to seems beyond her capacity."

Ashcon replies, "She is much more powerful than she realizes, of that I am certain. Sorenthor will be able to tell us if she is my seeker, and if so, her training will begin."

"And if not?" inquires Katrivus.

"Then I shall continue my search."

Katrivus sits back in his chair and sighs loudly. "So Skken is your True Guardian, I assume."

"That is correct. He has been with me ever since I started my training in the Fortress of the Invoker almost eight hundred winters ago."

"It doesn't seem to me like you need protection."

"That is part of the job of a runestar's True Guardian, sure. It's not the only reason the Star Gods bestowed barbarian True Guardians upon runestars." Ashcon finishes his wine and sits back down in his chair before continuing. "The life of a runestar can be a very lonely one. To walk through life an eternal being, for lack of a better term, can be trying, especially when you cannot tell anyone about your true self. True Guardians remain a companion of the runestar until their ascension to deity." He closes his eyes before continuing. "I have outlived everyone I have ever known, Katrivus. All but Skken. His constancy as my confidante has kept me going over the winters. I believe that was the real plan of the Star Gods."

"Does he have any magical powers?"

Ashcon studies Katrivus before responding. "His saber was blessed by the Star Gods, but other than that, no. He obviously will live as long as I do and that longevity comes from the Star Gods as well."

"Is he truly a master of all weapons as the legend states?"

"He is the most proficient fighter I have ever known, and yes, he is proficient in all known weapons."

Ashcon picks up the bottle to pour another glass but decides against it and places it down on the table. "Sapphyre doesn't know the entire tale, Katrivus."

Katrivus looks angrily at Ashcon and replies, "I will not deceive her, Ashcon. She is like a sister to me."

"I would not deceive her either, Katrivus. I have developed a deep respect for her."

"It seems to me you have more explaining to do, Ashcon," says Katrivus as he reaches into the cabinet for a second bottle of wine.

"We know, as do Skenn and Sapphyre, that she possesses magical abilities. She knows I am a runestar and I explained to her my powers and abilities."

"So what are you holding back and why?" asks an impatient Katrivus.

"I felt there was no reason to discuss her potential as my seeker yet." Katrivus is about to interject when Ashcon stops him with his hand and continues. "I told her the truth though, Katrivus. I told her she has an innate magical power with potential and we must travel to Sorenthor to figure out just how powerful she is and how to hone that power."

"So why stop there? Why not tell her the truth?"

Ashcon reaches for the bottle and pours himself another glass. "She is young, Katrivus, and just coming into her own. How am I supposed to tell her that she may become an immortal being and eventually a God?" Katrivus looks at Ashcon with a hint of understanding in his eyes. "I simply want to confirm her identity, Katrivus. What if I tell her about my suspicions that she is my seeker and then she turns out not to be? That could be devastating and it's not something I wish upon her." Ashcon stands up and looks at Katrivus and says, "Now do you understand?"

Katrivus, leaning back, smiles and says, "Ashcon, you surprise me. I didn't know you had a sentimental bone in your body. You really care about her don't you?"

"I have come to, yes."

"I'd like to ask you something," says Katrivus. "What is the answer you are hoping to get from Sorenthor?"

Ashcon looks down into his hands before responding. "If truth be told, Katrivus, I would like nothing more than to have Sapphyre as my seeker."

"That settles it then," says Katrivus as he rises from his chair. "I will keep our conversation in confidence and trust that you have Sapphyre's best interests at heart."

"Talon cannot know, Katrivus."

"Understood. He will not learn it from me, but that one has a way of finding out information on his own."

"Well, it certainly has been an interesting morning," says Katrivus as he rises from his chair. Ashcon just smiles in response and Kat says, "I think it's time for us to take our leave and have a bath. This evening after the meal, Talon and I have business to discuss with the leaders here regarding all the changes since I became a member of the Slight. I would suggest the three of you just get some rest after the sea voyage. As you heard, we will be here for a few days and there's not much to do on the island. I don't know your tastes, or that of Skken, but we keep a brothel here to keep the men from going mad."

"I stopped frequenting whores many winters ago, Katrivus," says Ashcon, "but I appreciate the offer."

"The barbarians also brew the finest ale in the world, and I've taken to keeping their finest selections here. There are three ale houses, and they all serve the best kendra can buy, and there's always a stasshire game to be found."

At the mention of the stasshire game, Ashcon's eyes light up and he says, "So fine ale and gambling. Sounds like my kind of island."

Ashcon then heads to the door of the library with Katrivus following behind him with a look of newfound respect on his face.

Chapter 29

THE final night in Flotine is similar to the first four nights. Katrivus and Talon are in meetings with the rulers of the little island while Ashcon and Skken enjoy the fine ale and the kendra from Ashcon's "lucky streak." Sapphyre spends the majority of her time in thought and studying the demeanor of the wizards on the island.

The fact that there are more than a handful of them comes as a surprise to Sapphyre. When she finds out there is a consortium of wizards who have a permanent structure on the island, it comes as a shock. The wizards took up residence on the northern side. There are over thirty wizards of varying degrees of power on the island at any given time. The residence is off limits to all but the wizards, and even Katrivus is only permitted with an invitation.

Of the three alehouses, the sailors frequent all, but only Dupreeze Fine Spirits has wizards in attendance. The elderly Dupreeze, the proprietor, has lived amongst wizards all his life, so in addition to the ale the sailors drink by the bucketful, he imports manka from the lands far to the south. Manka is a dark yellow liquor made from the leaves of the Great Mankalumis tree and is the preferred drink of wizards. Some believe it is simply a matter of taste, but Dupreeze knows better. Wizards derive their power from the elements and they believe that drinking manka will replenish their innate mana and keep their powers honed. Dupreeze doesn't care whether it's true or not; he makes a ton of kendra because the wizards believe it.

There are at least fifteen wizards in attendance at Dupreeze Fine Spirits this evening, as well as a handful of sailors. Sapphyre has her usual stool in the corner, where she can sip her plum wine and observe everything around her. There are always eyes upon her since she is an outsider traveling under the protection of Katrivus. The sailors look at her hungrily while the wizards do so more out of curiosity.

For the first time since she arrived on the island, a gnome wizard approaches her slowly and stands directly in front of her, looking at her with a bemused expression on his face.

"Can I help you?" asks Sapphyre.

"You came here with Katrivus?" asks the wizard. Sapphyre doesn't reply but rather just tilts her head to the side in response. "I suppose that was a rather redundant question. May I introduce myself? I am Lymer, a wizard of the consortium."

"Pleased to meet you," replies Sapphyre.

"Well, I assume if you wished to tell me your name, you would have." Since Sapphyre does not interject, Lymer continues. "Please join me by the fire so we can talk." He indicates an empty table with his hand. Sapphyre walks to it and takes a seat with her back to the wall.

As Lymer sits down opposite her, she takes a moment to take in his appearance. Lymer seems to be about forty winters old, but that can be deceiving since he's a wizard and even more so since he's a gnome. He stands an unobtrusive three feet three inches tall and has the traditional short white beard of a wizard. He is dressed in a nondescript grey robe, similar to all the other wizards on the island, and he has a light green aura surrounding him. Sapphyre sits up as Lymer sits down, realizing she is giddy with excitement at the prospect of picking the brain of a wizard.

"Thank you for joining me, Sapphyre," says Lymer as he sets his manka down on the table. In response to the look of surprise on her face, he chuckles and explains, "You've been here for four nights and it's not a very big island."

"So what is it like to be a magic user, Lymer?"

"You tell me, Sapphyre," responds Lymer to the shock of Sapphyre. "It's obvious to the wizards on the island that you have some type of magical ability, but we are all perplexed as to where that power derives from. I was hoping you could shed some light onto that."

"I can only do a few little things, Lymer. I have nowhere near the power you wizards wield," Sapphyre says in response.

"You're such a kidder!" exclaims Lymer, and to Sapphyre's shock, stands up on the table and does a quick pirouette, and then sits immediately back down.

Sapphyre laughs out loud as Lymer's actions put her at ease. "So the wizards have been perplexed by me? Have you all been talking about me?"

"You and your companions, yes," replies Lymer honestly. "The barbarian shaman-in-training raised some questions when he utilized magic on your inbound voyage. And there is something special about the yellow-eyed man. All of a sudden Kat introduces us to this Talon kid and tells us we're all part of the Guild of Slight. I mean, ballyhoo!" Lymer stands up on the bench, hoists his drink in the air, screams "ballyhoo!" one more time and downs his beverage in one gulp. Sapphyre can't help but like this little peculiar gnome wizard.

"So what have you wizard's been saying?"

"Just the normal chitter chatter. Who are they? Where are they going? Blah, blah, blah."

"That will remain confidential," says Sapphyre. "Katrivus assured us that our privacy will be maintained, but I'm starting to think he may be mistaken."

"I would never betray that confidence and you can be sure Katrivus will take all measures to insure your privacy. I was simply asking because not all travelers need to keep their destination a secret."

"We are not all travelers," replies Sapphyre as she takes another sip of her wine.

"No, you are definitely not the typical voyager."

Sapphyre, eager to change the subject, asks, "So I understand wizards derive their power from the elements."

"That is true. There are some wizards who can harness the power of the winds, others water, while others the ground we walk upon. That is why Katrivus employs us for his sea voyages. There is no better compass than a living wizard!" With that last exclamation, the little gnome stands up, does a somersault, and then sits right back down as if nothing happened.

"Where do you derive your power?" asks a chuckling Sapphyre.

"Like most of the wizards here in Flotine, I gather my power from the element of water. When I am in contact with the ocean I can direct its current, detect sea monsters, and even gather information about the wind. I can harness the power of water into a great weapon if I so choose."

"There is an entire table of wizards staring at us, Lymer," says Sapphyre with her eyes on a table on the opposite side of the room.

Lymer turns toward the wizards and then back at Sapphyre with a huge grin on his little face. He jumps up on the table and states very loudly so all can hear, "Pardon this interruption. Staring is not polite!" he states while pointing his finger at the table of leering wizards. "If you're going to stare, then how about staring at this!" Lymer spins toward Sapphyre and then lifts his robe up over his waist as he's bending down and exposing his bare ass to the table of astonished wizards. This brought the house down in laughter, even the wizards being mooned couldn't help but laugh at their little comrade.

"How did you end up here?" asks Sapphyre through her laughter as Lymer returns to his seat.

"Well, it's not really a choice, Sapphyre," replies Lymer. "Wizards are all trained in one aspect of our powers. When we are born, a high wizard determines our sign –"mine being that of the sea. Then we are trained until our powers are strong enough to be useful in our field. The High Wizard Consortium governs all wizards in Arstevia and they tell us where to go and what our instructions are."

"So you were told to come here and work as a navigator for Katrivus," says Sapphyre.

"It goes a little beyond that, but yes. Katrivus helps out the consortium in ways I will not divulge, and we return the favor."

"I can see a light green aura surrounding you, Lymer," says Sapphyre to her bemused companion. "I can see auras emanating from magic users and they vary in color. The light green emanating from you has a very peaceful tone."

"Thank you for sharing that with me Sapphyre," replies Lymer.

"The wizards who keep looking at us all emanate the same light green aura; however, there is something different about one of them."

Lymer turns to the table and then back to Sapphyre before responding. "What's different?"

"Well, the little man in the corner who has his head down," starts Sapphyre.

"That would be Steen," interjects Lymer.

"Steen then. His aura is also green but it is not constant like the others. It is flickering and I feel it's in a constant state of flux."

"Steen is new here in Flotine," says Lymer. "He harnesses his power from water, as most of us on the island, and from what I've heard there is no better navigator. He keeps mostly to himself and

I'm sure he was vetted by the high wizard as we all are. I wouldn't give him another thought."

Sapphyre nods in response and looks back to the table of wizards to see Steen rise and leave abruptly. She thinks nothing of it and returns to her conversation with Lymer. "The hour is getting late and I depart early on the morrow, so I regret I must take my leave."

Lymer stands in response and says, "It has been my pleasure, Sapphyre. I hope I have the honor of serving as a navigator on your trip."

"Well we sail tomorrow, so wouldn't you know if you were assigned to our ship by now?" asks Sapphyre.

"No. That is one of the safeguards that Katrivus uses to insure privacy. The wizards will not know they are assigned to a ship, nor its destination, until the morning of departure."

"But we were told that the crew only knew how to get to and from one destination," says Sapphyre.

"That is true in terms of the crew. They only know how to navigate to and from only certain ports of call. What good would a wizard be if we can only travel to and from two certain places?" asks Lymer.

Sapphyre nods, acknowledging the sense of his statement. "Well, goodnight then, Lymer," she says. "I do hope that you will be our navigator." She then exits Dupreeze's establishment with fourteen sets of eyes on her.

Chapter 30

To Sapphyre's dismay, the ship for this second leg of their journey looks smaller and less seaworthy than the Sweeping Swallow. She'd always heard the smaller the ship the more tumultuous the trip. Another week or so of seasickness is not appealing. The crew is just finishing loading the supplies while the companions watch from the dock. The forecast for the coming voyage is not very promising, even without big storms on the horizon. The problem is, the temperature has plummeted overnight and there is no respite in the foreseeable future. All in all, Katrivus assures his young friend she had nothing to be apprehensive about.

While she is contemplating the information Kat imparted to her, she spies two wizards boarding the ship and a small smile forms on her face as she recognizes the happy-go-lucky Lymer. The smile almost turns to a frown when she sees the second wizard is Steen, but remembering the assurances from Lymer about his ability as a navigator puts her mind at ease.

"It is time," states Talon to his newfound friends. "Once aboard please head directly to your cabins with your belongings. This leg of the trip looks like it will not be a much easier voyage. The winds are not as strong as they are south of Flotine but it is uncharacteristically cold for this time of year. We may need to travel further east then we would like to avoid the ice. We won't know for sure until we are directly east of Cornice."

"Will we be stopping in Cornice?" asks Ashcon.

"Doubtful," replies Talon. "If we were to travel directly to Cornice from here we would go north along the Stantin Strait, which is the only safe route due to the abundance of ice. Since we are going all the way north to Starkk, we travel east of Cornice and bypass it completely."

Ashcon nods in response and Talon turns to lead them onto the ship. The crew on this leg of the voyage only numbers about thirty, not including the workers in the galley. The cabins are surprisingly larger than on the Sweeping Swallow and look like they can accommodate more than the single passenger. Ashcon and Skken share a cabin, with Sapphyre only one door down. Katrivus and Talon each have their own cabins on the opposite end of the ship.

Sapphyre is stowing her belongings away when she feels the ship leave the dock and she braces herself for the pending sea legs. As her breathing gets deeper and she prepares herself for the seasickness, it takes a few minutes for her to realize that it's not setting in as before. She exhales quietly and smiles, hoping it lasts for the whole trip. Her clothes stowed, her bowl and feathers secure, and with Frostripper in her boot, she exits her cabin and walks right next door to talk with Ashcon and Skken.

"Enter," says Skken to Sapphyre's soft knocking.

Sapphyre walks in, closes the door behind her and looks around the cabin, which is only slightly larger than hers. It's all all furnished in simple wood with two cots, one large trunk and a small table with four chairs. She sits down in one of the chairs and watches as Ashcon and Skken finish stowing their belongings.

Ashcon looks at Sapphyre and says matter-of-factly, "Something is on your mind, Sapphyre."

She nods in response and says, "There are a few things I would like to discuss with you."

Ashcon walks over to the door and activates his Rune of Warding to make sure the conversation remains in the cabin. He sits down opposite Sapphyre, who is staring at him wide-eyed. In explanation to her stare, Ashcon says, "Katrivus knows I am a runestar," and he holds up his hand as Sapphyre is about to speak. "You trust him as a brother and I have decided to place my trust in him as well. The wizards are aware they will sense magic at various points throughout the trip. We are sustaining the ruse that Skken is a barbarian shaman in training and he will be conducting certain rituals along our journey."

"Why did you tell him?" asks Sapphyre.

"He knew I was lying when I told him that the magic on the way to Flotine emanated from Skken," replies Ashcon as he takes the seat next to Sapphyre. "He asked me if it came from you or I and I told him the truth, since he already knew you have certain abilities."

"So then why," starts Sapphyre.

"Your friend is very astute and, to be honest, he tricked me into revealing I have powers," replies Ashcon, to the laughter of Skken behind him. He turns toward his barbarian friend and continues, "That being said, we now have to trust him implicitly."

Sapphyre just nods in response and holds her hands together with her head toward her lap.

"Something is on your mind, Sapphyre," says Ashcon. Since she doesn't reply Ashcon continues. "You spent a lot of time on your own in Flotine."

"I was intrigued by the wizards, so I observed them most of the time we were on the island," Sapphyre says in response, to which Ashcon nods. "I never spoke with any of them until last evening."

"What did you learn?" asks Skken from behind Sapphyre.

"Well, I found out that the wizards derive their power from the elements, and the wizards on the island control water, which is why they are here to help with navigation. The wizard I was speaking with is named Lymer. He's one of the navigators aboard our ship," says Sapphyre. Skken walks around the table so he is now facing both Sapphyre and Ashcon who are sitting side by side.

"This Lymer troubles you?" asks Skken.

"No, not at all," replies Sapphyre. "I rather like him, actually. He spoke to me by name, which surprised me." This information caused Skken and Ashcon to exchange startled glances.

"What else does he know?" asks Ashcon.

"Well, he thinks that I'm travelling with a barbarian shaman in training and another odd companion. And he knows that I have some magic ability. He said he sensed something in me."

Ashcon stands up abruptly and starts pacing as Sapphyre continues in an effort to calm Ashcon. "He had a green aura about him and I could sense no hostility in him. I don't believe we have anything to fear from him."

Skken is staring at Sapphyre when she continues, "The other wizard aboard the ship is the one who troubles me." Ashcon immediately stops pacing and turns to Sapphyre, who continues. "His name is Steen and his aura is different. All the wizards I've encountered on the island have either a green or blue aura around them. Steen does as well, except his is in a constant state of flux. The only way I can explain it is to say that I feel he is exerting effort to hold that aura in place. It does not seem natural."

Ashcon and Skken exchange glances as Ashcon sits back down and turns to Sapphyre. "Does Lymer know the identity of myself or Skken?"

Sapphyre's eyes squint as she recollects the conversation with Lymer. "I don't believe so. I have never mentioned you by name and he didn't disclose that he was aware. But he did know my name and I didn't tell him."

His look of consternation quickly passes, and Ashcon stands up, smiles at Sapphyre, and says, "We will keep an eye on this Steen character, although I'm sure there is nothing to worry about. Just to be prudent, please tell Katrivus about your encounter with Lymer."

"I will," says Sapphyre as she rises from the chair. "'I'm feeling a little claustrophobic so I'm going to go abovedeck for a bit."

Ashcon and Skken nod to Sapphyre as she exits the cabin and then Ashcon turns to Skken and says, "We have been careless about our identity, Skken." Skken just nods. "We need to be more prudent. Even though it has been many winters since Drak'thonn has sent assassins, if the prophecies are truly in play we must take precautions and expect him to try and locate us."

"What should we do about the wizard?" asks Skken.

"Keep an eye on Steen. I doubt Drak'thonn knows of our whereabouts, but let us err on the side of caution."

The first three days of the trip pass without incident but the fourth day brings about an abrupt change in the weather. Sapphyre awakes with a start as the ship sways violently and almost knocks her from her cot. As she steadies herself, there comes a knock upon her door. She opens it to see Ashcon and Skken fully dressed. He gestures for her to follow them above deck.

As the trio climbs to the deck, the difference in climate comes as a shock. The sun is just starting to rise to the east, but they can't tell since the skies were dark as night. The winds are gusting hard enough to blow the sails about and it takes all the strength of the crew just to hold them in place. The two wizards take their places in the navigation hubs flanking the ship and both of them are in a state of deep concentration.

Katrivus and Talon emerge from belowdeck just seconds after their three companions. They all stand side by side watching the action on the deck. Sapphyre turns her attention to the wizards just as the aura around Steen dissipates and the green turns to a dark red. Sapphyre turns to Ashcon to alert him of the change when a black orb emanates from Steen's hand and slams directly into Lymer's chest, incapacitating the wizard.

With the other wizard out of commission, Steen turns his attention toward Ashcon. Ashcon and Skken immediately turn toward Steen as the wizard transforms in front of them. As the red aura grows around Steen, his white hair and beard vanish and are replaced by a bald head, charcoal skin, and black orbs for eyes. He holds his hands high and a spell in the language of the cursed warlock bellows forth from his black mouth.

As Ashcon and Skken approach the perch holding the warlock, the dark spell bursts forth from Steen's lips and the deck of the ship starts clouding over, a dense black fog rising from the planks. As the fog comes into contact with the crew, enveloping them, they start screaming in agony.

As soon as the bolt from Steen's hand strikes Lymer, Sapphyre makes her way to the fallen wizard. Ignoring everything around her, she attends Lymer to ascertain his injuries. Leaning over Lymer, she reaches down and feels a weak pulse and labored breathing. Not knowing why, Sapphyre cradles Lymer in her lap and concentrates on healing him.

Katrivus rushes to Sapphyre, both to avoid the fog below and to see what is transpiring. When he approaches the two, he finds Sapphyre cradling the unconscious wizard and is signaled by Sapphyre to stop his approach. Sapphyre's calm demeanor stuns him, and he stops to watch as she closes her eyes and holds her hands at her sides. She is suddenly enveloped in a light green sphere that shines even through the darkness. As the green orb grows in intensity, Sapphyre's hands start to glow a light blue and she places them on Lymer's chest.

As the cries of the crew pierce the darkness, Ashcon and Skken set their sights on the warlock. Skken stealthily makes his way behind the magic user to approach Steen from behind, while Ashcon activates his Levitation Rune to put himself on equal footing with the warlock. Steen turns to Ashcon and smiles a grisly smile before launching streams of shadow magic in his direction. Ashcon easily avoids the black missiles and counters with arrows of ice, each of which is blocked by the warlock's staff. The ice arrows continue raining down on the warlock as the Ice Rune that runs from the nape of Ashcon's neck down through the small of his back pulsates with each frozen bolt, visible only to those with the power to see. Skken, meanwhile, is silently making his way up to the warlock's perch while Steen and Ashcon battle back and forth with shadow and ice.

Ashcon notices Skken bringing himself into position to launch an attack and falls down to the deck hoping to raise in Steen a false sense of victory. Steen laughs as he watches Ashcon fall to the deck and raises his arms to launch a final attack. As Steen is calling forth a killing spell, Ashcon jumps up quickly and sends a shimmering bolt of liquid ice in Steen's direction. The bolt of ice flies by Steen's head and the warlock gets distracted long enough for Skken to approach from the rear. He swings Grizzclaw, now alive with liquid ice from Ashcon's last bolt, and de-capitates the warlock. Steen's body freezes from the strike as his head drops onto the deck below. A second swing from Grizzclaw shatters his body into thousands of shards of ice.

The weather immediately changes back to the clear skies and brisk cold of days past as the fog from the deck dissipates. The melted bodies of the majority of the crew cover the deck and the stench is overwhelming.

As Ashcon reaches down to grab the still-frozen head of the warlock, he sees Talon standing ten feet away with his mouth agape, staring at him. Skken shimmies down from the wizards' perch to stand beside Ashcon, his bloody saber by his side. Ashcon holds the decapitated head of the warlock in his hands when Talon says quietly, "I always believed runestars to be legend."

Ashcon is about to reply when Katrivus approaches the three of them and says, "You must see this." He then turns and walks toward the other wizards perch where Sapphyre is attending to Lymer.

As the four approach, they all stop in their tracks at what they behold. Sapphyre is enclosed in a transparent green sphere, sitting down cross-legged with Lymer's head resting in her lap. Her hands are upon the wizard's chest and are glowing bright blue. She looks up at her friends and a small smile appears on her face. She then looks back down at the wizard, whose eyes open briefly before Sapphyre shuts them with her fingers and continues her healing.

Katrivus turns to Ashcon and says simply, "I don't believe she is your seeker, Ashcon."

To which Ashcon nods, turns to Talon and says, "It looks like we have a lot to discuss, my young thief."

Talon looks down at Sapphyre and back to Ashcon and just nods.

Chapter 31

THE male companions are sitting around the circular table in the captain's chamber in silence while Sapphyre is tending to Lymer on the cot in the rear of the room. The green orb surrounding Sapphyre has long since vanished and Lymer is sound asleep and breathing normally. As Sapphyre is approaching the table, there is a rather abrupt knock on the cabin door. Katrivus rises from his chair and walks to the door while Sapphyre takes a seat. He has a brief conversation with whoever is on the other side, closes the door and returns to the table.

Katrivus sighs audibly and a cloud of smoke from the cold precedes his words. "There were seventeen sailors killed by the warlock. We must redirect to Cornice to get another ship and more crewmen. At the rate we'll need to travel, and with the ship in the condition it's in, it will take us two days at least to reach the island."

Ashcon interjects, "I don't think we have much of a choice." He stands up and starts pacing around the table as he continues. "If our enemies knew we were on the ship then they'll have people waiting for us in Stark."

"That is a safe assumption," says Katrivus. "When we arrive in Cornice we will pick a different destination port."

"That won't work," replies Ashcon. "He'll have people at the three major ports of call. We need a different destination."

Talon stands up quickly and loudly asks, "Who is he? Why is he after you? And what in the name of the light and stars just happened up there?"

Sapphyre stands up and slowly walks over to Talon and puts a loving hand on his shoulder. This seems to melt away the irritation he had built up inside, and he slowly retakes his seat. Sapphyre looks down at Talon and smiles warmly. He turns back toward her seat and says, "Yes, Ashcon, why don't you tell us what in the name of the light and stars happened up there?"

This brings a startled gasp from Skken who then burst out laughing, which in turn causes everyone to follow suit. With the mood lightened, Ashcon sits down and says simply, "We have much to discuss."

Katrivus stands up and walks toward the armoire in the front of the cabin. He retrieves five simple glasses and a dark amber bottle. He places the glasses on the table and proceeds to fill each to the rim with the clear liquid. Ashcon stands up and walks over to the door and activates his Rune of Warding. As Katrivus distributes the rum, Ashcon begins his tale.

He turns to Talon and begins. "Most of this will be for your benefit, Talon, as Sapphyre knows much of this and Katrivus even more. You mentioned you thought runestars to be legend. As you now see, that is not the case." He stands up, takes a small sip of the spiced rum, places the glass on the table, and starts to walk in no particular direction while he continues. "I am a runestar and Skken is my True Guardian. We have been together for over seven hundred winters and over that time we have been searching for my seeker." He realizes he has made his way over to where Talon is sitting and asks him directly. "Do you have any magical abilities that you are aware of?"

Talon looks up at Ashcon and says, "No."

Ashcon and Skken exchange glances and Ashcon continues. "Yet you were able to see my runes?"

Talon nods affirmatively.

"When we first came upon Sapphyre, we discovered that she can see my runes as well. It is because of this that we are on our current quest. Only extremely proficient magic users can see my runes and that is a very rare occurrence. One explanation is that she is my seeker." He turns to Sapphyre, and she looks at him with a startled expression on her face. "I'm sorry we didn't tell you, Sapphyre, but now we know that not to be the case. In fact, the only thing we know about you for sure is that you are not my seeker. It is now even more imperative for us to reach Sorenthor."

"What do you mean 'more imperative'?" asks Sapphyre.

Ashcon walks back to his chair and picks up his glass. He finishes it one gulp and places the empty glass on the table. He leans over with both hands on the table and slowly surveys his companions at the table. His eyes land on Sapphyre. He says, "Since we know you are not my seeker, Sorenthor is the one who may have the knowledge to figure out the origins of your magic."

"What makes you so sure I'm not your seeker?" asks Sapphyre.

"Well, for one, you are simply too powerful," answers Ashcon. "Seekers are untrained in magic and very rarely have the ability to perform even the most mundane of acts. The first time they realize they have any ability is when they meet their runestar for the first time and see the runes. It is then the runestar's responsibility to train their seeker. When we first met you, we knew you had some ability but were unaware of your true nature. Now that we know more of your powers, we are sure that you are not my seeker." Ashcon then stands up and turns to the young thief. "That's the first thing. The second thing that makes me sure you are not my seeker is a rather simple one. Every runestar has only one seeker." He starts walking the perimeter of the table. "And it looks like young Talon is mine."

Talon looks up at Ashcon and then back down at the drink in his hand. He takes a deep breath and takes a huge swallow of rum. "So what happens now?"

"I still don't understand how you are so sure, Ashcon," says Sapphyre. "Aren't you going to take him to Sorenthor to confirm his identity?"

"I am going to Sorenthor's, Sapphyre, yes," answers Ashcon, "but not to confirm his identity. I have other business with Sorenthor. In answer to your question, there is a bond that was formed the instant Talon saw my runes. I cannot explain it, but I knew immediately that Talon is my seeker."

As Sapphyre is about to reply, Talon interjects, "Sapphyre, it's true. There is no doubt that Ashcon is my runestar and I am his seeker." He stands up, places both of his hands on the table and exclaims, "And now that is out of the way, there is other business we need to discuss." He turns to Ashcon and says, "You know who planned the attack today."

"Yes," replies Ashcon. Ashcon then refills all the empty glasses and retells his entire tale, from the beginning, for the benefit of Talon and Sapphyre. Once completed, they direct the conversation back to the present.

"If Drak'thonn knew you were on this ship then he no doubt has people in each of the three major ports of call," says Skken.

"I agree," replies Ashcon. "We have to assume he does. We also have to assume he has people in Cornice."

Talon stands up and pushes his chair in. "He won't make a move in Cornice. He will see where we are heading and plan an assault after we land."

Katrivus says, "The problem is that we have a limited number of ships and even more limited ports of call. Where are we supposed to land if Starkk, Prospekt, and Thull are out?"

At this point Skken stands up and all eyes turn toward his intimidating frame. "There are isolated tribes up and down the coastline if you know where to look," he states. "I have not been back to the northern lands in quite some time and know not where these tribes are located." He then turns to Katrivus and states, "But you do, Katrivus."

"I know of one tribe, yes," says Katrivus. "How did you know?"

"The desk in your library in Flotine. The one you received as a reward for finding the high shaman's only daughter. I know of the Sashee tribe and I know them to be tied to the sea. I simply was unaware they still existed."

Katrivus looks at Skken with squinting eyes and says, "You were never in my library." Skken and Ashcon exchange grins.

Talon intervenes, "Okay, so do the Sashee have a port we can access?"

All eyes are on Katrivus, who replies, "It's not a port. It is a small, isolated small patch of beach surrounded by dense forest. They have a few fishing boats and we can approach in the smallest of our vessels." He stands up. "But the problem is that this tribe is hostile to outsiders and even though I gained favor with this high shaman, once I accepted his gift, the slate is wiped clean." He turns toward Skken and says, "I am not sure what type of reception we would get. He could just as quickly treat me as an enemy or as a friend."

Skken looks directly at Katrivus and says, "If you can get us there, I will take care of our reception."

"Very well," replies Katrivus. "It is located about two days travel south of Thull and north of Prospekt. We will take the quickest and smallest ship we have in port and run with a limited crew."

"How long will the trip take?" asks Sapphyre.

"Six days from Cornice," replies Katrivus.

"As far as anyone is concerned, our destination is Thull," continues Katrivus. "The first few days of the voyage is consistent with Thull being our port of call."

"How many crew will we need?" inquires Ashcon.

"The thinnest we can run with would be fourteen crewmen and one wizard."

"I believe I can fulfill the role of wizard," comes a shallow voice from the rear of the room. All heads turn toward Lymer as he sits up and exclaims. "This is so very exciting! To think I will be traveling with a runestar, his True Guardian, and a seeker! Oh, so very exciting!" He jumps up off the bed, stretches his legs, runs to Sapphyre's chair, and bows extravagantly. He then takes her hand, gives it a gentle kiss, and says quietly, "Thank you, Sapphyre."

Sapphyre nods at the little man, looks up at the group, and says, "It appears we have our wizard."

The men all know at that point that Lymer is the wizard, and since he obviously heard the entire conversation, there is no reason to object. The group spends the remainder of the night perusing maps and planning the next leg of the trip. By the time they retire for the night, they are all exhausted. The calm of the slowly drifting ship lulls them to sleep.

Chapter 32

It takes until sundown on the third day of travel for the ship to arrive in Cornice. Sapphyre stands on the deck looking at the island as they dock. It is smaller than Flotine and there are only two other ships docked at the port. There are four buildings in view and no wall to prevent assault as there was on the much larger island. The group disembarks and makes their way without interruption to the largest of the brick buildings. In fact, Sapphyre realizes they have not seen one other person since their arrival.

As Katrivus opens the door, the sounds from within come as an answer to Sapphyre's unasked question. The common room is rather large, with six tables that can seat up to six, a bar with seven stools, and a grand hearth that keeps the place warm. There are fourteen people enjoying dinner, one serving boy who looks about twelve winters, a bartender, and a cook.

Katrivus directs the group to an empty table kitty-corner to the bar, where the six of them take a seat while Katrivus makes his rounds. Sapphyre starts observing the room, wondering which of the strangers could be a spy for Drak'thonn. There is a table of dirty sailors, five wizards near the fire, two men sitting quietly in the corner, and a few men eating alone or enjoying a pipe. She starts to blush as she notices that most of the men are staring at her, and it hits her that she is the only woman in sight.

Just as Sapphyre is turning a light shade of purple, Katrivus rejoins the group and exclaims, "We are in luck. The Mermaid's Tale is one of the quickest clippers in our fleet, and it will be docking here tomorrow from Flotine." He takes a seat and pulls a swig from his mug. "It's also our smallest ship, and we can run it with a very few crewmen."

"How small?" asks Ashcon.

"We can probably get there with only four men and the six of us, but in order for them to return we'll need to bring six."

"You need to be extremely thorough in vetting the six who accompany us," says Skken authoritatively.

"I already know who will captain and he's a good man," replies Katrivus. "We'll have to see who arrives on the ship from Flotine and add them to the pool of possible crewmen."

Talon leans forward and says, "I wouldn't do that, Katrivus." All the eyes turn toward the young seeker as he explains. "This island is just a transfer point with no permanent residents. You can be quite certain that our spy will be on the ship arriving from Flotine tomorrow."

Ashcon leans back in his chair and says, "I agree with Talon. If there is a spy we have to assume it's one of the crew from Flotine. He'll report that we are going to Thull, where my brother will concentrate his efforts, which is what we want."

"We do have one problem that I cannot figure out how to bypass," says Katrivus as he refills his ale mug. "The six men whom we take with us will know where we landed.'

"It cannot be helped," says Ashcon. "By the time they return to Cornice and have the opportunity to pass on that information, we will be long gone."

At this point the serving boy emerges with a platter of grilled fish and fresh bread and places it on the table before retreating back to the kitchen. The six companions each help themselves to generous portions and continue the meal in relative silence.

Katrivus finishes the last of the ale in his mug, stands up and says, "If you'll excuse me, I'm going to start the vetting process right now. This building also serves as the barracks, and Cline will show you to your rooms." He makes his way to the table of dirty sailors just as the bartender comes around to introduce himself.

"I'm Cline. If you'll follow me," he says while gesturing with his arm.

The group follows Cline through the only other door besides the one leading to the kitchen. The hallway is thin and raw with a slightly mildewed scent and has doors on both sides. He stops about midway down the hallway and says, "Three on this side and two on the other."

Skken steps forward and says, "We need only four rooms and one with two cots."

"Fine," says Cline. "The last door on the left is for the double then. Breaking the fast is at first light. If there's nothing else, I bid you good night." Cline then heads back to the common room leaving the five friends in the hallway.

Sapphyre opens the first door on her left, takes a quick peek inside and turns back and says, "I'm retiring early. Good night."

Talon says, "Good night Sapphyre," and as she closes her door he turns toward Ashcon. "I think we need to speak alone before retiring."

Ashcon says, "I agree. However, as you will come to realize, Skken is always there. When you actually meet your True Guardian you'll see what I mean. In the meantime why don't we retreat to my room and talk?" He leads the way to the last room on the left.

The three men enter the room. Talon takes a look around as Ashcon activates his Rune of Warding. The room is bare with two lanterns, a plain oak table with four small chairs, and two cots along the right wall. There is a small fireplace on the rear wall, which is already lit when they enter, and a water basin with a few bowls beside it. Talon takes a seat at the table while Skken disarms himself by the second cot.

Ashcon turns from the door and takes a seat next to Talon. "I think we need to discuss some-thing before moving forward. There is a bond forming between us and we both felt it the moment you saw my runes. It's very similar to the bond I felt with Skken when I first met him. That bond has grown to the point where Skken and I not only trust each other with our lives, but we actually think the same way. What I mean is that we always come to the same conclusion when a situation arises. When we act we do so without having to communicate verbally." Ashcon stands up and starts pacing slowly and continues. "That is the type of relationship you and I will form. We have to not only be honest with each other at all times, but also trust each other with what we hold most valuable."

Talon looks at Ashcon and says, "I understand. There is much I need to tell you."

Ashcon sits back down. Skken walks over to the table and takes the seat opposite Talon.

"As you know, I've been a rather successful board member with the Guild of Slight for many winters," starts Talon. "I have committed my share of crimes from burglary to assassination. I know that this is in direct contradiction to the edicts of the Star Gods to whom you serve. What you must know is that I was ordered to become a member of the Guild of Slight. I was told to do whatever was necessary to gain the trust of the guild, no matter what the crime."

"Who ordered you to do this?" asks Ashcon.

Talon replies, "The High Priestess Ka'alshene."

Ashcon and Skken exchange startled looks. Then Ashcon leans back in his chair and stretches his arms up over his head, saying, "So you work for the high priestess?" to which Talon nods a yes. "I wonder if she knows you are my seeker."

"The high priestess told me you were coming to Thorenn and to take you to Sorenthor."

"So you were ordered by Ka'alshene to take us to Sorenthor's library?" asks Aschon.

"Yes. I can communicate with her through a ritual involving feathers I keep in this locket. A few nights before you arrived she summoned me and I spoke with her. She told me that two companions and a girl would be looking for the Lonely Hermit, the name by which I have always referred to Sorenthor. I asked her who you were and she told me it wasn't important. She then imparted to me a vision of a map with Sorenthor's Library noted on it. I can recall the map at any time in my mind's eye but I cannot transfer it to parchment."

"So Ka'alshene made sure that you had to come along on the journey. Interesting," says Ashcon.

"That leads me to believe that she may know some-thing of you being my seeker." He looks at Talon and says quickly, "Can you reach Ka'alshene at any time?"

"I only need water; however, I have never at-tempted contacting her without a summons from her."

"How does she summon you?" asks Skken.

"The locket heats up," says Talon simply. "I think you may be wrong about Ka'alshene know-ing I'm your seeker. I believe she just wants me here to be her eyes and ears."

"Have you reported in to her since we left Thorenn?" asks Skken.

"No, as a matter of fact, I have not. I assume that when she wants information, she will contact me," answers Talon.

"I would like you to contact her now. I want to find out how much she knows, plus she may have information to share. And if she does not know about you and me, then it is our duty to inform her."

"Very well," says Talon as he stands up and fin-gers the locket around his neck. He walks over to the basin in the corner, takes one of the wooden bowls and fills it up before returning to the table and sitting back down. He opens up the locket, takes the feather out and says, "Even though I don't need to communicate verbally with her, I will speak out loud so you can hear the conversation from my end. I'll ask any questions you have and relay her response." The two men nod affirmatively and Talon drops the hair into the water and closes his eyes.

"Good evening, m'lady," says Talon. "Please pardon the interruption but there have been developments I believe you need to be made aware of." Ashcon and Skken look on as Talon pauses and then continues the conversation. "I am well, m'lady, thank you."

Ashcon says, "Tell her you are here with me and Skken."

Talon nods slowly with his eyes still closed and says, "M'lady, Ashcon and Skken are here with me."

There is a long pause before Talon says, "M'lady, I understand it is improper but please know I would not have done so if it wasn't of the utmost importance."

Ashcon says loudly, "Ask Ka'alshene to tune us in."

Talon, still with his eyes closed, furrows his brow, and then to his astonishment, hears the high priestess talking to Ashcon.

"It has been quite a while, Ashcon," says the high priestess.

"It has, m'lady."

"Skken," says Ka'alshene in greeting.

"High priestess," responds Skken.

"Please tell me why Talon felt the need to divulge to you his relationship with me." asks Ka'alshene.

"With all due respect, m'lady, I must ask you a few questions first," says Ashcon.

There is a short pause before the high priestess replies with an irritated tone, "Very well."

"Why did you order Talon to help us reach Sorenthor?"

"As high priestess I have access to a vast amount of privileged information. It may be contained in ancient scrolls, it may come to me in a vision or in a moment of prayer. When I receive a vision, no matter the source, I act on it as an order from the Star Gods. I never question their motive."

Ashcon asks, "So you received a vision that ordered you to aide us in our quest to find Sorenthor?"

"Actually, I became aware of you before you went to Thorenn. I was alerted by the Star Gods when you first encountered Sapphyre," responds Ka'alshene.

"Why would Sapphyre and me meeting trigger a vision like that?"

"I was not sure at the time, but I assumed that you had finally found your seeker. When I ordered Talon to take you to see Sorenthor I was following the prophecy from an ancient tome that I was directed to read by the Star Gods."

"What did the prophecy say?" asks Ashcon.

"I cannot tell you, Ashcon, and let me explain. First off, the reason I had Talon aid you is because I may not become directly involved with subjects of prophecy. I can talk with you as we are doing now; however, I cannot directly aid you in your quest."

"Why did you find it necessary to insure that Talon had to join us on our trip?" asks Ashcon.

"How else was I going to keep an eye on you, my dear?" says Ka'alshene with a slight giggle.

"Then you do not know," says Ashcon quietly. "Sapphyre is not my seeker, Ka'alshene."

There is a short silence before she responds. "Are you sure? Isn't that the basis for the trip to see Sorenthor?"

"It started out that way, yes," replies Ashcon. "Then certain things unfolded and we saw that her abilities, however raw, are quite powerful and go beyond the ability of an untrained seeker."

"I still don't understand how you can be so sure," starts Ka'alshene before Talon interrupts.

"Excuse me, m'lady, but there is another, much more concrete reason we know that Sapphyre is not Ashcon's seeker. And that precipitated the reason for this contact."

"And what would that be my – ."starts Ka'alshene before gasping audibly and continuing at barely above a whisper, "Is it true? Are you his seeker, my young Talon?"

"It is true, m'lady," says Talon.

Ashcon interjects, "Can you believe the time has finally come, Ka'alshene?"

"When will you begin training?" asks the high priestess seemingly ignoring Ashcon's question.

"We are going to have to wait until we finish our business with Sorenthor."

"I am happy for you both," says Ka'alshene with genuine fondness. "And what has become of the young Sapphyre?'

"We still have no idea what school of magic Sapphyre hails from but she is definitely innately attracted to the healing arts," answers Ashcon. "We are hoping Sorenthor can shed some light on the situation."

"I am sure he will do what he is able," says Ka'alshene.

"There is another situation Ka'alshene," says Ashcon. "There was an attempt on my life recently. A warlock killed seventeen men and injured more in an attack aboard a ship before Skken decapitated him."

"So Drak'thonn knows your whereabouts and is actively hunting you once more."

"We are taking measures so he won't be able to track us, but yes, apparently he has taken an interest in killing me again."

"I will see what information I can obtain with regards to your brother," says the high priestess. "Contact me again right before you reach Sorenthor. Good luck in your quest and may the Star Gods light your way."

"You as well, m'lady," says Talon as the vision of the high priestess fades and the three men open their eyes.

The three men sit in silence pondering the conversation with the high priestess when Ashcon speaks. "It has been a trying few days and I suggest we all get some much needed rest." With that, Ashcon stands up as a signal to Talon that the evening is coming to a close and the young seeker heads to his own room for the night.

Chapter 33

THE speed of the Mermaid's Tale dazzles Sapphyre. It comes as no surprise to her when Katrivus lets everyone know they are making excellent time. The blonde, blue-haired beauty spends the majority of her time on the deck of the ship with Lymer discussing all facets of magic. It is acutely obvious to her companions that Sapphyre is getting more proficient with her magical abilities at an incredible rate. Lymer explains to Sapphyre how he manipulates the water and can sense the young girl drawing on the same power, although she is unable to harness it. As the two are discussing the scent of the air in relation to nautical properties, Ashcon steps to the front of the deck to converse with the two magic users.

"So what are the two of you working on this fine morning?" asks Ashcon.

"I am sharing with Sapphyre the correlation between the sense of smell and nautical deviations in regard to wind velocity," explains Lymer. Seeing the confused look on Ashcon's face, he continues. "In order to harvest the power of water one must utilize all of his senses. The sense of smell comes in handy when there is a subtle shift of the wind that is almost imperceptible to the sense of touch. If you are not sure which way the wind is blowing, any magic you implore to command the sea can have devastating effects."

"And how is Sapphyre doing?" asks Ashcon.

"You don't have to talk about me as if I'm not here, Ashcon," admonishes Sapphyre. "I don't necessarily understand the intricacies with which Lymer is explaining, but I do see how it is done."

Lymer interjects. "Sapphyre's magic is of a different school from mine and I must say it seems a much more complex one, and in a very strange way. Strange because it is so complex, yet simple for her to do. By merely explaining what I do, Sapphyre is able to harness her magic to do almost the same thing as I, but with no direct command over the water. I am just as excited as you are to meet Sorenthor and find out from which school of magic this young lady gains her power."

"We all do," agrees Ashcon. "Please excuse me as I need to speak with Katrivus. You carry on doing whatever it is you are doing."

Lymer just smiles at Ashcon and then does a backwards somersault into a pirouette to the amusement of Sapphyre.

Ashcon heads below deck to find Katrivus and Talon sitting in the Captain's chamber at the round table. "At what point do we change course and head for our real destination?" asks Ashcon.

Katrivus looks up as Ashcon takes a seat and replies, "According to my calculations, we should reach that point by mid-morning on the morrow. When we break the fast I will pull the captain aside and inform him of our plans."

"How will he take the news?" asks Talon.

"I think the only thing he will be concerned about is returning without a wizard on board. But since he won't be on any major trade routes, there shouldn't be much danger."

"Are you going to give him any specific instructions regarding our passage remaining secret?" asks Talon.

Ashcon leans forward and says, "Everyone in Cornice is under the impression that our destination is Thull. When we don't arrive in Thull,

Drak'thonn will certainly try to find out where we went. Are you going to have them return directly to Cornice, Katrivus?"

"Yes. If Drak'thonn has someone on Flotine and the ship returns to that port, he will only find out faster about our diversion. Returning to Cornice may buy us a few days more of a head start."

"Will the barbarians of this little tribe keep our passing a secret?" inquires Talon.

Skken steps out of the shadows to Kat and Talon's surprise and answers. "I guarantee they will." Talon just nods to Skken in acknowledgement.

"So once we divert our course, how long until we reach our destination?" asks Ashcon.

Katrivus stands up from the table, pushes his chair in and replies. "If the winds blow in their normal pattern we should make it there in two days' time."

"Talon, do you know how long the journey is to Sorenthor's Library?" asks Ashcon.

Talon looks at Katrivus, and then Ashcon and says, "From what I have been able to ascertain, we need to stay south of the Great North Road while going west. If we were travelling our original course from Thull, we would have headed directly west for three days to reach the road. From the road, it is still half a moonsign to the library."

Skken walks closer to the table and says to the three men, "Drak'thonn's men will most definitely stay to the Great North Road in their search for us. It is too dangerous for a small contingency of non-barbarians to roam the country side in the north."

"What if he recruited barbarians?" inquires Talon.

"Impossible," replies Skken. "The Great North Road will be too dangerous for us. I will lead us through the northern wild toward the DragonTooth Pass, which is southwest of where we land. Talon, where is the pass in relation to Sorenthor's library?"

Talon closes his eyes for a moment and replies, "It is southeast and looks to be about a ten-day journey to the library."

Skken places his hands on the table and says, "The Great North Road ends in the village of Redpost, which we will bypass. The road will not be an issue on our journey north after that point."

Katrivus looks at Skken and asks, "Are we going to stop in Redpost and see if we can find out if Drak'thonn has been inquiring of our where-abouts?"

Skken moves his head back and forth and replies, "No, that won't be necessary, nor is it wise. Redpost is as big as Prospekt and is the closest village to Dark Horde territory. They are certain to have it under watch. I will gain all the information we require from the small tribes we will encounter during the journey." He pauses and then takes a seat with his companions. "When we encounter the Sashee, let me do all the talking. They will expect us to spend the night with the tribe and it would be an insult not to. We will then start our journey west on the following morning." Skken stands up, nods to his companions, and steps back into the shadows by the further of the two cots.

"Do you agree with his plan of action, Ashcon?" asks Katrivus.

"Absolutely. It will be the safest means of pas-sage," replies Ashcon. Seeing the worried look on Kat's face, he continues. "I have travelled the lands of the north with Skken on many occasions, gentlemen and we have always come back."

Skken laughs quietly from the darkness, but Ka-trivus isn't satisfied. "I have been to the lands of the north many times and have heard the stories about the smaller tribes. The further you travel inland the more hostile they are to outsiders, and the more brutal they are in their tactics."

As Ashcon is about to reply, Skken emerges once again from the shadows and says, "If you were to travel alone, that would be the case, Katrivus. Trust me. I will take care of our safe passage." He turns to Ashcon, nods, and exits the room with Ashcon following signaling an end to the meeting.

Chapter 34

THE captain is navigating the small ship toward the land of the Sashee when Skken emerges on deck to the gasps of both his companions and the crew. Instead of his usual black billowing robes, Skken is awash in all colors of the spectrum. Atop his bald head lies an intricate band of woven threads interspersed with feathers and long sharp tusks of ivory rising six inches up into the sky. His face is painted so there is no hint of his skin peeking through. There are light blue ovals surrounding his eyes and mouth, with vertical lines of green and yellow from the top of his head to his neckline. His black robe is gone and his only garb is a loincloth and boots made of fur. Bracelets adorned with gold and lapis cover both his arms, but the most striking part of his appearance is the four tattoos that appear to be glowing on his torso. Above his right breast there is an image of a green cyclone, so vivid it seems to be moving. Above his left breast is a blue wave so intricate one can see the foam at the crest. Side by side on his abdomen are a small flickering flame that is almost smoking and a light green orb representative of the land so realistic one can almost smell the grass.

While most of the crew is simply staring with their mouths agape, Skken ignores them and makes his way over to where his companions are standing on the deck, saying,. "As we make our way to the shore, I will stand at the front of the ship so they will see me upon our arrival. You will see the tribe react somewhat strongly to my appearance, but do not be alarmed and do not say a word. When we do arrive on land, I will leave the ship with Ashcon and talk with the high shaman. Under no circumstances are you to leave the ship before you are summoned." He turns to address Katrivus. "Inform the captain that his crew must go belowdeck immediately and stay there until further notice."

Katrivus nods and walks in the direction of the captain as Skken continues. "From this point on, remain toward the rear of the ship. We will summon you shortly after our arrival." His companions nod affirmatively and silently make their way to the back of the ship.

While Katrivus, Talon, Lymer, and Sapphyre look toward the shore from the rear of the ship, Skken situates himself in the very front with Ashcon directly beside him. The barbarians notice the ship arriving and have assembled along the shore. As they come into view, the four companions to the rear of the ship step back apprehensively almost in unison. There are dozens of barbarians along the shoreline, each one of them armed with bows aimed at the incoming ship. The gasps were not in reaction to the scantily clad barbarians but to their companions.

Behind the line of archers are dozens more of the tribesman, each with a white wolf beside them. The wolves are huge, their heads aligned with the barbarians' chest, and their bodies stretching back almost six feet. The extra fur to fend off the cold adds to their already tremendous girth lending an even more menacing presence.

The ship slowly makes its way to within a hundred yards of land, and the barbarians part their ranks for someone to make his way forward. As the leader of the tribe makes his way toward the shoreline, Skken turns to Ashcon and nods.

Ashcon steps forward besides Skken, closes his eyes, and activates his Rune of Levitation. To the shock of the barbarians looking on, both Ashcon and Skken start hovering and proceed toward the shoreline, which is now forty feet away, gliding ten feet above the water.

The barbarians are staring in shock as the two strangers approach and as a few of the tribesman are nocking their bows, the high shaman makes his way to the front of the shoreline and has his men hold fast. Skken finally comes into focus and the high shaman holds his arms to the air. A booming voice comes forth in a language the companions on the Mermaid's Tale do not understand. Within seconds, every tribesman places their weapons beside them and get down on their knees with their heads firmly planted in the sand, their arms outstretched. Even the high shaman is in the same position in obvious reverence to Skken.

The four companions look at each other in silence and then back to the shore to the unraveling scene. As Skken and Ashcon approach, Ashcon lets his Rune of Levitation fade. The two walk on the sand toward the High Shaman of the Sashee. Skken places his hand on the head of the kneeling leader and says something quietly. The high shaman stands up, faces Skken, kisses each of his palms and embraces the True Guardian. He then turns toward Ashcon and bows slightly. The runestar returns the gesture. The high shaman then announces something to his tribesman and they all return to their feet.

Sapphyre and her companions watch Ashcon and Skken make their way inland with the high shaman. To their surprise, the archers immediately get back in position, and the tribesmen with the wolves assemble directly behind them. As they watch the tribesmen, Katrivus turns to the others and says, "I knew that True Guardians were revered among their people, but I never realized to what extent. I have never seen a high shaman on his knees before."

Talon turns to Kat and says, "Now we know why traversing the lands will be less of a problem than we anticipated."

"I only worry word will spread that there is a True Guardian travelling the lands of the north," says Katrivus solemnly. "It is quite an honor to be visited by one."

Sapphyre replies, "Skken told us not to worry about word spreading, and after all I've seen, I tend to believe him."

Just as Katrivus is about to respond, Ashcon emerges on the shore with a barbarian female. She gives some instructions to the armed tribesmen, who nod in unison. As the bowmen remove their bows and make their way inland, the men with the wolves turn in a different direction and run north along the shoreline. Seconds later, a slew of barbarians jog to the shore, towing small fishing vessels. They maneuver them expertly into the water and two boats with two men each row to the Mermaid's Tale. Sapphyre and Talon make their way down the side of the cutter into one of the waiting boats, while Katrivus and Lymer get into the other. The captain looks at Katrivus from the deck and says, "I will stay with my crew and await further instructions." Katrivus nods and the boats retreat back to the shore and the captain heads below deck.

The two small boats find their way to the shore, and Ashcon and the barbarian female greet the four friends. Ashcon says, "I believe the high shaman is the only one who speaks the common tongue. Do not attempt to communicate with any of the others. If they offer you something, take it and then bow your head in thanks. For greeting a simple nod is expected. Nod to the female and she will lead us to the high shaman's dwelling."

They follow Ashcon's instructions. The barbarian leads the way inland at a slow pace. Sapphyre looks at the natives who are following and staring but staying at a comfortable distance. The temperature is far below freezing yet the weather doesn't seem to bother the barbarians. Most of the tribesmen have only fur shoulder straps, headgear also made of fur, a simple loincloth and fur boots. All of the barbarians have some type of jewelry on one arm only, and it looks random to Sapphyre as to whether it is on the right or left. The women are dressed identical to the men with their breasts exposed and the same adornments on their arms. There are males and females interspersed amongst the archers and the wolf trainers, so it is obvious that gender does not play a role in this society with regard to defense. No man amongst the tribe stands less than six and a half feet tall. The women are a mere inches shorter.

Following the female, they make their way through the heart of the village, which has fire pits every few dozen feet. The dwellings seem to be made of some sort of mud, though they have a slight sparkle as they rise the ten or twelve feet to their summit. Sapphyre counts fourteen of these huts and they step toward the largest and most inland when the female stops at the entrance and moves to the side. She bows her head slightly to Ashcon. He returns the gesture, and the five companions enter the hut single file.

Whatever these structures are made of, they are certainly not flammable as there is a fire in the middle of the bare hut and torches along the walls. Upon their entrance, Skken and the high shaman turn toward the door and the high shaman speaks. "You are welcome in the land of the Sashee. Enter my dwelling and partake of my triumphs."

Ashcon nods and says in response, "Thank you, High Shaman of the Sashee. May your triumphs eclipse those of your people past." He then proceeds to where Skken and the high shaman are standing with the other four following.

The high shaman turns to Katrivus and says, "I never thought to see you again, Soui Toofen."

Katrivus replies, "I too did not think our paths would cross, but the fates have made it so." He turns to Sapphyre's puzzled stare and the others who also have confused looks on their faces. "Many winters ago I rescued his daughter from a rival tribe. Soui Toofen is a Sashee name of endearment."

The high shaman laughs lightly and moves to stand directly in front of Katrivus. He opens his palms and Kat slides his hand into the huge mitts of the barbarian. He grips his hands, closes his eyes, speaks in his language and then opens his eyes and the two embrace.

"Please let us sit around the fire and share a drink in honor of the visit of the Ta'adaal," says the high shaman as he takes a seat beside the fire.

Skken speaks while sitting down beside the high shaman. "Ta'adaal is the tribal name of a True Guardian. It is the only word in the many dialects of the tribes of the north that is universal."

"It is the honor of any tribe to be visited by Ta'adaal," says the high shaman. "The last time this tribe had the honor was over four hundred winters ago. In our tribe, the title of high shaman is hereditary and a high shaman can be either male or female. The high shaman at the time was a female by the name of Jienna. Her story of her meeting with Ta'adall has been passed down from one high shaman to the next. So I have heard the tale, and it is my pleasure to welcome you back to the tribe of the Sashee after so many turns of the moon."

The high shaman than looks at the runestar and the True Guardian with frank reverence in his eyes and asks, "Skken, Ashcon, may I have the honor of relaying to my heir this most holy of visits so that it may honor the tribe of the Sashee for all eternity?"

Skken looks to Ashcon and back to the high shaman and then replies, "You may honor your heir and your tribe, but you must wait until the time of your passing when you grant your heir the title of high shaman."

The high shaman beams with pride and replies enthusiastically in the language of his tribe, "Raankal tovin standee, Ta'adaal." Skken nods. The high shaman turns to the entrance of his home and raises his voice in the language of his people. Three young males enter and fill ornate ceramic goblets from the cistern by the fire. They distribute it to the companions before leaving without a word.

Ashcon speaks first after the high shaman blesses the warm wine, confiding in him and addressing him by name. "Fareen Makuu, we are on a quest travelling west and wish our traversing your lands to remain in confidence. That is the reason for our visit."

The high shaman nods in understanding but remains silent.

Ashcon continues, "For your own safety and that of your people, we must keep our destination a secret."

Again the high shaman nods but remains silent.

Skken intervenes, "As Ta'adaal, if we encounter other tribes, I will demand their silence of our passing."

The high shaman looks down into his hands, and frowns. Raising his eyes to Skken, he says quietly, "May I ask, with all due respect, when is the last time you visited the lands of the north?"

Ashcon and Skken exchange glances and Skken replies, "Almost two hundred winters."

The high shaman looks back and forth between the two men, and then around at the other companions by the fire, his eyes pausing slightly at the little gnome with a permanent grin on his face. "Much has changed over time," he starts and then pauses to take a sip of wine. "Once the trade with the south began in earnest with young

Katrivus, the changes were inevitable. In all of the three major cities there are taverns constructed for your sailors. At first they were confined to the docks and run by your own men." He stands up and shakes out a cramp in his leg, pauses, and continues. "There is now active trade between Redpost and the coastal cities and it is not confined to barbarians."

Katrivus looks to a stunned Ashcon and Skken and asks the high shaman, "What of the tribes between here and Redpost?"

"As has been over time, they keep to themselves and are nomadic in nature. As long as the strangers do not attack them directly or attempt to move them off the land they claim for a brief time, they leave them alone." He then takes a sip of wine and in his native tongue addresses Skken. "Ta'adall." Skken immediately corrects his defeated posture and sits straight up, looking directly in to the eyes of the high shaman as he continues. "I'm afraid that it will be impossible to keep your passing through the lands secret on your journey west."

Ashcon is about to object, but the high shaman turns to him and raises both hands to his lips. The runestar keeps silent as Fareen Makuu continues.

"There have been tributaries constructed off of the Northern Trail to accommodate the traders in their travels." He pauses for affect. "Most are run by humans and dwarves."

The faces of Ashcon and Skken pale in disbelief, and Ashcon clears his throat before admitting out loud, "It seems as if we need a change of plans."

Sapphyre stands up and, with authority suggests, "I believe we need to retire and in the morning reconvene with fresh minds." Nods of acquiescence fill the dwelling and, after the proper salutations are exchanged, the companions retire to their assigned quarters.

A few hours have passed when Katrivus sits up, grabs his bearings, and makes his way to the high shaman's dwelling. The two barbarian males standing guard bar his entry until they hear a voice from within commanding them to allow him to pass.

Katrivus walks in and finds the high shaman in the same position by the fire. He bows in greeting and speaks. "I am sorry for the intrusion, High Shaman." The barbarian nods. "I may have found a solution regarding our passing."

Katrivus then walks over to where the high shaman is sitting and looking up with a sparkle in his eyes. He takes a seat beside the high shaman and asks quietly and deliberately, "Is there anyone preparing for their Jaa'neet Torvol?"

The high shaman stares at Katrivus wide-eyed, unable to hide the shock at the mention of the deeply religious rite, and articulated in his native tongue. Katrivus immediately explains. "I have an extensive library, including ancient scrolls from thousands of winters past. Some are from the times before the mountains grew from the land, and our ancestors lived amongst each other."

The high shaman looks at Katrivus with a new-found respect in his expression, and the two remain silent for a few moments. As he is gazing into the eyes of the young man, his expression changes from one of contemplation to one of sudden understanding. "There are two who are of the age, Soui Toofen."

He then stands up slowly, prompting Katrivus to jump to his feet. The elderly barbarian turns to Kat and places his right hand in a fatherly gesture upon his shoulder, saying, "I believe you may have found a solution."

Chapter 35

THE morning arrives abruptly with a bitter cold wind screaming in from the ocean and dark storm clouds filling the horizon both east and west. Katrivus and the high shaman are sitting beside the fire within the leader's dwelling. A male and a female barbarian quickly exit and escort Skken, Ashcon, Sapphyre, Talon, and Lymer inside.

The look of confusion on Ashcon's face elicits an explanation from the high shaman. "Soui Toofen came to me in the night with a revelation on how best to fulfill your quest. Please be seated and we will explain."

As the companions take the same positions as the night before, Katrivus bows his head to the high shaman. The old barbarian begins. "What I am about to impart to you is not known to many beyond our people. It is one of the most sacred rites we observe and I ask for your confidence before I continue." The old man locks his gaze with Katrivus who nods before continuing around the circle until each has agreed.

His voice gains strength as he proudly continues. "When a member of our people reach a certain age, they are given the opportunity to go on a sacred quest. It is known as Jaa'neet Torvol." The high shaman looks at Skken, whose eyes slowly blaze with understanding. The old man grins slightly and continues. "No one is under any obligation to partake in the ritual and only the sons and daughters of the highest ranking members of our people are expected to do so." He shifts his weight, takes a deep breath and continues. "The ritual involves a journey westward into the Marsh of Sorrow where they are tested by the spirits of our ancestors."

Talon leans forward and asks humbly, "With all due respect, how does this aide us in our quest?"

Katrivus immediately intervenes, "If I may?" he asks the high shaman, who nods affirmatively. In response to the looks of his companions, Katrivus explains, "I have a scroll from ancient times which depicts this ritual and it gave me the idea." He pauses briefly and then continues. "The Marsh of Sorrow is the western border of the barbarian lands and runs from the Myth Mountains all the way north to the Sea of Tears. Part of the rite of Jaa'neet Torvol is the sacred journey west to the Marsh."

"When participating in the ritual of Jaa'neet Torvol, my people are under the protection of the ancient gods," says the high shaman. "While under their protection, they may not be preyed upon by rival tribes. In fact, it is the duty bound honor of any tribe to insure safe passage through their lands of any partaking in Jaa'neet Torvol."

Katrivus sits up excitedly and says, "So not only are they guaranteed safe passage, but it would cause dishonor to any tribe if harm was to befall them on their land. So the rival tribes actually protect them as they venture west."

The high shaman clears his throat and says, "Those who partake in the ritual travel in holy garb which assures safe passage. They are expected to travel with members of their tribe, which number no more than twelve. You will travel west under their protection, in the guise of tribesmen, with four additional members of our tribe."

Ashcon asks quickly, "Why must we take four additional men?"

The old barbarian looks at Ashcon and replies deliberately, "The two who are making the journey are doing so both for their own honor and to aid the Ta'adaal. They have every inclination to fulfill their rite of Jaa'neet Torvol. When you reach the point where you part ways, my tribesmen will accompany the two who are on their holy journey as you make for your destination."

Ashcon looks down into his hands and then directly at the high shaman before speaking. "I am sorry, Fareen Makuu, I meant no disrespect. I was thinking only of our quest and did not give consideration to your most holy of rites. Please accept my apology."

The high shaman nods in response to Ashcon.

Sapphyre speaks for the first time, "Who has the honor of fulfilling their rite of Jaa'neet Torvol and allowing us to accompany them west?"

In response, the high shaman closes his eyes. Within seconds, two barbarians with their heads covered in damp dark blue cloth are escorted inside. They are standing side-by-side, both adorned in the same garb as all of the other tribesmen: fur boots, loincloths, bare torsos, and their left arms adorned with bracelets. The only difference is the cloth hiding their identity.

The high shaman stands up. All eyes are on him as he walks toward the front of his home, resting beside the two newcomers. "To honor his father, reigning first warrior, and to test his resolve to hold that title after his father passes from this land, Ayatana Saayan has proudly affirmed his right to attempt Jaa'neet Torvol." The man standing beside the high shaman removes the cloth from his head to reveal a sixteen-winters-old barbarian beaming proudly and standing at attention.

The high shaman moves to stand beside the smaller female. "To honor the tradition of all High Shamans of the Sashee, and to test the wisdom of her mind and the compassion in her heart, Laven'lei Makuu has proudly affirmed her right to attempt Jaa'net Torvol." The girl removes her cloth to reveal delicate features for a barbarian: slightly slanted hazel eyes, subtle lips, and shoulder length, jet-black hair against flawless bronze skin. As the only daughter of the high shaman beams with pride upon the announcement, she steals a quick glance at the slack-jawed Soui Toofen.

Chapter 36

IT has been two days of terrible weather since Stolor, captain of the Mermaid's Tale, set off from the land of the Sashee back to Cornice. The latest barrage of waves and hail damaged the cutter to a point that the captain had to make the decision to reroute to Thull in order to make repairs to the ship. Even though he is under strict orders from Katrivus to sail directly to Cornice, he deemed this detour absolutely necessary.

The Mermaid's Tale pulls into the docks at Thull just as the sun is setting on the horizon. Most ships have to moor off-shore and send in a few sailors with a request to dock, but Katrivus owns the Mermaid's Tale, so there is always a dock available immediately.

Stolor takes care of arrangements to have the cutter repaired and makes his way to his favorite watering hole right off the docks. Thull is a hotbed of activity and has tripled its population in less than ten winters. The overwhelming majority of the inhabitants are the native barbarians, followed by humans, dwarves, and the occasional elf. The barbarians have always been a neutral party to the ongoing undeclared war between the humans and orcs. To the dismay of the human population, orcs are welcome in Thull. Not only are they tolerated, but also they have carved out a section of the city not far from the docks where they have formed some permanent residences.

The barbarians who live in Thull live a much different lifestyle than those who live out in the wild. They are still a tribal society but instead of remaining secluded from one another, they live amongst each other in peace. There are many marriages between different tribes, and the females always become a member of the male's tribe once they finalize their union.

The high shaman of the Takani tribe rules and has for as long as anyone can remember. The Takani are the only pure tribe left in Thull, as they are prohibited from intermarriage. The high shaman from the other dozen or so tribes who inhabit the city form the ruling council; however, the final word of the leader of the Takani is law.

As long as the Takani remain in the gods' favor, no changes are expected.

One would expect there to be violent outbreaks in Thull due to the diversity of its inhabitants, but the opposite is true. There are minor skirmishes here and there, but the barbarians make sure to keep the peace. There are always patrols of barbarians with their huge hounds in all the areas of the city and they deal harshly with any crime. The brutality of their law enforcement is what keeps Thull a relatively peaceful place.

If someone steals in Thull, not only is the perpetrator's hand cut off, but also so are the dominant hands of their children if they have any. If there are no children, the spouse gets their hand cut off. For those unfortunate single thieves, they lose both their hands. Any second infraction with the law is banishment with a standing order of death upon return. Any brawls that break out result in fingers being removed from all perpetrators. Murder results in the death of the criminal and his youngest relative, as well as the banishment of every surviving relative in Thull. As one would guess, crime is almost unheard of.

When Stolor stumbles out of the Hair of the Dog a little past midnight and is making his way back to the Mermaid's Tale to sleep, he is shocked when three huge, green orcs apprehend him. As his arms are grabbed from behind and he is trying to comprehend what is happening, an orc slams a mallet against his head knocking him unconscious. One of the orcs slings the human onto his shoulder and carries him off to the east end of the docks and into orc territory.

When Stolor awakens, he is tied to a chair in what he perceives to be a basement. He is alone with one torch on the far wall. Glancing around the dark chamber, he notices the cement walls are seeping with mold. It is both wet and extremely cold. It is only then that he notices that he is stark naked and bound to the chair by his arms, legs, feet, and neck. He has ample room to turn his head to the right and left. He starts to squirm in his chair and test the bindings. The chair is bolted to the floor and situated in the middle of the square room. There is no way to tip it in any direction. The bindings are secure, and even moving his fingers is a challenge.

He hears someone enter the chamber from behind him and does his best to try to maintain some level of courage and dignity. The door closes behind him and someone speaks.

"You are the captain of the Mermaid's Tale, are you not?" asks the stranger.

Stolor give no answer. Two orcs who stand at least seven feet tall walk on either side of him and turn to face him. He looks up at them and notices they are looking behind him, apparently at the leader of the group. They hold two weapons each: a mallet and a rusty sword. Without warning, the orc to his left slams the mallet onto his left kneecap, shattering it on one blow. Stolor's shrilling screech echoes through the chamber and just as he is about to pass out, a bony hand from behind passes in front of his face, which causes him to remain awake.

"You will not pass out on me no matter what I put you through," says the stranger, barely whispering into Stolor's right ear. "And what I put you through will be pain you simply cannot imagine." The stranger then makes his way around to the front of his captive and Stolor glances up to see who has taken him prisoner.

The man is wearing all black, and it is too dark to see his features underneath his hood. He looks to be extremely skinny with bony fingers peeking out from the long black sleeves. Grasped in one hand is a strange staff that has a dagger hilt protruding from a human skull. The sight of it sends chills down the captain's spine.

"The orcs can only provide so much torture and pain, and only in a brute force sort of way," the stranger continues. "What I can do is much different and much more painful. I will ask you questions that you will answer honestly. If you don't, I will know it, and you will suffer. Are we clear?"

Stolor speaks for the first time, his words coming out like gasps. "I guess we will find out."

The stranger turns to the orcs and commands, "Leave us." They exit the chamber and Stolor can hear the door closing behind them. "We are deep below Thull in a chamber of my design. Only a handful of my trusted orcs even know of its existence, and it is soundproof, so no one will hear you scream."

The stranger walks behind Stolor and reappears to his left. He continues walking around his captive before he finally asks again, "Are you the captain of the Mermaid's Tale?"

Stolor replies truthfully since he is sure that his jailer knows who he is or he wouldn't be in this predicament.

"Very good," says the stranger who makes his way around to face Stolor once again. "I expected you to be in the company of Katrivus and a few honored guests, but you showed up with only five other crewmen and no wizard. Would you care to explain this?"

Stolor hesitates before responding, "Katrivus was not on board and –" Before he can continue, the stranger cuts him off with a quick slap to the face.

"I don't think you understand what is happening here," he says, "so I will give you a small demonstration of what I mean by real pain." The stranger looks down at Stolor and chants in a language the captain does not understand. The eye sockets in the skull adorning the staff start to glow dark amber. Stolor feels a sensation in his left hand and his fingers start to contract and spasm. The stranger finishes his chanting and looks down at Stolor. "Please keep watching your hand."

Stolor looks down. Without warning his fingers begin to melt away, bone and all, until he is looking at nothing but a stump at his wrist. The pain is so unbearable that he can't scream, even though his mouth is wide open and he is gasping and crying. Sweat is pouring out of every pore in his body. He starts convulsing from the pain. The stranger chants another indecipherable spell, and the pain subsides.

"I can bring back that pain at any time but I don't believe I will need to, will I?" taunts the stranger in a monotone voice. "Because if you don't answer me truthfully, you will lose an ear in the same manner. Then I will move on to your nose and finally I will take your manhood."

The stranger steps behind Stolor. He reappears seconds later with a second chair and he sits. "Was Katrivus with you?"

Stolor immediately replies, "Yes, he was."

"Very good!" Sleeth replies enthusiastically. "Were there others with him as well?"

A slight hesitation by Stolor causes Sleeth to point to the stump. The pain immediately returns.

"Yes," screams Stolor, "there were others." The pain subsides and Stolor takes long gasping breaths.

"How many others?"

"Five, including the wizard."

"What were their names?" asks Sleeth.

"I only know a girl by the name of Sapphyre. I was never privy to the others' identities."

Sleeth stands up eyeing the captain and says quietly, "We will see." He starts another spell and the familiar glow in the eye sockets of the skull cause Stolor to shake violently knowing what is coming. Seconds later, Stolor can smell his left ear burning as it melts away. The excruciating pain seems to go on forever. Sleeth speaks again and the pain subsides.

"What were their names?" asks Sleeth one more time.

"I don't know," replies Stolor through muddled gasps.

"Maybe you don't, maybe you don't," says Sleeth. "Describe them to me."

Stolor goes into detailed descriptions of Ashcon, Skken, Talon, Lymer, Katrivus, and Sapphyre. He is asked many times to go back over the details about Ashcon and Skken. Stolor does his best to recollect everything he can. Once Sleeth is satisfied, he moves on to his next line of questioning.

"Where did you drop them off?" he asks.

A slight hesitation causes Sleeth to stand up and prepare the staff for another round of unbearable pain when Stolor replies. "We dropped them off at a small barbarian village about three days travel south of here."

"Excellent," says Sleeth. "I knew you would come around. Does this village have a name?"

"I don't know," he replies. "I truthfully do not know." Tears roll down his cheeks. "I was never permitted off the ship. None of us were. We dropped them off and left the next morning."

Sleeth seems satisfied with his answer and continues. "I want you to envision in your mind exactly where you dropped off your charges. I will be looking into your mind's eye and will be able to see what you envision. I will also know if you are being truthful. If you wish to ever use your manhood again, you should be honest and forthright. Do you understand?"

Stolor nods his head vigorously up and down and asks, "Should I do so now?"

Sleeth replies, "Yes. You will feel a slight tingle as I join you but it should not cause you any pain. You will keep the vision in your mind until I tell you to release. Now close your eyes and begin."

As soon as Sleeth is convinced he has enough information from Stolor's recollection of the landing point, he opens his eyes and tells Stolor to do the same.

"Thank you for your time Stolor. You did well. Unfortunately you will die now in a most unbearable way." Sleeth then lifts the DarkFlame Staff and starts another incantation, his voice drowned out by the screams of his victim. He looks down at Stolor one last time and grins as he watches his limbs, his head, and finally his torso start to melt away, until there is nothing left to show that Stolor ever existed.

Sleeth then looks at the door. With a quick spell, the door opens. The two orcs guarding the door enter and stand to the side. Sleeth nods to them and exits the chamber. The orcs wonder where the prisoner went but know better than to question their master.

Chapter 37

Iᴛ has been four days of miserable travel through the forests west of the land of the Sashee, rain pelting the companions, leaving them all drenched with no respite from the downpour. Lymer is truly ecstatic with the rain and literally dancing his way through the barbarian lands of the north. The little wizard's extravagant gestures and prolific frivolity keep a decent humor amongst the companions despite the weather.

The pelting storm doesn't seem to bother Katrivus or the young Laven'lei Makuu who spend the entire time enraptured with each other and in constant conversation. They do nothing to hide their affection for each other and it doesn't bother Katrivus when the other men tease him. Apparently being called a barbarian's wife doesn't rouse Katrivus in the least, much to the dismay of Talon.

While Katrivus spends all his time with the high shaman's daughter, Ashcon, Skken, and Talon do everything together. Although Talon's instruction does not begin in earnest until after their current mission has been completed, Ashcon wants Talon to understand the history of runestars and prepare himself as best he can for what he will be facing. Talon has always had a thirst for learning and has excelled at every task he has ever attempted. He is not at all ashamed about telling this to Ashcon and Skken. Instead of taking it as a boast, Ashcon looks at it as a positive aspect of the young man's character.

Sapphyre spends her time in the rain with the little gnome wizard. Lymer is never one to keep his mouth shut and Sapphyre enjoys listening to him ramble with a story or a song. His voice has a musical quality to it that enables him to sound like he's in an a cappella band although he is, of course, just one wizard. Sapphyre has kept her part of the bargain with Ashcon and has not tried to do anything at all that could be perceived as magical, and it really hasn't been a chore. The entertaining little wizard has kept her mind occupied with the mundane and the hilarious, all a welcome at an opportune time.

The barbarians accompanying the two honored tribesmen lead the way through the dense forest. The warriors are well aware that a rival tribe is watching them when they announced that they will stop and set up camp for the night. Skken approaches the lead Sashee scout to ask if it is safe to camp while under the watchful eye of a rival tribe. After conversing in the local language, Skken nods and looks at his companions and starts to set up camp for the night.

As has been the short tradition over the past few days, Ashcon, Skken, and Talon tend to clearing the sleeping grounds and preparing a fire. The warriors of the Sashee take up scouting points around the perimeter while Katrivus, Sapphyre, and Lymer tend to the mounts and start preparing the evening meal. The two honored barbarians who are on their Jaa'neet Torvol head to the westernmost part of the small camp and prepare for their evening prayer ritual.

Sapphyre, Lymer, and Katrivus finish with the horses and are nearing the fire with rations for the evening meal when one of the Sashee warriors approaches them. He makes a gesture with his hand and the three follow him toward where Skken and Ashcon are finishing preparing the fire. The warrior then speaks to Skken, and the large barbarian nods in comprehension. The Sashee warrior retreats to the camp perimeter once again.

Skken looks at his companions and says, "You can put the food away." As they gaze up at him with a surprised look in their eyes, he continues. "We have been followed the majority of the afternoon by a local tribe known as the Atani. They have seen the garb worn by our honored Sashee and would like to make an offering of a meal to bless this most sanctified of rites. The high shaman and his three wives will be joining us shortly."

"Three wives?" inquires the young Talon.

"Different tribes have different customs. Many of the nomadic tribes such as the Atani believe that the high shaman should have many offspring with many different females. It is an honor to be chosen as a wife to a high shaman," Skken explains.

Katrivus continues, "The custom is almost exclusive to the nomadic tribes and as you get closer to the populated cities, you see less of it."

Skken looks at the companions and continues. "When the high shaman arrives we will be situated by the fire and we will rise yet remain in your position. He will address each of you in his native tongue and you will simply bow your head in response. Do not speak. Do not smile. Do not extend your hand in greeting. Although it will be obvious that we are not of the Sashee, there is no reason to give any clue at all to our identity. Once the high shaman has greeted all of us he will proceed to the western side of the camp and spend the remainder of his time with our honored guests. We will then sit down and his wives will serve us our meal."

"Won't he be suspicious since he will know we are not of the Sashee?" asks Talon.

Skken replies, "It will be a puzzle, yes, but the high shaman would never question someone who is on Jaa'neet Torvol. It is assumed that those who accompany the honored ones are chosen by the Gods, and one simply doesn't question the Gods."

The answer seems to satisfy the companions and as they approach the fire, Ashcon takes Sapphyre aside and whispers, "Please make sure your little wizard friend behaves. Challenge him to a game of who can stay still the longest or a silence contest or something like that."

"He's not a twelve winters old child, Ashcon," says Sapphyre a bit louder than she intended.

"Make sure he behaves, Sapphyre," orders Ashcon with a tad more force than necessary. He turns abruptly and walks to his place by the fire. He takes his seat, and his companions follow suit.

Within a few moments of them sitting down, the warriors of the Sashee approach with torches lit, followed by the Atani guests. The warriors come in from the east and when they get to within ten feet of the fire they stop and part to the side allowing the guests to come through.

Sapphyre gasps audibly at the sight of the High Shaman of the Atani as he approaches slowly with his wives following. He is no older than twenty-five or twenty-six winters and the most stunning male specimen Sapphyre has ever laid eyes on. He stands almost seven feet tall with a mane of pure white hair extending below his waist. His striking blue eyes are in direct contrast to his bronze flawless skin, and his physique is what you would expect of one who survives as a nomad: lean and muscular without a hint of fat. The loincloth adorning the midsection and the fur lined boots are the only similarities between the Atani and the Sashee.

The high shaman approaches Ashcon first and stands two feet away. He places his palms up in front of him and speaks in a booming, baritone voice in a language Ashcon doesn't comprehend. He just nods, and the high shaman moves onto the rest of the party. The high shaman continues through Katrivus and Talon. When he glances down at Lymer, he takes a step back in surprise at his size. The little gnome's head barely tops the kneecap of the barbarian. Lymer hasn't been able to close his mouth since the high shaman made his appearance. Ashcon looks over, hoping that the wizard keeps his cool, thinking that the scene would be hilarious in most any other situation.

The barbarian is looking down at Lymer inquisitively and turning his head from side to side before finally straightening up, placing his palms up, and reciting the same verse as before. Lymer nods slowly, his mouth remaining agape but his tongue luckily remaining inside.

The high shaman steps to his right and situates himself in front of Sapphyre. He is gazing at her and examining her intently from head to toe, obviously pausing at the blue streaks in her hair. The moment seems to go on forever and Sapphyre had to avert her eyes in embarrassment twice. Finally the high shaman holds his palms up in front of him and in his booming voice recites the same passage as before.

He makes his way to Skken and stops abruptly, gazing into the True Guardian's eyes. The two are locked in a stare until the high shaman drops to one knee and utters just one word. "Ta'adaal." Skken touches the barbarian on both shoulders and speaks in a tongue unfamiliar to his companions. The Atani high shaman stands up to his full height and Skken walks with him toward Laven'lei and Ayatana, deep in conversation the entire time.

After a few moments, the wives of the high shaman approach each of the friends one at a time. They are garbed in green vests and grass skirts that extend below the knee, much more conservative than the Sahsee from the east. Without a word, they give each of them a plate of roasted boar, raw carrots, and local berries. As they dine on the gift of the Atani, the wives retreat to the perimeter of the camp awaiting their husband.

Sapphyre is just finishing up her meal and looks up to see the high shaman walking back toward the fire. The wives get in line into the same position they were in when they approached the camp. The high shaman walks over to Sapphyre, who stood up to greet the holy man. He looks down and smiles once more, closes his eyes, nods, and then turns around and walks briskly to where his wives await. Without further ado, the high shaman and his wives are escorted out of the camp by the warrior scouts leaving the companions to camp for the night.

The friends didn't even notice that the weather changed for the better and it stopped raining before they ate their evening meal. They about getting ready to retire for the evening in relative silence when Skken decides to address the stares of his companions.

"We have nothing to fear from the Atani. He asked only if I would bless his people and ask those on Ja'anaat Torvol to ask the gods to do the same. He will keep our passing in confidence." Skken then proceeds to prepare for sleep. With no further discussion, his companions do the same.

Chapter 38

S LEETH exits the portal from the Demon Realm into his private quarters in the basement of the Temple of the Dark Gods, fresh with the knowledge of where Aschon and his companions began their trek somewhere to the east. As he always does when he enters his chambers, he removes the ward protecting the ancient tome and removes the sacred book, placing it upon his desk. He always laughs to himself for putting a ward around the book, knowing that it isn't going anywhere it didn't wish to be.

The Tome of Eternal Night, as he found the book to be called, has been a dream come true for Sleeth. Thanks to the tome, Sleeth now has the ability to enter the Demon Realm to travel great distances in a fraction of the time it would take conventionally. Sleeth was a bit skeptical before he entered the portal to Thull on the first day of the current moonsign and emerged at his destination only two days later. A trip across the continent at this time of year would normally take fifty times as long!

It has been hard to conceal his excitement while at the same time only telling Drak'thonn what he wishes him to know. He knows he can't conceal everything from his mater but picking and choosing what he will tell him has been the challenge. He doesn't want to lie directly to his face, because regardless of his personal feelings, the burned one is in the favor of the Dark Gods.

As Sleeth prepares his thoughts for his pending meeting with Drak'thonn and Selentha, he prepares to open the Tome of Eternal Night to see if it has revealed anything else. He slowly opens up the book to the page he left off on and gently turns it over. As symbols begin to appear on the previously blank page, Sleeth pounds his fist in excitement and starts interpreting the symbols as quickly as they become visible in the book. Page after page is written in front of his eyes, and just like that it ends. Sleeth takes a deep breath and sits back in his chair contemplating what he just read. He then sits up, page marks the tome, closes it gently and returns it to its resting place. He puts his protective ward back into place and sits back down in his chair. Sleeth leans back and clasps his bony hands behind his bald head grinning from ear to ear. He has a meeting coming up with Drak'thonn, and he just learned something the burned one will love to hear. Although that news is pleasing to Sleeth, it is what he will be holding back from Drak'thonn that puts the smile on his face.

As Sleeth makes a leisurely trek via horseback to meet with Drak'thonn and Selentha, he looks around at the huge army covering the vast territory. The smell from the orcs' camp is simply vile and the prospect of having these disgusting creatures finally commence with their invasion is a most welcome one. Once the orcs and the dreggans start pilfering the south, Sleeth will no longer have to tolerate the various rituals these petty species participate in. All day long, they battle amongst themselves while the thralls of spectators cheer on until one dies. They make up games about the human and dwarf slaves. Some of the green creatures actually taught the dreggans the best way to cook them and which parts were safe to eat raw. This spectacle was a constant distraction to Sleeth, who had far more important things to do and looked forward to telling Drak'thonn he may commence with the invasion of the Kingdom of Martel.

Drak'thonn and his bride look up when Sleeth makes his entrance, but neither speaks as the warlock makes his way to his chair opposite the two. He sits down and lets the DarkFlame Staff come to rest on his right, holding it so the skull is above his head standing straight up. As is always with these meetings, there are no pleasantries exchanged. Sleeth jumps right in and tells all he has learned.

"The time has come for the invasion of the kingdom to commence," says Sleeth without introduction.

"The tome has told you so?" inquires Selentha.

"Yes." Sleeth has learned that direct answers to direct questions is not only what the two required, but also allows him to be both brief and vague. Unfortunately, the one-word answers do not placate the burned one every time.

"What exactly did the tome say?" asks Drak'thonn.

Sleeth keeps his frustration to himself as he has had to explain this concept to him on numerous occasions. "The tome never actually says anything. It reveals symbols to me of an origin I do not recognize yet I can ascertain the meaning. The most important thing to remember is that the tome does not reveal anything to me until it is ready to."

"You have mentioned this before," says Drak'thonn. "How do you know when it is ready?"

"When the tome is ready, it simply fills in more pages with symbols, and then stops when it feels I have enough information. I do not know whether it is brought about by the passage of time or if there is an act that precipitates it." Drak'thonn shifts in his chair, and the flames around his eyes grow larger. Sleeth knows he is getting frustrated and continues quickly to try and pacify the chosen one. "What I have learned today is truly amazing, and it signifies pending war."

This news makes Selentha sit upright in her seat and the flames around her arms jump in excitement. "Explain yourself High Warlock," she says forcefully.

Sleeth leans forward, elbows on the table and slowly removes his hood before continuing quietly. "The tome has bestowed unto me the ability to travel through the Demon Realm to cover great distances in a very short time." Before either of them can interrupt, he continues. "What this means is that our armies will not need to travel by sea to reach the kingdom. The armies will march south to the Myth Mountains and I will create a portal to the Demon Realm. The armies will enter the Demon Realm and emerge on the other side of the mountain range in less than two days' time." Sleeth sits back with a small grin on his pale skull letting the two burned ones digest this information.

"Instead of marching south to the mountains, you will open the portal to the Demon Realm here. There is no reason to delay the invasion any longer," says Drak'thonn with authority.

"With all due respect, Chosen One, the plan the tome revealed to me is very precise," says Sleeth. "The tome wishes the armies to march south to the mountains. I doubt it would allow the portal to be opened here. We must follow its instructions implicitly."

Drak'thonn accepts the warlock's answer with a sigh before responding. "Very well. We will trust the tome and we will march south to the Myth Mountains." He stands up and addresses his wife. "Gather all the leaders and have them prepared to march at first light." He turns to Sleeth and says, "You will march with the armies and establish the portal when they arrive."

Sleeth interrupts one more time, hoping not to draw the ire of Drak'thonn. "The tome has other instructions for me, Chosen One." Drak'thonn looks over to Sleeth while flexing his fists, fire flying off his body in frustration, waiting for the warlock to continue. "I have been instructed to await further passages from the tome and to be alerted when the armies arrive at the Myth Mountains. At that time, I will travel through the Demon Realm to join them and prepare the portal for the invasion."

Drak'thonn seemed to contemplate his answer before responding. "Very well." He looks at his wife and addresses her directly. "You will lead the armies south. Kreel will accompany you. I will wait with the warlock in case there are further instructions from the tome. When the time comes for the invasion, I will travel with Sleeth unless I am ordered otherwise."

Drak'thonn then nods to Sleeth and turns toward his private chambers, implying to the warlock that the meeting has come to an end. Selentha exits the building without a departing word to Sleeth, which is just fine with him, leaving the warlock to retreat back to his chambers and contemplate his next move.

Sitting down in the temple, Sleeth listens to the sounds of the armies preparing to march and smiles. Not only did he get rid of the vile creatures that comprise the army, but that burning bitch of a leader is going with them. Sleeth also succeeded in convincing Drak'thonn that he need not be disturbed until the forces of the army were at the mountains, which should be a minimum of half a moonsign. He certainly doesn't need the fifteen days to achieve his objective but welcomes the time alone nonetheless.

As he slowly descends the steps to his private quarters to retire for the night, Sleeth recounts what has transpired in the past few hours. He told Drak'thonn the truth regarding the army; however, he had to come up with a lie rather quickly when ordered to create the portal here in the Dark Fortress. He actually wasn't sure if it was a lie since the tome did show him where the invading army would enter the portal. Whether he could have called forth the portal here and now is something he will thankfully never know.

The fact that Drak'thonn never once asks Sleeth if he learned any more from the Tome of Eternal Night leads credence to the warlock's belief that the chosen one is a poor leader. He automatically assumes all of his followers are dedicated to him and his cause and no one would ever betray him. It is a fault which has led to the collapse of many kings before, and if Sleeth has any say, one that will eventually lead to Drak'thonn's destruction as well.

He doesn't even have to lie to hide the most important information from the burned one. Not only can Sleeth travel through the Demon Realm, but he also has the ability to bring creatures from within the realm to do his bidding. He smiles as he lies down upon his bed, thinking about the destruction he and his demons can bring forth upon the land.

Chapter 39

IT has been three days since arriving back from Thull and three days of constant study of the Tome of Eternal Night. Sleeth believes he has conceived a plan. The tome explains in detail what types of creatures one would encounter and all the powers each of them possess. Sleeth has learned how to enter the Demon Realm and exit on the other side with a small army of creatures from nightmare. In only four pages of symbols, Sleeth has acquired thousands of years of knowledge hidden within this ancient scripture. Each time he masters one concept, the tome reveals another to him. Three days have passed and the tome has finally stopped writing. Sleeth takes a deep breath and leans back in his chair as his plan slowly comes into focus. Smiling, he rises and makes his way to his quarters to get some rest. Tomorrow he will find out exactly where Ashcon and his companions are heading.

The warrior scouts of the Sashee look on in surprise from the camouflage of the brush to the strange object that is glowing on the beach to the north. The sun is rising to their right, just making its way over the horizon, leaving the beach in a dusk light. The three scouts creep north along the coast, keeping to the tree line of the dense forest and stop about forty yards southwest of the object. Just as they situate themselves the object starts to glow red around the rim and black as night in the center. The darkness in the center ripples like water in moonlight and without warning a man in a robe steps out from the middle wielding a glowing staff.

He takes a few steps forward and black shapeless forms like mist start assembling behind him. The man walks a few steps further and turns to look back at the object from which he came. At least twenty ghost-like creatures exit and assemble in two lines in front of the black-clad man. The man holds the staff up in his right arm and aims the skull at the strange rippling object from which they came and it quickly dissipates and what is left gets sucked up by the staff. The man looks at the ghostly beings for a few moments and then turns and marches south along the beach toward the unsuspecting Sashee tribe.

The scouts arrive first but only moments before the uninvited guests. The Sashee warriors have not had time to set up a defensive wall with their archers and their huge hounds. The high shaman has already made his way to the forefront with a small contingent of warriors to see who has trespassed his lands. As he sees the ghostly creatures approach, he sighs deeply, sensing both the evil and his pending doom.

Sleeth has his creatures hold fast about twenty yards from the tribe and continues to approach himself. He stops a few feet from the warriors and locks his eyes with the high shaman. "Do you speak the common tongue, Barbarian?"

The high shaman looks at the man, his face still hidden behind the hood of his robe. "I speak the common tongue. Why do you trespass on Sashee land?"

"I come seeking the travelers who passed through here only days ago."

The high shaman looks at the stranger and replies, "You are mistaken."

Sleeth turns to the ghostly creatures he left behind and then back to the high shaman. In a blink of an eye, the shapeless forms are all beside the leader. He speaks. "I don't have time for this. I will show you my power and you will then decide how to continue this conversation." Sleeth takes a step back and looks at the creatures as one of the creatures attacks the warriors surrounding the high shaman. Attack may be the wrong word. Consume may be more appropriate. The demons attack from the front and use their entire ghostly form to adhere to the barbarians from head to toe. They then proceed to "eat" them from front to back. The entire process takes only a few seconds until the barbarians that were once there simply are not. And not one has the chance to scream.

The same could not be said for the Sashee who witnessed the entire scene from behind the high shaman. The chilling screams pierce the night as the demons surround the perimeter of the tribal grounds.

Sleeth moves forward to stand before the high shaman. "If you wish any of your tribe to survive, you will answer my questions," he says to the high shaman, whose resolve appears unshaken despite the occurrences of the last few minutes.

"Very well, I will start by ordering the shades to consume your women. Believe me when I say I have the means to get my answers. And then I will kill all of you." Sleeth looks at the high shaman, who says nothing and then looks at his demons preventing any of the barbarians from escaping. He grabs the old man by his hair and shoves him toward the center of the camp, where he throws him down to the ground.

"This is your last chance," says Sleeth as he pulls his hood back to the gasps of the Sashee. The high shaman brushes the dirt from his face and stands up defiantly.

"Very well," says Sleeth as the DarkFlame Staff begins to glow. "As you watch your women slowly consumed, I will be melting your extremities piece by piece." He then chants a spell in the language of the warlock and points to the high shaman's right hand that slowly starts to melt away. The high shaman does not even let out a gasp as his fingers become molten fire. This only enrages Sleeth, who turns to his creatures and holds his arms up to the sky.

Some of the demons attach to the women and slowly bring them to the center of the village so they can consume them in front of the high shaman. The barbarian warriors are being held at bay by the remaining shades, and the hounds have long since retreated to the forest in fear. Some of the creatures attach themselves to the backs of the women first so the old tribal leader can stare into their eyes as they are consumed by the shadows. Sleeth is slowly melting body parts from the high shaman and fending off futile attacks by the barbarian warriors. Any time a warrior gets close to Sleeth, a shade appears as if out of nowhere to consume the warrior and protect the warlock.

Sleeth leaves one ear and one eye alone on the face of the high shaman so he can see and hear what he wishes him to. Half of the Sashee are simply gone, and the others are being kept at bay by the demons or have simply gone mad from the attack.

Sleeth walks through the throng of barbarians and stops in front of what appears to be a boy of about twelve winters. He grabs him by the arm and brings him to the center of the slaughter so the high shaman can see. He has the boy kneel in front of him and holds one arm on his head while the other wields the DarkFlame Staff. He closes his eyes and chants slowly, commanding the boy's young, weak subconscious to answer his questions in his mind's eye. Sleeth probes his mind but has a hard time communicating with the young barbarian. He decides on a different approach and seeks pictures instead of words. He finally sees a vision of nine people leaving the land of the Sashee on horseback. The child only knows these people as holy people, but the warlock knows that the one he seeks is among them. When he probes for the destination of these holy people, he is given a vision of a place he knew. It is unmistakable: the dark green rivers leading to the only mountain on Arstevia with peaks of gold and green. To the barbarians it is the holiest of mountains. To Sleeth, it is the answer he is searching for. Ashcon and his companions are heading to the Marsh of Sorrow and the Mountain in the Middle.

Sleeth releases the boy who slumps to the ground before a demon immediately consumes him. Sleeth walks to the high shaman and bends down to look into what is left of his face and speaks. "I now have the answers I seek. You could have spared your people. Now they will all die. And you will watch as I melt the last of you away." Sleeth orders his demons to dine on the remainder of the tribe while he sits down in front of the high shaman and watches him slowly melt away.

The High Shaman of the Sashee keeps his emotions in check throughout the entire ordeal. The physical pain is bearable since he has long ago taught his mind to ignore the worst of it. The most difficult part of this trial is allowing the warlock to leave with his destination being the Marsh of Sorrow, knowing he is probably sacrificing his daughter for the holy mission of the Ta'adaal.

Once the destruction of the entire Sashee tribe is complete, the shades, none of which are any larger after the feast, make their way back to Sleeth. He looks around at the now uninhabited beachfront and the structures within and holds the DarkFlame Staff up once more. He turns and faces the vast ocean and the eyes in the skull of the staff glow deep amber. Sleeth chants in the warlock tongue and the shades disappear, sent back to the Demon Realm.

Sleeth looks around the desolate beach at the empty shelters and the doused fires, taking pride in the complete destruction of the Sashee and wondering just how strong his powers will become. Shades are some of the least intelligent demons and the easiest to control, but with the knowledge imparted by the tome, the warlock was confident that what he was about to try will succeed.

He takes a deep breath and faces eastward over the vast ocean, opening the portal to the Demon Realm. The center of the portal shimmers as Sleeth enters the cursed land once again. Within seconds he emerges back on the beach followed by an entity from the Demon Realm.

Sleeth turns back toward the demon, which does not seem to be a very menacing creature, but Sleeth knows its true nature. The demon does not have much substance and has the same transparent quality as the shades; however, there is no question as to what it resembles. It looks like a large eye, stretching about six feet wide and two feet high, and it hovers about five feet above the ground. There is energy crackling all about it, but when it moves it is practically invisible.

Sleeth grins showing his pointed teeth as he looks at the Eye of Zorn, telepathically giving the creature its orders. As the demon speeds off to the west on the trail of Ashcon and his companions, Sleeth calls forth the portal, anxious to get back home and to the Tome of Eternal Night.

Chapter 40

"So you actually trained at the Fortress of the Invoker?" asks Talon as they maneuver the horses carefully through the thick brush with the sun at their back.

"Yes," replies Ashcon, "It should be a brisk yet sunny day." He pauses and then continues. "When I was ordained a runestar, as you know there were no seekers. I had to spend fourteen winters at the Fortress of the Invoker until I learned to harness my power."

"So what happened after seekers were introduced?"

"Once seekers were introduced, their training changed and will be what you go through." Ashcon laughs rather loudly and says, "It will be new for me as well, as I have never trained a seeker of course."

"So what happens next?" asks Talon.

Ashcon pauses, deep in thought, and then responds. "What's supposed to happen is that we are to present ourselves to the high priestess at the Temple of the Star Gods. Since Ka'alshene knows that you are my seeker, I'm certain she has everything prepared for our arrival. Unfortunately, we have much to do before we may travel to the temple."

They travel along in silence, Talon glancing back to see Sapphyre giggling as usual, riding with the silly gnome holding on to her waist from behind. Behind the two of them are Katrivus and Laven'lci deep in conversation with their horses so close they might as well be touching. Talon glances longingly at Sapphyre one more time before facing front and looking at the back of Skken about ten yards ahead. He knows the four warrior scouts of the Sashee are out there somewhere, although he can't see them, which means they are good. There have been no run-ins with other tribes since the visit by the young high shaman and his harem two nights past.

Talon shakes himself back into the moment and asks Ashcon, "Is my training going to be similar to what you went through in the Fortress?"

Ashcon looks to the young seeker and replies, "Yes and no. When you leave the Temple of the Star Gods you will have power over the four common runes amongst runestars that we discussed."

Talon nods, speechless, and looks at Ashcon, almost begging him to continue.

"It will take you many winters to learn to command even those four runes, Talon. That is the beginning of your formal training. After you have total command of the four common runes, you will gain access to more runes with many more powers, all of which are specifically attuned to your innate talents. I would expect that the runes that will be affixed to your body will correlate with your already peaked talents from your previous profession."

Talon is about to speak when Ashcon holds his hand up and interrupts. "I remind you this is pure speculation on my part, but if you had runes with the ability to become invisible or pick locks I wouldn't be surprised."

Just as Talon is about to answer, a deafening shriek pierces the morning and the party comes to a halt as everyone turns to the high shaman's daughter, who is keeled over grabbing her stomach and crying intensely. Ashcon, Talon, and Skken all dismount and make their way over to where Katrivus is beside the hysterical barbarian trying to console her with no luck.

"What happened?" asks Talon just as the warrior scouts of the Sashee approach the group with saddened expressions on their faces. They tend to Laven'lei and the son of the first warrior, using their bodies to block off the others. Laven'lei lifts her head up briefly, touches Katrivus's cheek gently, seeing the pain in his eyes due to her condition. She drops her hand, turns to the other Sashee, and walks the two feet over to them, leaving the saddened Katrivus behind.

Katrivus turns toward where Ashcon and the others are looking on and makes his way to join them.

"I don't know what happened," says Katrivus. "One moment I was telling her how it was to ride aboard a ship and then her eyes went dark and she burst into tears."

Just as Skken is about to speak, one of the warrior scouts makes her way to the group and addresses the barbarian in her native tongue. Skken listens to her and nods and turns to his companions. "The high shaman's daughter wishes to speak with us." The group starts to walk to where Laven'lei is sitting with Ayatana.

She looks up at the group and settles her eyes on Katrivus before speaking. "My father is dead. As is my younger sister. The others sense the destruction of their families as well. That is eighteen souls that we no longer can feel. We must assume the worst and realize we are the last of the Sashee."

For what seems an eternity no one speaks, until Laven'lei stands up, gains her composure, and issues an order to the warrior scouts, who bow and depart to the perimeter. She then turns and faces the first warrior's son, and they hold a brief conversation in their native tongue. Ayatana takes both of Laven'lei's hands into his, nods to her with reverence, and kisses her palms. He turns to walk away. The slender barbarian turns to Katrivus and the others and says, "We must continue our quest. It is more important than ever for the two of us to complete Jaa'neet Torvol. Then we will rebuild the Sashee." She hustles over to her mount and sets atop the large horse as the group shuffles to get back on course.

Katrivus makes his way to be by Laven'lei's side as Ashcon signals for Talon and Skken to slow down. They allow some distance between themselves and the others before Ashcon speaks.

"We must assume that our enemies are on our trail once again. There is no other explanation for the massacre of the Sashee."

"I disagree, Ashcon" says Talon. "One uses torture to gain information and once that information is ascertained, there is no longer a reason to continue. If he did get what he was looking for, there would be some survivors. He would have stopped once he got his prize."

Ashcon nods his head and replies, "You are making the assumption that Drak'thonn is human. I doubt he has been human, at least our definition of human, for centuries. He is all about destruction, and he would kill the tribe just for sport. We must take the position that we have enemies on our trail and prepare."

Talon nods as does Skken before the seeker proposes a question. "So does he know where we are going?"

Ashcon and Skken look to each other, and Skken is the one to speak. "We never told anyone of the Sashee our final destination, and that includes the high shaman. Drak'thonn did not find out from the Sashee where we are heading," he says matter-of-factly.

Ashcon nods and says, "He must know we headed west, so Skken, I need you to talk to the scouts and then take up position at our rear."

Skken nods and urges his mount westward at a gallop toward the scouts. Talon and Ashcon catch up to the party and situate themselves behind the horse carrying both Sapphyre and Lymer. Talon sways back and forth on his horse, deep in thought, looking ahead at Katrivus riding beside the high shaman's daughter, obviously in intense conversation.

The mood of the group has soured considerably, and even the always cheerful gnome has tears in his eyes and a frown upon his face. Sapphyre talks briefly to the little wizard and they trot forward to where Katrivus is riding beside Laven'lei. She addresses him.

"Kat, will you please trade places with me and ride with Lymer?" she starts. "I would like to have a private word with Laven'lei." Kat looks to the high shaman's daughter who nods and the two exchange places.

They ride in silence for a while before Sapphyre speaks. "I am sorry for your loss." Laven'lei simply nods in response. "I feel we must speak because if we never came to your land, your people would still be alive." Laven'lei is about to speak but Sapphyre cuts her off and continues. "We all feel terrible about it, but none more so than Katrivus."

"The gods have predetermined our fates long before you came to the Sashee," says the beautiful barbarian. There is a long pause before she continues. "You love Sooui Toofen, yes?" she asks.

"I do," replies Sapphyre. "But not in the way you do. He gave me a life a long time ago and he is more of a brother to me. You, however, care for him deeply."

Laven'lei nods in confirmation without looking at Sapphyre before speaking. "When I was a child, I was abducted by a rival tribe and Sooui Toofen rescued me. I never thought to see him again and then you arrived with the Ta'adaal, and I felt the gods brought him back to me." She pauses and looks back at Katrivus who is in deep conversation with Lymer, but his eyes never leave Laven'lei. "It is unfortunate that we cannot be together."

This stuns Sapphyre who asks, "Why can you not be together? It is obvious that you love each other."

"He is not of the Sashee," she replies matter-of-factly. "And now that we must rebuild our tribe, it is my duty to wed Ayatana."

"Does Katrivus know?" asks Sapphyre.

"Not yet. Please do not tell him. I wish to be the one."

Sapphyre nods in response and the two women continue on in silence as the morning sun retreats behind darkening clouds, signaling an incoming storm.

Chapter 41

ONLY a few days remained before the group is to split up and the barbarians will continue west to the Marsh of Sorrow to fulfill their Jaa'naat Torvol. Those heading to Sorenthor's Library will make a sharp turn to the north. The storm has not lessened at all, and the group finds the shelter of a cave along the western bank of the Lilly River where they can gain some respite from the weather and catch up on some much-needed rest.

Two of the barbarian warrior scouts insist upon keeping the first watch, and there is no objection from the exhausted party. They prove they have superior tracking skills and Ashcon and Skken are confident they will have any advance warning of a pending attack. So the tiny cave is virtually silent and all are sleeping when Talon's locket heats up for the first time in quite a while.

He sits up and re-associates himself with his surroundings before waking Ashcon to inform him of the summons. Ashcon nods and wakes his True Guardian and the three exit the cave to answer.

They are approached by one of the Sashee scouts, again proving their efficiency at their task. Skken reassures the barbarian that all is okay, and the three trod a bit downriver before attempting to contact Ka'alshene.

As soon as Talon makes contact, the high priestess brings in both Ashcon and Skken and her voice fills their minds.

"Unfortunately we have much to discuss," starts Ka'alshene. Hearing no reply she continues. "After the attack upon the ship I have made many inquiries and have news. First off, have there been any other attacks?"

Ashcon replies, "No direct attacks on us, m'lady, but it appears Drak'thonn has destroyed the barbarian tribe of the Sashee in an attempt to learn of our destination."

"I know of the Sashee," she replies with a sadness inconsistent with the notoriously stoic manner of the high priestess. After a pause, she continues. "Although I am confident he is behind the attacks, Drak'thonn has not left the land of the Dark Horde in quite a long time."

Talon speaks for the first time. "So his minions were responsible for the massacre, but I don't understand how that changes anything."

"The manner in which they were massacred is what troubles me," says Ka'aalshene.

"How are you aware of the manner in which they were killed, m'lady?" asks Skken.

"As you know, I have eyes and ears in all corners of the world," she starts. "I ascertained that you diverted from Thull and after some prodding I figured out where you landed. Once I was told that the entire village was deserted, I decided to see for myself."

Talon asks, "So you were already in the barbarian lands when we arrived?"

"No, dear one."

"So what was the manner in which they were massacred?" asks an impatient Ashcon.

"When I visited the land of the Sashee I was immediately taken aback by the scent of demons."

"I was under the impression that demons were banished from this world after the War of the Sanctum," says Ashcon.

"That is true, which is why this is most troubling," answers the high priestess.

Talon interjects, "So are you saying Drak'thonn has found a way to bring demons back into this world and do his bidding?"

"Drak'thonn gets his power from the Zagador in the form of the element of fire," says Ka'aalshene. "No matter how powerful he is, one cannot change the nature of his magical powers."

Skken asks quickly, "Are you saying Drak'thonn was not responsible for the massacre? I find that hard to believe."

"How is your knowledge in regard to the history of the followers of the Zagador?" asks Ka'alshene, seemingly ignoring Skken's inquiry.

Ashcon replies, "I only know what I have been told in order to come up with the best way to defeat my brother. I do not recall any demons being brought up in my teachings."

"Before the Zagador anointed your brother the leader of the Dark Horde and the chosen one of the Dark Gods, their followers were led by warlocks," explains the high priestess. "Before the War of the Sanctum ended, warlocks were able to enter the Demon Realm and bring forth demons to do their bidding." No one interrupts so she continues. "After the followers of the Zagador were defeated, all of the knowledge on how to reach the Demon Realm was destroyed."

Talon quips, "Apparently not."

"We know that Drak'thonn has warlocks in his ranks," says Ashcon referring to the attack on the ship. "It seems as if one of these warlocks has learned the secret of the Demon Realm."

All is silent for a few moments before Ka'alshene speaks again. "Yes, it appears so. Most likely it is the high warlock, who is the spiritual leader, confidant, and advisor to Drak'thonn, as well as the most powerful practitioner of the dark arts."

Ashcon stands up and starts pacing back and forth as he speaks. "This still doesn't change our objective. If anything, it makes it even more imperative to get to Sorenthor to see if he can shed some light on this."

"It does not change your objective, that is true," she replies. "You must get to Sorenthor's Library, both to find out how this has come to be, and ascertain any information you can on how to defeat demons." She tilts her head in thought and continues. "Have a word with the little wizard in your party as he may have some information on demons."

"If I may interject for a moment, please," implores Talon. "Forgive my ignorance, but from what I understand Sorenthor is a former seeker. We have many questions and the answer to all of them seems to be to ask Sorenthor. Is he so wise and powerful?"

It is Ka'alshene who responds to the inquiry. "Sorenthor is a fine practitioner of magic as well as an accomplished apothecary. However, that is not why we seek him out. His library is home to over thirty thousand volumes of history, lore, and prophecy." She pauses before saying, "And Sorenthor has read every one of them. He can also recall each passage, so if you are seeking information on a specific prophecy, he knows every book that may mention it."

"Incredible," whispers an astonished Talon.

"Truly," says Skken loudly, getting the attention of the party. "M'lady, by your tone I feel that you have more to impart to us."

"I do," replies the high priestess. "Drak'thonn has mobilized his forces and plans to attack the Kingdom of Martel with his army. They are marching south to the Myth Mountains and should arrive their within half a moonsign."

Ashcon says, "It will still take him quite a while to march to the west and reach the kingdom by ship. I'm guessing it will take more than a moonsign until they arrive."

Ka'alshane responds. "That is the interesting part, Ashcon. Instead of marching southwest, which would make sense if they were taking to the sea, they are marching southeast. If they stay on the course they are heading now, they will hit the Myth Mountains directly north of Antoine."

"That is almost as far east as the Marsh of Sorrow," says Skken. "Are they planning on traversing the Marsh and invading via the DragonTooth Pass?"

"That is what I thought first, Skken," she replies. "But the Marsh is impenetrable for leagues north of the Myth Mountains. If one wishes to cross the Marsh from the west, the only available route starts from the northwest of the swamp. If that was their intention, they would be marching northeast, not to the southeast." Silence follows and she continues. "I also don't believe that the Dark Horde wishes to do battle with the barbarians, which would be inevitable if an invading force traverses the marsh."

"So have you ascertained their intention?" asks Talon.

"I have not," admits the high priestess. "So when do you believe you will arrive at the library?"

"We are only one day ride from Redpost, which we will bypass to the north, and it looks like another eight days from there," replies Ashcon. "What will you do?"

"I will meet with the prince regent and the leaders of the Imperial Army in Thorenn in hopes of getting them to mobilize their forces. I should meet with little resistance and we can expect they will quickly head west." She pauses and continues. "Then I will meet with the king of the dwarves of the Myth Mountains and hope to gain their assistance."

"You don't sound very confident, Ka'alshene," says Skken.

"Except for trade with the barbarians, the dwarves of the Myth Mountains have basically cut themselves off from the rest of the world," explains the high priestess. "They rarely care about what transpires above ground. Since the Dark

Horde seems to be marching directly to the Myth Mountains, I am hoping that will spur them into action. We can only hope."

"We should waste no more time and head directly to Sorenthor's" says Ashcon.

"Sorenthor will contact me when you arrive and, if I am able, I will meet you there," says Kaa'alshene. "Please be careful and make haste." She closes her eyes and the line of communication is broken. The three companions look at each other with concern. They turn and march in silence back to the cave, hoping to steal a night's sleep before continuing on their quest.

Chapter 42

ASHCON puts his hand gently over the gnome's mouth and with his right hand nudges Lymer awake. The startled wizard tries to speak as Ashcon calms him down with both a finger to his lips and whispers in his ear. "Shhh, we need to talk. Follow me quietly."

He stands up and exits the cave with Skken in tow and Lymer following sleepily, kicking Katrivus in the kneecap on the way out. Ashcon waves at the Sashee scout who just watches from afar as the three walk twenty feet up river before coming to a stop.

"It is important you don't repeat any of this, Lymer. Is that understood?" asks Ashcon, looking down at the gnome.

"Of course, Ashcon. I may be small but please don't treat me like a child," retorts Lymer. "So why did you interrupt my dreams?"

"As you are aware, Drak'thonn has warlocks in his ranks." Lymer nods affirmatively in response. "It appears as if at least one of them has the ability to bring back demons from the Demon Realm."

Lymer looks down in despair, lets out a deeps sigh, and replies, "The Sashee?"

"Yes."

"I see."

"I was led to believe you may have some knowledge on demons and what we may be facing," says the runestar.

"Wizards who attend the academy all study the Second War of the Sanctum because of the profound affect it had on all wizards for all time," starts Lymer.

Ashcon interrupts the longwinded gnome. "We have limited time, so give me the short version."

"Of course," Lymer replies. "The type of demon brought back from the Demon Realm varies in power in direct correlation with the skills of the warlock. Assuming that the warlock is somewhat proficient, you can expect to fight beings that are virtually immune to conventional weapons. Magic is the only means to defeat them."

Ashcon lets out a deep breath and asks, "What are their means of attack?"

Lymer shakes his head back and forth and replies, "That is the problem. Until you face them you really have no idea. There are so many possible demons with diverse powers that it is impossible to say. The wizards were used to combat the demons, and eventually succeeded, but at a great cost. It is unknown how many wizards perished."

Ashcon patiently lets the gnome sit in thought for a few seconds, and then he clears his throat and continues. "Wizards were the primary means of combating the demon hordes. For some reason wizards' magic worked better than some of the other practitioners. Barbarian Shamen were very useful, as was the occasional sorcerer, but wizard magic seemed to work best."

"Was all other magic useless?" asks Skken.

"No, not useless. Just not as effective," replies Lymer. "Due to this, many wizards perished and the war was being lost, so something needed to be done."

Both Skken and Ashcon wait for Lymer to continue.

"Some of the wizards decided to make the ultimate sacrifice," says Lymer sadly. "The twelve most powerful wizards of the time each took a weapon and transferred the entirety of their power into it. By doing so they lost all of their magical abilities for all time." Tears start to form in Lymer's eyes, but the gnome recomposes himself and continues. "These magnificent weapons could be wielded by non-wizards to defeat the demons. They were given to the twelve most able warriors. The weapons worked even better than anyone imagined, and the tales tell of warriors with these demon banes taking down dozens of demons with one swing."

"So we were victorious in the Second War of the Sanctum thanks to these courageous wizards," says Ashcon with true reverence in his voice.

Lymer pauses for a few second and continues. "Once the war ended and the demon horde was driven back, these weapons were deemed too powerful to be left in the hands of man."

"They destroyed them?" asks Skken.

"No, actually," replies Lymer. "The twelve wizards who sacrificed themselves each took the weapon they imbued with their power and went off to destinations unknown to die with the weapons by their side. No one knows where they went and the weapons have been lost to the world ever since."

A dire look overcomes the faces of both Ashcon and Skken before Ashcon speaks. "There is no need to alert the others about demons since Drak'thonn doesn't know our whereabouts as of yet." He starts back to the cave and signals Lymer and Skken to follow. The three return to the cave to find the rest of the party awake and packing up the camp.

"Decide to take a quick stroll?" asks Talon teasingly.

Ashcon just glares at him in response and starts to pack up his belongings. "The weather has not improved. I suggest we continue north along the western bank of the river until we are well north of Redpost. We should get there by midday."

Skken replies, "I concur. After the noon meal we will turn west." He turns his head to the left and addresses Ayatana. "We will have two days riding west before we must part ways."

The son of the first warrior nods but does not speak. He then glances toward La'avenlei who is locked in a tearful stare with Katrivus. It is Katrivus who breaks the stare, looks down at his feet, and exits the cave.

Chapter 43

KATRIVUS'S melancholy only deepens as the evening of the second day of travelling west is upon them. The weather seems to match the mood of the love-stricken Soui Toofen, as it has gotten steadily worse. The sun has been behind dark clouds for three days straight. Only the little wizard is happy with the rain. In fact, he absolutely delights in it, shifting side to side in his saddle, catching drops on his tongue. Laven'lei rides with her betrothed while the others of her tribe scout ahead. Sapphyre is riding next to Katrivus, and both she and Lymer have attempted at conversation with him but to no avail. Talon and Ashcon are whispering as usual with Skken taking up the rear of the party.

The group slows down as two of the Sashee scouts gallop back signaling them to halt. One of the scouts addresses Ayatana while the other continues to the rear to consult with Skken. Skken looks to the young Ayatana, who locks eyes with the Ta'adaal. They both nod and give orders to the scouts.

Skken trots up to the main party and says, "There is an abandoned farmhouse not far to the west. We will spend the night under a roof, with a warm fire." Only Katrivus seems immune to the happy news, and they continue toward the shelter without another word.

The farmhouse is indeed abandoned, but rather large with six stalls, and most importantly, about three quarters of the roof was intact. It sits amidst a field that once served as farmland, now giving way to the infringing forest. To the delight of the party, the Sashee scouts already have a fire started. There is enough room to keep the horses dry and after the scouts tend to the horses, they surprise everyone with a slew of rabbits for the fire.

Sleep comes easy with full bellies and a roof over their heads for the first time in weeks. That is, it comes easy for everyone except Katrivus. Ever since Laven'lei broke his heart, he has been lost. If she didn't love him, it would be easy for him. That is something he could accept. But she loves him with all her heart, and that is why the pain is unbearable.

Katrivus sits up and glances around the room, his eyes coming to rest on the silent form of the high shaman's daughter. He sighs as he stands up and decides to take a walk.

The scout sees Katrivus pull his hood up over his head and leave the farmhouse. He starts to make his way over to him when Kat stops him with an icy glare. The scout nods and returns to his post. Katrivus continues eastward into the dense forest.

The rain is still pouring down in buckets, penetrating the trees that fill the dark sky, hiding the stars and moons. Katrivus slows down after moving at a rather quick pace, finally coming to rest leaning his left side against a tree trunk three times as wide as himself.

A static-like noise crackles from the west, back toward the farmhouse and immediately snaps him to attention. He starts to slowly backtrack to the west.The noise is getting louder, hence closer, but the pelts of rain obstruct the view. Now, with a few hundred yards left of forest before he hits the clearing, Katrivus turns to his right and stops dead in his tracks.

Less than twenty feet away is an eye the size of a barbarian, staring at him, or through him. The eye lacks substance, yet crackles with transparent electricity. Without warning the eye changes its shape before the stunned Katrivus. In its place is a large, oval object standing ten feet tall by five feet wide. The outer rim is glowing dark amber, pulsating like lava, the tube-like structure encircling the darkness within. The center is black as night, yet rippling like a faltering tide. Katrivus edges backwards, a tree trunk stopping him, mouth agape starting straight ahead. He glances to his right, less than a few hundred yards from the farmhouse, and is about to make a run for it when something emerges from the portal. Katrivus makes the mistake of pausing to look.

A head appears first and takes a deep breath of air. Two red arms, each rippled with muscle and easily the size of Kat's thigh, follow the head and grab the outer lava ring as leverage and lurch the rest of his body into the forest.

Katrivus is backing away in awe, staring at the creature standing over twelve feet tall, dwarfing the largest of barbarians. The demon stretches while Kat surveys the situation from less than twenty feet away. The head is huge, with six inch horns sprouting from above the eyes and extending upward toward the sky. The eyes resemble black orbs and slant slightly downward toward its wide nose, and while it's adapting to its surroundings, opens its mouth to nothing but blackness. It's turning its head from left to right, still unaware of Kat directly in front of him. As its stretching its arms outward, the span easily ten feet wide, it opens its eyes and locks them on Katrivus. As he's looking at the shocked Katrivus, the beast fluidly moves his right arm to his leg, and duplicates the motion with his left. He then stands to his full height and stretches his arms, revealing both a mace and an ax, dripping with a blood red liquid. Katrivus races to his right just as the demon bellows an ungodly roar, alerting anyone within earshot.

Katrivus is running full speed toward the farmhouse hoping to outrace the creature in pursuit. The demon moves with the speed of a Dreggan. Just as Katrivus reaches the outskirts of the farm, the beast swings his mace toward Kat's back.

The Sashee warrior scout has his spear and shield out and is racing north attempting to cut off the demon before it gets to the farmhouse. The demon whips the mace back in his right hand just as the barbarian makes his way to intercept. The burning mace is arching around his body just as the spear of the barbarian hits the demon in his right ribs, bouncing off his scaled body but distracting the beast just enough to alert Katrivus to the attack. Kat glances back over his right shoulder to see the mace, ducks, and rolls to his left, the weapon barely missing his head.

The demon looks to the right and in the blink of an eye swings the ax in his left hand, decapitating the unarmed barbarian who saved Kat's life. Kat is on his feet and running toward the farmhouse where the rest of his party made their way outside, not sure what they would be up against.

Ashcon and Skken are already on the move, running straight at Katrivus who is less than one hundred yards away. Laven'lei is right on their heels while the barbarians get their weapons ready.

The demon is gaining headway on Katrivus as he scrambles through the mud, seeing his companions for the first time through the torrential downpour. Laven'lei sees him and instinctively screams, "Soui Toofen!"

Kat pauses as he hears her voice, and it is just long enough for the demon to take advantage.

The demon leaps forward with his ax held high in his left hand. Katrivus's head is an easy target. With the ax inches from Kat's head, an ice bolt slams into the hilt, and the weapon drops to the ground.

The demon adapts immediately and eight-inch talons replace his blade. All five of his razor-sharp claws slice their way down Katrivus's back and he falls face down in the mud just as Laven'lei lets out a horrific scream.

The demon steps over the fallen body of Katrivus and faces off against the remainder of the party. It looks back and forth among the companions and starts to advance slowly. It then lifts both arms to the sky and screams before jumping to the right where two barbarian warriors lie in wait.

Aschon starts barking orders as Skken charges toward the demon with Grizzclaw in hand. "Conventional weapons don't work," screams Ashcon. "Magic is the only thing that will harm the demon. If you don't possess magic, stay out of the way and tend to the wounded."

The barbarians are doing their best against the demon but he deflects their weapons as if they are toys. The demon kicks one of the Sashee which sends him rolling ten feet until he stops face up, the hoof print of the demon emblazoned upon the dead warrior's chest.

Ashcon is levitating toward the demon and launching ice bolts at the hideous creature. The bolts penetrate its scaly armor and slow down the creature's attack, but don't incapacitate the monster. Skken is fluidly dodging attacks from the demon's mace and ax, all while countering with slashes from Grizzclaw, injuring the demon but only for seconds and with no permanent damage.

Talon knows he can't do anything without magic and makes his way over toward the body of Katrivus. He gets down on his knees, placing his ear upon the downed thief's mouth and is astonished to hear laboring breaths. He reaches down to his arm and feels a pulse and then looks around hoping to find Sapphyre.

Laven'lei steps into the forefront and raises her arms, and leaves and rain start to swirl about her. Her arms keep moving around and around, tightening the globe in front of her and gaining momentum. She steps toward the demon and launches the globe at its back.

As it touches her foe, it erupts, and the power of the wind within blows it forward and the demon stumbles and reaches out with his right arm to balance itself. Skken takes advantage of the opening and swings his magical saber severing the eight foot long barbed tail of the beast.

The demon howls in rage, but turns completely around to face the female barbarian. Ashcon floats between them and launches ice bolts from both hands, distracting the demon from Laven'lei as she makes her way over to where Talon is tending to Katrivus.

Skken continues his assault from behind, but the demon is too quick this time and slaps Skken away like a fly with the back of his right hand. Just as quickly the demon brings his left arm around and swipes Ashcon out of midair, sending him tumbling through the mud, his head crashing upon a damp rock.

The demon bellows forth a growl and raises his arms in triumph just as Lymer steps from the shadows and bellows at the demon with a booming voice echoing through the rain. Lymer is standing about fifteen feet from the demon when it turns to face the little gnome.

Without warning, Lymer raises his arms and starts moving his hands above his head, apparently amusing the staring demon. The palms of the wizard are suddenly alive with cyclones, formed from the pelting rain and gusty winds. Lymer shoots his arms forward and the cyclones move at the speed of light and pierce into the unworldly creature. One of the cyclones hit it on its left shoulder, piercing a hole straight through, while the other penetrates the right thigh, doing the same damage.

The demon screams in rage, looking down at the damage done by the little gnome. Lymer is starting to chant another spell and gather more power from the weather when Skken jumps at the demon hoping to take advantage of the wounded beast.

The distracted demon takes a slice from Grizzclaw in its belly as Skken jumps away after leaving his mark. Lymer launches two more cyclones at the demon, one missing its mark but the other going straight through the right side of his chest.

The demon stands straight up and looks back and forth between Skken and the little gnome. Ashcon finally gets back to his feet and walks over to Lymer just as the beast stands up in defiance. Its severed tail starts to grow back as the astonished onlookers stare with their mouths agape. It stretches its neck just as the holes that Lymer's magic caused heal themselves and the demon is whole once more.

The demon locks eyes with Lymer. The gnome is frozen in place, since his confidence is shaken after watching the beast regenerate from his attacks. Ashcon steps in front of the wizard and urges him backward toward the farmhouse, ready to stand up against the demon when Sapphyre finally emerges from behind the beast.

Ashcon levitates and launches ice bolts at the demon's chest, hoping to keep all the attention on himself. The demon starts taking deliberate steps toward Ashcon just as Sapphyre unsheathes Frostripper for a pending attack. As soon as she removes her dagger, the demon stops and turns to face her.

The companions look on in disbelief as the demon starts backing away from the young woman, fear evidenced in his movements, his eyes locked on Sapphyre's dagger. Then it stops and defiantly holds its ground and lets out a thundering roar before charging at Sapphyre.

Calm as ever, Sapphyre waits for the demon's approach with the courage of a thousand elite warriors. Ashcon is about to intervene when Lymer grabs his waist and holds the runestar fast.

The demon is now only a few feet from Sapphyre and lifts his mace to make the first strike. He simultaneously strikes his mace high from right to left, aiming at her head while bringing the ax in a swinging motion along the ground, expecting Sapphyre to parry the blow by rolling from the mace. To the surprise of all, Sapphyre jumps high into the air, easily avoiding the strikes, the momentum of the demon almost turning it completely around.

Sapphyre takes advantage and while landing, attacks with Frostripper severing the tail from the demon, who lets out an ungodly scream. The severed tail bursts into flame, and it's obvious that this dismemberment will be permanent.

The demon turns to face Sapphyre, who is once again standing upright, looking at it, fear returning to the face of the demon as it stares at the weapon. Frostripper's blade has extended from twelve inches into a full-blown sword, black as night and pulsing with power.

The demon goes into a berserker rage at the sight of the weapon and charges at Sapphyre with reckless abandon, swinging both weapons, hoping to score any type of killing blow. Sapphyre reacts with dazzling speed, pirouetting out of the way, countering each missed blow with a gash into the demon's skin, Frostripper piercing through its flesh like butter. Her party is mesmerized watching the young woman dance out of the way of each blow and countering with the expertise of a prized swordsman.

While Sapphyre is parrying strike after strike, slicing into the demon's skin, Lymer is next to Ashcon, eyes closed, preparing for an attack of his own. The wizard opens his eyes and the storm clouds have all converged into one bustling ball of electricity and situated itself directly above the battling demon.

Lymer points his hands to the sky and lightning erupts from the cloud, bolts reaching down and striking the demon, holding him in a net of static electricity, rendering him unable to move.

The demon is howling in rage, aware of his predicament as Sapphyre approaches the beast, holding up Frostripper inches from its face, the demon unable to move. She brings the point of the magical blade up to its eyes, and then in one fluid motion, steps back and strikes, slicing the beast from its left shoulder down to its right hip. Without stopping she repeats the motion on the other side forming an X on the demon's chest. The demon looks down in disbelief as his chest is now wide open and with one final thrust, Sapphyre plunges Frostripper straight into the middle of its torso up to the hilt.

The demon tries to scream but no sound escapes from its lips. Sapphyre removes Frostripper just as Lymer releases his spell and the creature's body explodes. The only remnant of the demon is the black sludge in the six-foot crater where it met its doom.

Chapter 44

SAPPHYRE sheaths Frostripper, which has returned to its dormant state, and locates where Talon is tending to Katrivus. She walks over purposefully, ignoring the wide-eyed stares of all her companions. She leans down and takes the unconscious head of her oldest friend into her hands when Talon speaks.

"His breathing is labored and there is a slight pulse. I've done what I can to dress the wound but it seems to be festering already."

Sapphyre gently turns Katrivus on his side on her lap to inspect his back. She slowly traces her fingers along the dressing, all the while holding his head in her palm. She's about to speak, but Laven'lei does so first, her voice strong despite the state of Soui Toofen.

"I added some cooling herbs to the dressing," she starts. "I also had him breathe some cho-chi, but it did not seem to have any affect."

Sapphyre closes her eyes and with one hand cradling Katrivus's head, the other starts moving gracefully over his fallen body. After a few seconds, a green sphere starts to surround both Sapphyre and Katrivus and once they are completely enveloped, Sapphyre ceases her motion and opens her eyes.

All of the companions are speechless, watching this spectacle as Sapphyre rests Katrivus head onto the bottom of the sphere and walks out to join the others.

"I do not have the ability to heal him of the wounds he suffered at the hand of the demon," she explains. "His condition will not deteriorate while he is in the sphere, but it also will not improve."

Ashcon is the first to speak. "How long can you keep the sphere up, Sapphyre?"

"I am not sure, though it is not terribly trying. I'm assuming as long as I am close to him, I should be able to keep it intact."

"Good," says Ashcon. "Let us prepare a litter for Katrivus and get on our way as quickly as possible. We will discuss what has transpired on the road."

This spurs everyone into action and the group started their preparations for the pending travel. Lymer took the opportunity to engage Ashcon in conversation.

"Does Sapphyre even recall what transpired?" asks Lymer.

Ashcon looks down at the little gnome and replies, "I think so. We will find out shortly." As if on cue, Sapphyre strolls over to the two and joins in.

She stands directly in front of both Ashcon and her new little friend, Lymer, and for a few moments there is complete silence. Sapphyre sees that her friends now view her in a totally different light, especially Lymer, whose eyes are sparkling with reverence. In response, Sapphyre takes a few steps forward and places her left hand upon Lymer's right cheek, smiling brightly.

"I'm the same person, my friend," she says quietly.

Lymer grins from ear to ear and exclaims, "Of course you are, Sapphyre!" and he wraps his arms tightly around her waist while the three friends laugh, the tension gone.

Lymer takes a step back and looks up at Sapphyre and asks, "Do you remember what happened?"

Sapphyre responds immediately, "Of course."

"So you realize your dagger is more than it appears," says the little gnome.

"Yes, and by the look in your eye it seems as if you know what that is."

He glances down at her boot and the hilt of the weapon and asks, "May I?"

In response Sapphyre reaches down, unsheathes Frostripper and hands it hilt first to Lymer. He holds it in his little hands and runs his fingers along the blade, spinning it over and over in his palm. He is admiring the gem encrusted hilt when Sapphyre asks, "What is it, Lymer?"

Her voice breaks the trancelike state Lymer found himself in inspecting the dagger and he looks up to Sapphyre and replies. "During the second War of the Sanctum the demon horde was on the offensive and their victory seemed inevitable. It was at that time when the twelve most powerful wizards of the day imbued all of their power into twelve demon banes – weapons with the power to defeat the demon horde. These weapons were wielded by chosen warriors who defeated the demons with them."

"How is that I have never heard this story?" asks Sapphyre.

Lymer replies, "What you must understand is that when the twelve wizards imbued the weapons, they transferred all of their power into them, therefore becoming mortal men. They paid the ultimate sacrifice of giving up their powers to defeat the demons."

Ashcon and Sapphyre let Lymer reflect without interrupting and he continues. "The tales you hear about Forborn the Destroyer wielding an ax of liquid gold and destroying demons by the score are all true. Over time, the man became the legend, as was intended." He pauses and looks up at his companions. "Can you imagine the battles that would take place and the wars that would be waged to gain ownership of such powerful weapons? Safeguards were put in place to ensure that word never got out about the true nature of the demon banes."

"So how is it that I am in possession of one?" asks Sapphyre.

Lymer looks up at Ashcon and back to Sapphyre and says, "I don't know, my dear. When the war was over and the demons were defeated, the twelve wizards took their respective weapons and banished themselves. They each made an oath to find a place in which to die, and hide their weapon, never to be wielded again."

Ashcon intervenes, "Apparently, this one made it to the surface and somehow ended up in Sapphyre's possession."

Lymer says excitedly, "As you can see, the wizards added many precautions in case the weapon did find its way back into the hands of man." As he is still grasping the weapon, he holds it up and continues. "It disguises itself as a simple, yet ornate dagger. If you never encountered a demon, we would never have realized its true nature. Once the weapon sensed the demon, it transformed into its true form."

Ashcon asks, "So I'm assuming the dagger also has the ability to turn the wielder into a world class swordsman?"

Lymer laughs and says, "Apparently! The wizards who imbued the weapons were extremely proficient in their abilities. I cannot begin to fathom just what this weapon can accomplish."

He is about to give the dagger back to Sapphyre and grasps the blade lightly and extends it hilt first to Sapphyre before he freezes and pulls it back.

"What is it?" asks a startled Sapphyre.

"There's a mark," explains Lymer. He holds the dagger inches from his eye, inspecting the area where the hilt meets the blade. "There is a symbol here. It is miniscule but it appears to be a serpent with three heads." He holds it up for Sapphyre to see. "Look. There are tiny pearls as eyes, and if you look closely, you can see the serpent etched into the blade."

"Yes," she replies. "I have never seen that mark before. I am certain."

Lymer takes it back down to eye level, glances at it again, and says, "Perhaps the mark became visible once the blade was exposed to the demon." He places it in Aschon's outstretched hand.

Ashcon inspects it and says, "That makes sense. It looks as if it is a maker's mark."

Sapphyre asks, "Do you mean the wizard who imbued the weapon marked it?"

"That's exactly what I'm saying," says Ashcon as he hands the dagger back to Sapphyre. She puts it away. "It's the only thing that makes sense.

Maybe there will be a reference to it at Soren-thor's."

Lymer interjects, "I doubt it, Ashcon. The wizards are a secretive group and I would venture to say that the only reference to the weapons are closely guarded and known to few."

"We'll see," says Ashcon. He looks to the rest of the party that is preparing to depart and motions for the two to follow him.

Laven'lei has been sitting by Katrivus's side, holding his hand through the healing sphere. Ayatana walks over to his betrothed and puts a loving hand on her shoulder. She looks up at him and smiles. She leans in and gently kisses Katrivus on his forehead and whispers, "Be well, Soui Toofen." She rises, nods to Ayatana, and the two go hand-in-hand to join the remaining warrior scouts.

Laven'lei walks slowly over to Sapphyre and the two embrace in a hug that lasts a few precious moments. Teary eyed, Laven'lei turns to Skken and bows reverently. Skken responds in kind and without another word, the daughter of the High Shaman of the Sashee returns to her tribesmen, and they journey west in search of their destiny.

Chapter 45

SORENTHOR senses the visitors' approach long before the group sees the tower that houses the famed library. Anyone who comes within a few leagues of the Lost Seeker's residence cannot traverse the lands without him knowing. He has been waiting in anticipation ever since he felt their presence with the sunrise and expects them as soon as the sun goes down. Glancing up at the sky from the top floor of his library, he sees that their arrival is imminent.

The litter that carries the injured Katrivus doesn't delay the group as expected. Sapphyre is correct in assuming that as long as she remains close to her friend, keeping the healing sphere in place takes little effort. Sorenthor's Library comes into view in the late afternoon of the seventh day of travel since the battle with the demon.

As the tower comes into focus the group comes to a sudden halt. Talon, Lymer, and Sapphyre staring wide-eyed at the looming structure when Ashcon speaks. "It has the same effect on all who behold it. It is quite an intimidating sight."

The three nod and continue staring. From a distance, the tower seems as if it climbs as high as the clouds and is a menacing dark grey. Sharp, jagged edges run the length of the pyramid-shaped structure with no windows visible to the naked eye. The perfectly cylindrical base appears to stretch at least twenty yards into the air creating the guise of a fortress wall. The air surrounding the library is a thick fog, an eerie combination of green and grey lending a more ominous feel to the lair.

Skken urges them on and says, "Not all is as it seems, my friends. Let us continue." His companions look at him with a confused expression, but all urge their mounts on as Ashcon lets out a short chuckle.

Talon looks inquisitively at Ashcon and then Skken before stating accusatorily at the True Guardian, "You are obviously familiar with the Lost Seeker's lair, yet you claim to have never been here. Would you mind explaining yourself?"

Skken looks at Talon with raised eyebrows. He glances at Ashcon, who is still chuckling softly. "Ashcon and I visited Sorenthor's Library over two hundred winters ago," explains the barbarian.

Aschcon intervenes and continues, "The Lost Seeker moves his entire lair about every fifty or so winters. No one knows how he does it. One day it is in one place and the next somewhere else." He glances over at Sapphyre and says, "When Skken and I met Sorenthor for the first time, his library was in the same region as where we met you, near Meer."

Skken then looks back at Talon and says, "There is your explanation, thief."

Lymer interjects for the first time. "Incredible. Truly incredible." He then stands up in the saddle behind Sapphyre, puts his arms on her shoulders and yells, "Can't this thing go any faster?" to the amused laughter of his companions.

A short time later the group is traversing the fog they saw from a distance and emerge from it with a collective gasp from all but Ashcon and Skken. What looks like a dark, uninviting fortress from afar is gone, replaced by a splendid garden of tropical plants and exotic trees radiating vibrant colors of the rainbow. The garden stretches the perimeter of the library that reveals its true self.

The ominous structure is gone and replaced by a much smaller yet intricately designed pyramid. It is a beautiful mix of yellow and green that layer upon each other, cascading up to the apex. The material is nothing any of them have ever seen before. Despite the time and the darkness of the hour, the entire area around the library is awash in light and the pyramid-like structure reflects that light upon the garden and the grounds surrounding the library.

The companions dismount and start walking their horses toward what appears to be the rear of the building when they are greeted by a voice from behind.

"Welcome, friends. I've been expecting you," says Sorenthor to the startled group.

They all turn around at the same time to behold the famed Lost Seeker. Sorenthor is wearing his usual blood-red robe, resting loosely on a six-foot, slender frame accentuated by his broad shoulders. His sleek, bald head and clean-shaven face give off a sense of warmth, which matches his velvety baritone voice. The bright blue eyes contrast sharply with his olive skin. While he exudes the intelligence of an elder statesman, physically he appears to be a man of only thirty or so winters.

As if in response to the looks of surprise, Soren-thor quickly explains. "The mirage you saw from a distance is a little trick I put in place to keep out undesirables. If people believe the famed Lonely Hermit is an evil sorcerer who performs black magic in his castle, so much the better." He waves his hands to his right and a stable appears where there was nothing a moment ago. He glances over at Katrivus, enveloped in the green sphere, and states, "Please join me inside and I will tend to your injured party member." He then proceeds toward his library without another word, leaving the companions to care for the horses.

Talon and Skken finish tying off the animals and the two of them carry Katrivus in his litter, following the others to the main house. Sorenthor leaves an opening for them to enter. Calling it a door would be inaccurate since once closed there is no way to figure out where it once was.

Ashcon enters first, followed by Sapphyre and Lymer, and then Talon and Skken with Katrivus in tow. Sorenthor is standing in the center of the cylindrical main floor as the companions approach, his eyes on the injured Katrivus the entire time.

He makes his way toward the litter just as Sapphyre is removing her hood. As it falls away revealing her unique features, Sorenthor stops dead in his tracks. His mouth agape and at a loss for words for the first time in centuries, he stares at the blonde, blue-haired beauty as tears form in his eyes.

"By the Star Gods, can it be?" he asks both softly and rhetorically. No one responds as Sorenthor walks over to Sapphyre and looks down at her and smiles. "You look just like your mother. And you have your father's eyes."

Sapphyre is stunned and looks up at Sorenthor just as he reaches down and touches the blue streak in her hair. Without a word, she starts crying hysterically and falls into the arms of Sorenthor, who holds her tightly with his eyes closed.

After a few moments, Ashcon interrupts. "Well, Sorenthor, it has been quite a while."

Sorenthor looks up at the runestar, nods affirmatively and says, "It certainly has." He then looks over to the True Guardian, nods, and says, "Skken."

Skken responds in kind. "Sorenthor."

"Ka'alshene foretold your coming, but she didn't tell me you would be joined by so many interesting characters," the Lost Seeker says, still holding Sapphyre in his arms.

"We have much to discuss," says Ashcon.

"You simply have no idea, Ashcon," replies Sorenthor as he pulls back from Sapphyre and looks down into her eyes. He then takes Sapphyre by the arm and gestures for the others to follow as he says once again, "You have no idea."

Chapter 46

THE group follows Sorenthor and Sapphyre to the far end of the room where he stops and turns back to the companions. "Please bring the injured man forward." Talon and Skken approach with the litter and stand in front of Sorenthor, Talon on his left and Skken to the right. The Lost Seeker raises his arms and the litter falls away leaving the green sphere holding Katrivus levitating in front of him. As he moves his hands, the sphere rotates, moving Katrivus around, allowing Sorenthor to inspect the injured man. As the back of Katrivus becomes visible, he reaches through the sphere and with one motion of his hand, the bandages covering the wound melt away. The wound has remained in a constant state since Sapphyre enveloped her friend within, yet it is a gruesome sight, nonetheless.

Sapphyre lets out a gasp as she sees his back, while Sorenthor leans closer to inspect it further. He asks, "First off, who has been healing this man?"

"I have," replies Sapphyre.

Sorenthor looks down at Sapphyre, when Ashcon interjects. "Sapphyre has some incredible powers and healing seems to be among them."

Tears form in his eyes and he says softly, "Your name is Sapphyre." His eyes sparkle for a moment and he continues with a smile. "Of course it is."

He turns again to Ashcon, his face stern once again and asks, "What caused this wound?"

Ashcon says simply, "The claws of a demon."

Sorenthor has to do a double take before confirming. "A demon. You are sure?"

"Absolutely," states Ashcon.

"I take it you dispatched the demon," he says matter-of-factly to Ashcon.

"Actually, it was Sapphyre who destroyed it."

Sorenthor cannot hide his surprise as he looks down at Sapphyre, wide-eyed and mouth agape.

Sapphyre blushes and says softly, "It was more due to Frostripper than myself." She notices Sorenthor's confused stare and explains,

"Frostripper is my dagger," instinctively touching the hilt of the weapon.

"I told you we had much to discuss," says Ashcon to the stunned Sorenthor.

"More than either of us has imagined, I would presume," replies Sorenthor.

Sapphyre interjects impatiently, "Can we please tend to Katrivus first?"

Sorenthor replies, "Of course, my dear." He looks at the stricken man once again, closes his eyes, and continues. "Sapphyre, can you keep the healing sphere in place for a while longer?"

"That shouldn't be a problem," she replies.

"Good," says Sorenthor. "Let us adjourn to the study where I can tell you what I know regarding demon wounds." He walks to the opposite end of the main room and through a granite door as the others follow right behind.

Sorenthor's study is a round room, consistent with the theme, with an intricate oval table in the center. He waves his hand and six ornately carved chairs appear around the table. He gestures for each of the companions to take a seat. He closes his eyes for what seems like many minutes as the friends look on without speaking. He opens his eyes and takes a seat at the table, looking at each of the people at the table in turn before speaking.

"Are you all aware of my gift of Consummate Recollection?" he asks the group and Ashcon responds.

"I explained to each of them your gift, yes. But if you would like to elaborate, please do."

"Very well," says Sorenthor. "Once I read something I have the ability to draw upon it at any time. In my library, I house thousands of volumes of texts, prophecies and so forth. I have read almost every one. I can recall complete phrases or complete volumes, if necessary." He pauses and glances at the companions, landing finally on Lymer who is looking at him with his mouth agape, his tongue hanging down, causing the Lost Seeker to smile to himself. "I have gone through my memory on everything I have read regarding wounds inflicted from a demon and I will impart to you what I know. I'm afraid it is dire."

This brings a collective sigh from the group, but an especially grief-stricken look comes across the face of Sapphyre, which prompts Sorenthor to continue. "It is not a lost cause, Sapphyre, although it will be rather difficult to cure your friend."

"I will do whatever it takes," Sapphyre says authoritatively.

"Please tell us what you know," says Talon, locking eyes with Sapphyre.

"'Very well," says Sorenthor. "The unconscious state that your friend is in is what is referred to as the Demon Sleep." He stands up and squints his eyes, preparing his words. "His body is here, yet his soul is right now in the Demon Realm and will remain until rescued or until death."

Sapphyre asks, "Rescued?"

"I'm afraid so, Sapphyre. Demons gain their power from souls they destroy when they enter other realms. Since your friend was not killed, but rather wounded, his soul is entrapped within the Demon Realm. The demon who caused the wound is simply waiting for your friend to die and it will then feast on his soul and add to its power."

Talon interjects, "But Sapphyre killed the demon, Sorenthor."

Sorenthor looks to the young seeker and replies, "The demon was killed in our world, but it still exists within the Demon Realm. The only way to utterly destroy a demon is to do so in its home realm."

Ashcon says, "How do you rescue a soul from the Demon Realm?"

Sorenthor sighs before replying. "After finding the trapped soul within the Demon Realm, it must be freed, for lack of a better term."

Lymer interjects with a question, "How big is the Demon Realm?"

Sorenthor replies, "The Demon Realm is huge, but that is only one problem we face. Only warlocks of incredible power have the ability to open a portal to that accursed place. Without a portal, there is no way to get to your friend."

The silence that follows is deafening as the companions contemplate the fate of their companion. Lymer stands on his chair and asks the Lost Seeker, "How long do portals stay active?"

"Portals stay active until they are destroyed or closed by a warlock."

Talon interjects as he sees where Lymer's train of thought is heading. "The demon we faced had to come through a portal, correct?" The group all nods and he continues. "That portal may still exist."

Sorenthor looks to the group and says, "I assumed you destroyed the portal when you dispatched the demon."

Ashcon replies, "We never saw a portal. The first time we saw the demon it was chasing Katrivus."

Sorenthor closes his eyes for a few moments and then speaks. "If that portal does still exist, it will greatly enhance our ability to rescue Katrivus's soul. Besides being able to enter the Demon Realm, the portal will most likely lead to an area within the realm close to where the demon you met resides."

Ashcon looks around the table and asks, "How long can Katrivus remain in this state, Sorenthor?"

"Indefinitely."

"Then I suggest we complete all of our business here and then we can discuss a way to rescue Katrivus," says Ashcon.

Sapphyre is about to interject before Sorenthor cuts her off, "I know you are anxious to rescue your friend, but Ashcon is right. We have much to discuss and learn before we can attempt to enter the Demon Realm."

Sapphyre looks around the table before sighing and agreeing, "Very well."

Sorenthor then stands up and says, "Good. I have much to discuss with each of you. I would like to start with Ashcon and Skken, but not before you all gain some sustenance and some rest. I have prepared a feast in the main room and the guest rooms are ready for you. Please enjoy the food and then get some rest."

The companions all nod to Sorenthor, realizing in unison just how hungry and tired they are. They exit the study to find an elaborate table set up in the main room, piled high with roasted meats, fresh vegetables and hot bread. Not one of them asks where it came from as they sit down to dine.

Chapter 47

Ashcon gets out of bed and looks over at Skken, who is fully dressed and waiting by the door even though the sun is still hours from rising. Without a word, Aschon dresses, walks over to the water basin, and splashes his face with the cool water. The two then depart the room and head toward the main chamber.

They enter the study, the large round table gone and has been replaced by a smaller octagonal desk with only three chairs around it. Sorenthor is sitting reading a scroll and glances up at the runestar and true guardian and gestures for them to take the two open chairs. Skken and Ashcon patiently wait for Sorenthor to finish what he is reading, although they are eager to engage in conversation.

Sorenthor breathes deep and leans back in his chair says, "Well, we have much to discuss and I was contemplating where to start."

Ashcon replies, "Why don't we begin with our reason for seeking you out?" he says and then pauses before continuing. "Or rather our many reasons for seeking you out."

"Very well."

After Ashcon and Skken complete the tale, Sorenthor stands up and starts to pace, recapping the important points out loud. "Let me start with Sapphyre. So, you met her in a tavern on the western portion of the continent. She was able to see your runes and you thought she may be your seeker." He pauses to look at Ashcon and Skken, who have questioning expressions on their faces. Sorenthor explains, "Oh, please pardon me. Although I do have the power of Consummate Recollection, it only applies to the written word. I wish to make sure that I have all the facts correct before I render my opinions or make suggestions."

"Very well, please continue," says Ashcon.

"Over time you realized that Sapphyre had some powerful abilities and it became less likely she was your seeker. Then Talon was able to see your runes and the connection was made between the two of you, confirming immediately that he is your seeker and therefore Sapphyre is not."

He looks over to Ashcon seeking confirmation before continuing. "Sapphyre has powerful healing magic, of that we are certain. She also has shown you she has the ability to listen from afar and can detect auras on both people and objects. She also wields a magical dagger which has the power to destroy demons." He pauses and turns toward the men. "You all are wondering where her power is derived from and from what school it hails," he says.

They both nod affirmatively.

Sorenthor continues. "I will be able to shed some light on that issue, but not quite yet." Ashcon is about to interrupt, but Sorenthor holds up his hand and says, "Please Aschon, indulge me."

The runestar nods reluctantly and the Lost Seeker continues. "Drak'thonn has made numerous attempts on your life. The Zagador have always had warlocks in their ranks, but none have been powerful enough to enter the Demon Realm and bring forth creatures in thousands of winters." He closes his eyes in concentration and then opens them and looks at Aschon and Skken. "There are many prophecies that appear to be coming in to play. Some are false, as prophecy often is, but a few speak the truth. When I say the truth, that may be a bit of a misnomer," Sorenthor explains. "A prophecy does not predict the future, it predicts many possible futures depending on the actions taken by the subjects of the prophecy."

"We know how prophecy works, Sorenthor," says Ashcon impatiently.

"I apologize, Ashcon," says Sorenthor. "I tend to be longwinded." He pauses, deep in thought before continuing. "What I believe is this regarding Drak'thonn. You and your brother will face each other on the field of battle and one of you will emerge victorious."

"That has been my understanding for a long time, Sorenthor" says Ashcon, quickly losing his patience.

"What I mean is that the time is almost upon us. Now that I have met Sapphyre and understand who she is and that the warlocks are summoning demons again, the prophecy's many puzzles are starting to fall into place. Meeting your seeker at this juncture is no coincidence either. These simultaneous events all point toward the culmination of your existence. You and Drak'thonn will fight for the future of all of us."

Ashcon leans back in his chair and replies. "I always knew I would have to defeat Drak'thonn, but please elaborate when you say the future is dependent on it."

"I didn't realize that either, until today. I don't have the time to show you all of the texts that I have on the subject, so I will sum up." They both nod to Sorenthor. "Basically, it comes down to this, Ashcon. If you defeat your brother, the other battles will be won by your allies, and the followers of the Star Gods will emerge victorious." Ashcon and Skken exchange glances and Sorenthor continues. "If Drak'thonn defeats you, his allies will win their battles, and the world will be enveloped in darkness and we will all worship the Zagador."

"So, I guess it is a bit more than a brotherly squabble then?" Ashcon asks quietly to no one in particular.

Sorenthor takes his seat. The three sit in silence for a few moments until the door to the study opens and the men turn to see Ka'alshene standing outside with Sapphyre beside her.

Chapter 48

THE three men stand in unison as the women enter the room. Sorenthor says, "Welcome, ladies." He makes his way over to Ka'alshene, kisses her on both cheeks, and points to two chairs that just appeared.

"I see you have met Sapphyre," says Sorenthor.

"Indeed," replies the high priestess. "I had no idea, Sorenthor. Did you?"

"No, I did not. It came as a shock, but it is all starting to make sense." He looks at the other three and apologizes. "I'm sorry." He looks at Sapphyre. "I believe that things will be much clearer in short order."

"I hope so," says Sapphyre softly.

Sorenthor stands up and starts pacing before speaking. "As you are aware, Sapphyre, Ka'alshene and I knew your parents. Your father was my runestar, Kentin, and your mother was his true love, Nestair." He walks over to Sapphyre and places his hand upon her shoulder. "I loved them both dearly." Sapphyre looks up at him quizzically and sees tears forming in his eyes. He looks down at her and his head tilts to the side. He exclaims, "Of course!"

The companions all look at Sorenthor for an explanation when he holds his hand out to Sapphyre and says, "Sapphyre, please come with me. I have a hunch about something and it will take only a moment to confirm." She looks at him, smiles and takes his hand.

Ashcon stands up as the door opens to reveal Lymer and Talon with hurt looks on their faces. Sorenthor and Sapphyre race toward the opening as the Lost Seeker says, "We will only be a moment. Please come in and have a seat." He points to two chairs that suddenly appear and exits with Sapphyre right behind.

"I'm sorry about that, Sapphyre. I should have thought of this earlier," he starts as they walk toward the round staircase. Sapphyre glances up just when Sorenthor takes her hand and they walk behind it and through a door that Sapphyre has never seen before. They enter a small square room with a few chests scattered about. "Only days before his Ascension Day, your father bestowed upon me one task and one task only."

Sorenthor looks down at Sapphyre, walks to the opposite side of the room, reaches down, and takes hold of a small, ornately carved box. Holding it in his hands, he walks the three feet back to Sapphyre. Holding it in front of him, he explains.

"I was to hold this box until the time has come," he says.

"What is inside?" she asks.

"It is a large, dark blue stone. I am not aware of any magical abilities within, nor am I privy to the secrets it may hold, if any. When I pressed Kentin on how I will know when the time has come, he just smiled and said 'It will shine.'"

"What does that mean?" asks Sapphyre.

"Why don't you open the box, Sapphyre?" asks Sorenthor as he holds the box in front of her with both of his hands.

She looks up into his eyes, and he gives her a supportive nod. Tracing the ornate carvings of the box she asks, "What is this box made of?"

"It is a derivative of mythril that I made mixing mythril ore from the Myth Mountains with emerald dragon scales. It is unsuitable for armor due to its inflexibility, but perfect for storing valuables."

Sapphyre turns it horizontally in Sorenthor's hands, and with one hand on each side, lifts the lid off to glance at the stone within. Her breath is caught in her throat as she sets her eyes on the wondrous gem. The dark navy blue seems to travel in waves through a fourteen-sided stone that is larger than the most valuable of diamonds.

After a few seconds Sapphyre says quietly, "I don't think it's –" Her voice stops as the gem begins to give off rays of light. As if in recognition of the young woman, the stone rises from the box and hovers in front of her. It starts spinning in the air, all of the colors of the rainbow shining brilliantly, illuminating the small room.

Sorenthor is laughing out loud at the wondrous sight and Sapphyre is standing quietly with a small grin on her face when the gem stops spinning. The two watch as the lights that illuminated the room project into one beam ending in an expanding globe.

The globe of light expands and shapes begin to appear within. There is a garden extending as far as the eyes could see, although the room only goes about fifteen feet. In the distance they could make out animals running in a dense forest and to the west is a lake with a waterfall extending to the heavens.

Sorenthor and Sapphyre exchange startled glances when a voice speaks and they both look to the scene revealing itself a few feet away. "Sapphyre," is the one word spoken as the form of a man takes shape at the forefront of the garden.

"Father," says Sapphyre, trying her best to compose herself, her hands shaking by her side.

"Sorenthor," says Kentin.

Sorenthor bows down on one knee in response when Kentin says, "Please stand up, Sorenthor."

"But you are a God," says the humbled Lost Seeker as he slowly gets to his feet.

"I am always your runestar first, Sorenthor. Now, stand up." Kentin pauses, looks to Sapphyre and then back to Sorenthor and says, "Thank you for keeping my gem in safety. Nestair and I put our history within the stone so when Sapphyre came of age she could learn of her heritage."

He looks to Sapphyre and says, "My daughter, you must take the stone and join me here in the garden. Once you enter, you will meet the shades of both your mother and myself. Although we will not be with you in flesh and blood, we will be in spirit. The memories we stored within the stone will come to life within this world. You will learn much and leave with many answers. You will also leave with more questions."

Sapphyre tilts her head to one side and says to her father. "How long will I be with you and mother?"

Kentin smiles and replies, "That is impossible to answer in any real terms. For the sake of your question, you will be gone from your companions for a mere half day."

"Then I am ready, Father," Sapphyre says as she steps toward him.

"You must bring the gem, Sapphyre," says Kentin, pointing to where it is resting in its box.

Sapphyre walks to it and places the lid on, taking the box in her left hand when Kentin interrupts. "Please leave the box, Sapphyre. Just take the stone." Sapphyre removes the stone and places the empty box onto the floor.

She looks at Sorenthor, smiles and starts walking toward Kentin when he says to his former seeker, "Protect the gem always, Sorenthor." He nods in understanding as Sapphyre steps forward into the garden leaving Sorenthor standing alone in the once again empty, dark room.

Chapter 49

SORENTHOR returns to his study to the confused looks of all at the table and says, "I am sorry for the outburst, but it turned out to be worthwhile." The faces of his companions entice him to continue. "Kentin left me with a keepsake to bestow upon Sapphyre, although I didn't know it at the time."

"Enough with the riddles, Sorenthor. Where is Sapphyre?" asks an exasperated Ashcon.

Sorenthor takes his seat at the table and admonishes the runestar with a stare. "Days before his ascension, Kentin charged me to hold onto a particular box and keep it safe until the day had come. There is a gem inside the box and when it beheld Sapphyre, it started to glow. That was an indication that the time has come. Kentin came to us"

Lymer jumps up onto the table and interrupts, "There is a Star God amongst us?" He starts glancing around the room, wide-eyed before Sorenthor cuts him off.

"Kentin is not with us, Lymer. Please sit down." The wizard takes his seat, blushing, and silence fills the room in anticipation of Sorenthor's next words. "The stone apparently holds certain memories of both Kentin and Nestair. Sapphyre has entered a different realm to learn of her past."

"When will she return?" asks Ka'alshene.

"She should rejoin us for the midday meal," replies Sorenthor. "In the meantime, I would like to discuss what transpired with this demon."

The faces of the companions all take on a dire look as they rehash the battle. Sorenthor and Ka'alshene listen intently as Ashcon takes the lead in the retelling of the events, with tidbits added by the others.

"What happened to the barbarians of the Sashee who were killed?" asks Sorenthor.

"The Sashee burned the remains and took the ashes with them to offer to their gods when they complete their Ja'annat Torvol," answers Skken. "They will tell the gods they died with honor in the hopes they will transcend to the afterlife and the hall of heroes."

Sorenthor nods to Skken and then stands up and starts to pace. He stops behind the little gnome, places his hands upon the back of the chair, and states, "Lymer, please tell me what you know of these so called demon banes."

Lymer stands up on his chair and addresses the group, most of his attention on both Sorenthor and Ka'alshene. He recalls the tale of the demon banes and how the weapons were forged during the Second War of the Sanctum. When he finally finishes his story, Sorenthor stands up and paces once again, obviously recalling information from his vast memory.

"So, you are saying that the stories being passed down over the generations about the heroes of the war driving back the demon horde were just that – stories to protect the true reason for victory, which is that these magnificent weapons that were supposed to be lost forever?" asks Sorenthor.

"Yes," is the one word reply from the little gnome.

Sorenthor looks down at the little gnome and asks, "How do you know of this, Lymer? It's obviously one of the consortium's darkest secrets."

Lymer shifts uncomfortably in his seat in response to the inquiry. He looks back and forth between the eyes of Ashcon and Ka'alshene before landing on Sorenthor. He speaks as his head falls down toward his chest. "I am a descendant of one of the twelve wizards who imbued their power into the demon banes."

"And you held this information back why?" asks Ashcon angrily.

"Please be easy on Lymer, Ashcon," admonishes Ka'alshene.

"We are sworn to secrecy as soon as we are imparted with this information. When I turned eighty winters –" starts Lymer.

Talon sits up and interrupts, "Did you say eighty winters?"

Lymer looks to Talon and says, "Yes, young friend. Although I may look to be about forty, I am nearly as old as Sorenthor. I am approaching my three hundredth winter."

The startled looks at the table urge the little man on. "When I turned eighty winters, the High Wizard of the Consortium bestowed upon me my legacy. The information I was imparted was for one reason only. If the demons were to find their way back to our world, there must be some who know the truth about how to dispatch them."

"But all of that is moot since we don't know where these weapons were hidden away," says Ashcon.

Lymer says, "We were imparted with the information so we can understand the method used to imbue the weapons, not so we can search for and find the demon banes. I also assume we were told so we can understand our legacy."

Ka'alshene looks to Lymer and asks, "Who else is aware of the power of the demon banes?"

"My understanding is that the only one who knows of the demon banes is the high wizard himself, and any chosen descendants of the twelve," responds Lymer.

"Do you know of the true meaning of the symbol which revealed itself on the hilt of Frostripper?" asks Skken.

"I do not," answers Lymer. "The high wizard may be able to shed light on that."

Talon looks at the little wizard and says, "I still don't comprehend how your understanding of the demon banes and their true nature will help in future battles against the demon horde."

They all turn to Lymer for an explanation when Sorenthor answers in his stead. "I believe that the reason is a simple one, young Talon." He looks at Lymer who nods at the Lost Seeker while closing his eyes, urging him to answer the inquiry. "The wizards were aware that the demons might not be lost to time forever and might need to be banished once again. If that is to be the case, Lymer and the other chosen descendants will be called upon once again to make the ultimate sacrifice."

The look on the little gnome's face is all the confirmation they need that the Lost Seeker's explanation is right on the mark. They sit in silence, contemplating the latest turn of events, anticipating what other startling discoveries may come to light.

Chapter 50

SLEETH is pacing back and forth within the library in the Temple of the Dark Gods, astonished at what he has just learned while awaiting the impending arrival of Drak'thonn. Today is the day foretold by the Tome of Eternal Night for the leader of the Dark Horde to meet his troops, prior to the invasion of the kingdom. Although it appears the Zagador are granting the burned one even more extraordinary gifts, Sleeth vows to continue to consolidate his knowledge and power until the moment when he will take control.

The door bursts open and Drak'thonn storms through in full battle regalia, exclaiming, "It is time to join the armies. Prepare the portal. We leave now."

Sleeth nods reverently to Drak'thonn before replying. He phrases his words carefully and starts. "Burned One, the Tome of Eternal Night and the

Zagador have decided to impart to you a most dark gift." Drak'thonn tilts his head encouraging Sleeth to continue. "I have been up all evening as the tome came to life once again, and even I am astonished as to what lies within." He points to the chair opposite his and Drak'thonn takes a seat, enthralled with the tale.

"Do you understand from where demons derive their power?" asks Sleeth.

Drak'thonn sits up, places his hands on the table, and responds, "Assume nothing and tell me what you have learned."

"Very well," says Sleeth. "When a demon slays a foe, the soul of the dead becomes trapped in the Demon Realm, fueling that demon's power for all eternity." He pauses, cringes, and continues. "Or until the demon is slain. The more souls a demon has accumulated, the greater its power."

Drak'thonn leans forward and says impatiently, "I assume you have a point, warlock."

"Most certainly," Sleeth says, leaning forward. "The tome has told me that a rather powerful demon has offered its services to you." Drak'thonn comes instantly to attention just as Sleeth says, "You must make an offer to the demon that would entice it to work for you. The demon would agree to subjugate itself to your will. It is a difficult thing for a demon to do. You are forcing it to act in direct contradiction to its most basic desires. Consider this, as the offer must be so remarkable that the demon will subject itself to this unprecedented act. The tome says not what you must offer the demon. It does say that if the demon refuses your offer, you will perish in the Demon Realm and all is lost forever."

Drak'thonn stands up and starts to pace back and forth when Sleeth interjects once more. "If you wish to meet the demon, you must do so before this day has run its course."

Drak'thonn comes to a sudden halt and exclaims, "I know what I will offer the demon! Open the portal. We will meet him now," instructs Drak'thonn to the Sleeth's surprise.

Sleeth starts to tell Drak'thonn of what will transpire both inside the Demon Realm and when they emerge on the other side. Sleeth then stands up and puts the Tome of Eternal Night back into its resting place, gesturing to the stairs with the DarkFlame Staff.

Drak'thonn rises, his frame seemingly larger with the knowledge of the power he will soon yield. He follows Sleeth up into the temple where the high warlock situates himself in the middle of the room and starts chanting with the staff in hand, creating the portal to the Demon Realm.

Sleeth looks to Drak'thonn and asks, "What do you intend to offer the demon, Dark One?"

Drak'thonn looks down at Sleeth and replies, "I intend to offer him a one-of-a-kind feast." The burned leader of the Dark Horde then steps into the Demon Realm, followed by the high warlock, who is less than confident about emerging alive.

Chapter 51

SELENTHA and Krull have the armies camped for the second straight night about two leagues north of the Myth Mountains. The vast armies have tents pitched for leagues in every direction, burning fires dominating the landscape. The orcs and the dreggans have kept up the daily jousts between themselves and the fatality rate is consistently between three and four hundred a day. The human and dwarf slaves do all of the cooking, and any injured slave becomes a meal rather quickly.

It is approaching the final hour of the day when Dark'thonn and Sleeth are supposed to join the army, so Selentha calls her War Stack to order while Krull gathers his officers. Just as the two are preparing to engage in yet another invasion contingency plan, storm clouds start to converge to the north of the camp and a black oval begins to form. Selentha and Krull look to each other and walk to the north, standing in front of the armies who have gathered behind.

The black oval is still growing as the clouds above sparkle with dark electricity. Just as Selentha is starting to wonder just how big this portal is going to get, it stops growing at what is easily fifty feet in circumference. The blackness within the amber rim ripples and Drak'thonn steps out, followed seconds later by Sleeth.

He looks about at his armies, who have all burst into a cheer upon his arrival. He holds his arms up and a relative quiet takes over. He holds his hand out to his bride who walks the fifteen yards to stand beside him. He turns toward the high warlock, nods and leads Selentha away for a private conversation. Sleeth takes the DarkFlame Staff, waves it in the air, and nods back.

Sleeth addresses the armies, his voice loud and clear for all to hear. "The time has finally come. In short order you will emerge on the south side of the Myth Mountains and lay siege to all you see." Roaring cheers fill the night as Sleeth holds his hand up to silence the crowd. He turns towards the orcs and says, "Krull will be leading your chain of destruction to the south." Krull beams with pride and the orcs all scream with joy until Sleeth cuts them off.

Sleeth continues to explain to the orcs and dreggans exactly what to expect when they enter the portal while Drak'thonn speaks to Selentha off to the side.

"The tome has facilitated a change of plans," Drak'thonn starts without preamble. "Krull and your War Stack will lead the armies south. You and I will return to the Skeed Towers where the tome will continue to reveal itself to us."

Selentha nods and asks, "What about the high warlock?"

Drak'thonn looks over to Sleeth, who is expertly controlling the crowd with his speech. "He will lead the army through the portal and then return to continue to interpret the tome." Selentha stares at Drak'thonn and he says, "You have never trusted Sleeth. I trust no one."

"He has aspirations of power. That is dangerous."

The chosen one of the Zagador looks over at Sleeth who is obviously basking in the attention of the masses. "As I said, I trust no one. He is useful now. When he is no longer useful we will kill him."

"Very well," replies his bride.

Sleeth silences the crowd and looks over to Drak'thonn, who nods to the high warlock. He turns to his bride and says, "We have gained a most powerful ally." He starts to walk toward Sleeth, leans close to Selentha and says, "I have made a deal with a demon who is lending his services to our cause."

This causes Selentha to stop in her tracks and ask, "What kind of deal?" In response, Drak'thonn rushes to Sleeth and turns to the vast armies, holding his burning arms up to raucous cheers.

"I need one hundred warrior volunteers," Drak'thonn states to the crowd and thousands rush forward for the honor. He looks to Krull, who nods and with his legionnaires pushes the crowd back, randomly choosing one hundred warriors, a mixture of both orc and dreggan. The War Stack proceeds to push the crowds south, in the opposite direction of the large portal still looming behind Drak'thonn and Sleeth. The warriors are given an area one hundred yards long and wide to assemble.

Drak'thonn starts to speak once again and all eyes turn to him. "As you know, I can control fire." He bellows forth a howl that can be heard for leagues in every direction and shoots his arms from his sides and launches fireballs in every direction over the armies. He turns to the west and streaks of fire spew forth from his hands, burning everything within fifty feet. The crowd is cheering their leader, enthralled with the spectacle, and he puts his hands up to silence them.

"I control an army of orcs and dreggans that will bring living hell upon all of the Kingdom of Martel!" The cheers are joined by the occasional scream as overexcited orcs maim a nearby slave.

He holds his arms out once more and the crowd quiets. "I have one more exceptional gift bestowed upon me by the Zagador. I have entered the Demon Realm and I have returned with a slave to do my bidding." Sleeth looks at Selentha with a startled look on his face, while the queen smirks back. While Sleeth thinks it a dangerous game to state it so, Selentha sees Drak'thonn's genius. There is no better way to achieve loyalty than to scare it out of your subjects.

Drak'thonn then raises his arms to the sky and the portal behind him turns from shimmering black to living flames of fire. An arm, black as night, extending at least ten feet in length explodes through the portal, its enormous claw landing besides Drak'thonn who stands unfazed. A head starts to emerge and the eyes are the first thing the crowd notices. Slanting downward sharply toward the bulbous nose, each eye is at least two feet in length with shadows enveloped within. As the demon stretches its neck, it brings forth its left arm to land on the other side of Drak'thonn.

The armies are slowly backing up in fear, as the demon's head is only a few feet above Drak'thonn's still outstretched hands, its torso extending into the portal where the legs have yet to emerge. Their leader speaks. "Behold, Kulag!"

At the mention of his name, the demon howls deep into the night, and each and every member of the Dark Horde falls silent. It then jumps out of the portal, into the air and lands just a few feet in front of the volunteers.

The demon stands almost twenty-five-feet tall and bears no weapons. Its sheer skin is flawlessly black and burning with demon fire. As it paces back and forth, gazing at the vast armies, allowing them to wallow in fear, it leaves footprints similar to those of their leader in its path Drakthonn addresses the warriors in front of him. "Defeat the demon and you will earn a seat on my council."

He then throws his arm into the air and exclaims, "To the death!"

Kulag then stands to his full twenty-five feet and turns back to look at the army which has backed up to allow sufficient room for the demon to demonstrate its powers. The orcs and the dreggans who volunteered for this task huddle together to try and implement a strategy.

They start to fan in an attempt to surround the demon, just as Kulag lets out a thunderous laugh that shakes the very ground upon which they walk. With a tremendous sweep of his right hand, the demon strikes at twelve orcs creeping toward his right, scooping up three while crushing the other nine. The orcs and dreggans watch in shock as the demon bites the head off of one orc while crushing the two in his opposite hand, letting their insides drip onto the ground below.

The demon hunches down and on all fours charges the twenty or so dreggans directly in front of it. With blaring speed, it is upon the front line, opening its mouth and eating the dreggans whole, crushing others under its arms. The demon stands to its full height in front of the thirty orcs who stand defiantly in front of it. Twenty more comrades join the orcs in a futile attempt at solidarity.

The demon turns to the twenty or so remaining participants who are lined up behind it, preparing to attack. Kulag roars and holds his arm up, and a wall of demon fire emerges between them. The orcs and dreggans look back and forth among each other as the black fire pulsates, its unworldly heat acting as a sturdy barricade.

The demon turns to face the numerous dreggans and orcs who steadfastly hold their ground. Saying nothing, it lowers its head until its face is eye level with the foes. With thirty yards between them, a group of twelve orcs launch an offensive at the demon, charging straight at the creature. The demon waits for the charge and lifts up onto its two hind legs just as one orc jumps and lands on its shoulder. Easily kicking the orcs aside, he plucks the one off his shoulder before looking down at the three orcs who are still alive after the brief offensive. Kulag holds his huge hand palm out and a ball of demon fire blasts forward, incinerating the orcs. With each death of an orc or dreggan, Kulag takes the time to take a deep breath and savor the flavor of a new soul to empower him.

The orc and dreggan warriors who are on the same side of the wall of demon fire look back and forth to each other in desperation as Kulag approaches. He still has the screaming orc in the grip of his right hand when he stops about ten yards in front of the stunned warriors.

He howls in rage and, taking the orc in his hand, brings it up toward his face. Kulag speaks for the first time and everything falls silent. "Behold," is the one word he speaks and it echoes throughout the camp. He closes and then opens his eyes and forces the orc in his hand to gaze into them.

The orc's face turns pale white and his eyes gloss over as he stares into the depths of the eyes of Kulag. A smile creeps across the face of the demon while the orc sees the souls of each and every creature Kulag uses to fuel his power. The number of souls is seemingly endless, as Kulag has existed for thousands of winters.

After a mere thirty seconds, he drops the body of the orc onto the ground and steps back, eager to have the orc comrades inspect the creature. The orcs and dreggans rush forward to their fallen comrade and turn away in shock. The orc is still alive, but the eyes hold no color. The once heavily muscled body is shriveled down to mere skin on bones. The labored breathing of the orc suddenly turns into violent spasms and the others back away in shock.

The stricken orc is turning black as pitch and starting to burn with a black fire. The shrieks of the creature fill the silence that has taken over the camp. Kulag stands and roars just as the orc explodes in a ball of demon fire, immediately cremating it and three other warriors standing close by.

The onlookers all gaze toward Drak'thonn, wondering if they should intervene. Drak'thonn looks toward Kulag, who, now satiated, nods back at the burned man.

Kulag then turns back to the wall of demon fire, and at his howl, it dissipates. He walks back to Drak'thonn on his rear two feet, his full, intimidating height drawing the eyes of all around him. Selentha leaves Sleeth's side and joins Drak'thonn just as Kulag situates himself in front of them.

With everyone looking on, Kulag hunches down so his head rests upon the ground, enabling Drak'thonn and Selentha to climb upon his back. The two jump onto the right shoulder and make their way up to the small of his neck, the demon's skin doing no harm to the two chosen ones.

The demon is now standing on all fours, facing the vast armies, the leaders of the Dark Horde atop this beast from the Demon Realm. Drak'thonn breathes deeply, turns to his wife and smiles.

Drak'thonn looks to the vast armies and addresses them once more. "Kulag will join me on the field of battle and bring the forces of the Star Gods to their knees!" The crowd breaks out in raucous cheer once again, already over the carnage that took place mere moments ago. He looks to Sleeth and nods to him, indicating it is time to open the portal for his armies.

Sleeth then steps into the area that was occupied by the earlier bout and begins a chant with the DarkFlame Staff in hand. A portal, much smaller in size than the one behind Drak'thonn, begins to appear.

Krull and the War Stack assemble the armies before it as Drak'thonn urges them forward. "Destroy the armies of the Star Gods!"As the orcs and dreggans continue into the portal by the thousands, those remaining keep cheering with the shouts of their leader. As the final group of orcs and dreggans enters the portal, Krull turns to his leader one final time. Drak'thonn rises to his full height atop the shoulder of the demon and states, "For the glory of the Zagador!"

Krull raises his battle ax to the sky and screams, "For the glory of the Zagador!" He then turns and enters the portal to face the unknown.

Drak'thonn and Selentha sit down comfortably on Kulag's shoulders when Sleeth approaches. He's about to speak when Drak'thonn cuts him off. "Go now, high warlock. I expect you back in two nights time to continue your work on the tome." The tone of his voice silences any reply and Sleeth merely nods and then turns and follows Krull into the portal.

Now that the two are alone, Selentha turns toward her husband and says, "So what kind of deal did you make with this demon?"

"It is quite, simple, my warrior wife," he replies. She looks at him, prodding him to continue. "I promised Kulag he can dine on the soul of a un-estar for all eternity."

At the mention of runestar, Kulag howls into the night and stands to his full twenty-five feet. The demon then turns around and looks at the portal pulsating in the night, and, with a nudge from Drak'thonn, launches into the Demon Realm once again for the return trip to the Temple of the Dark Gods.

Chapter 52

THE companions are finishing up the midday meal and anticipating the return of Sapphyre when the sound of a door behind a staircase opens. All head turn as the beauty with the blue streaks in her blonde hair makes her way around the bend with a content look upon her face.

Talon is the first to make his way to her and she puts her hands in his and smiles. She leans forward and kisses the young seeker on the cheek, leaving a crimson stain that seems to linger.

Sapphyre walks to Sorenthor and looks up into his eyes and says, "Thank you. I am aware of the love you had for my parents, as well as the sacrifice you made for my father." Sorenthor nods to the young lady and smiles while closing his eyes.

Sapphyre looks at the table with the colorful fruits and, turning, she smells the freshly roasted boar and realizes just how hungry she is. "I need sustenance, and then we can discuss a plan of action," she says as she walks toward the table.

Ashcon chuckles softly as Sorenthor replies, "Very well, Sapphyre. Let me tell you what has transpired in your absence." Sorenthor gives Sapphyre the important points about Lymer's heritage while she eats quickly, glancing frequently in the direction of the little wizard.

Upon finishing her meal, she rises and the companions all follow suit. Sorenthor leads them into the study where the large oval table from the previous evening has reappeared. They all take their seats around it.

All eyes are on Sapphyre, so she leans forward and speaks. "I know all of you are curious as to what I may have learned. Let me say that I have discovered much about my family history and I understand why my parents put me in the care of the Oracle of Anon." Sorenthor and Ka'alshene exchange knowing glances as Sapphyre continues. "I understand the powers the two of them wielded, so I have a bit of knowledge on what to expect with regards to my abilities. I do not know when I will come into my full power, nor if I ever will." She pauses and then looks at each of them and says,

"Please understand this is all I wish to discuss. The rest is intensely personal." She slowly lowers her head toward her chest, takes a deep breath, exhales, sits straight up, and opens her eyes.

Sorenthor takes over immediately. He looks to Sapphyre and gives her a loving nod and says, "Very well, Ka'alshene please tell us what you have learned."

The high priestess nods and says, "Since I have met with the prince regent, the kingdom's armies have been amassing at the garrisons directly south of the Myth Mountains. They are concentrating their efforts from the DragonTooth Pass west, with the largest contingency along the coast by Tekken as they still anticipate an attack by sea."

Ashcon intervenes, "You can't blame them, Ka'alshene. Even though they are marching southeast."

Ka'alshene holds up her hand and interrupts him. "They are through marching. They set up camp a few leagues north of the Myth Mountains, directly north of Antoine."

Ashcon looks at her with surprise before continuing, "Unless they plan on marching directly through the mountains, they either have to go to the DragonTooth Pass or head west to the ocean."

Sorenthor is about to speak when Lymer jumps up onto the table and says, "Hold on. If they have a warlock who can open a portal to the Demon Realm, they may be able to transport their entire army south of the mountains."

Skken says, "Why would they bother marching then? They could just open a portal, enter the Demon Realm, and then show up anywhere and attack."

To the surprise of the group it's Sapphyre who replies. "They marched south so they can be as close to their destination as possible." All heads turn to her as she continues. "Traversing through time in the Demon Realm takes a toll on the warlock and his ability to continue to call forth portals. Creating a portal to transport thousands of souls through the Demon Realm is very trying to say the least. The shorter the distance, the easier it is on the warlock. The Demon Realm is also a test of courage, so to speak, so many will perish on the journey. They are camped directly north of where they will appear in the kingdom. I know not when they will traverse the Demon Realm, nor how long the journey will take, but that is where you need to prepare for battle."

Ka'alshene is about to question Sapphyre when the young woman turns to the high priestess and says simply, "The transformation of the dagger has bestowed upon me knowledge of demons and the Demon Realm. I do not know how vast the knowledge is, but I do know what I speak to be true."

Ka'alshene nods to Sapphyre and then addresses the group. "Then I must inform the prince regent so he can muster his forces in preparation for the attack."

Sapphyre speaks and all eyes turn to her. "My first priority is to rescue Katrivus."

Sorenthor is the one to respond. "I understand your need to save your friend, Sapphyre, but we must keep the big picture in mind. Drak'thonn's ability to enter the Demon Realm and return with allies takes precedence over the life of one person, no matter how dear he may be to you."

Sapphyre is about to reply when Talon reaches over and takes her hand in his. The two exchange a loving glance. He is about to speak when Lymer interjects for the first time.

"If we are to do battle against demons, then we need the assistance of the wizards. I will travel to the consortium and meet with the high wizard to inform him of the impending attack."

Sorenthor nods to the little wizard and sneaks a glance at Ashcon who also nods and then speaks. "I think it would be wise for Sapphyre to join you, Lymer." His gaze turns to Sapphyre. "The high wizard can probably shed some light on the demon bane you wield and provide us with valuable information on how to defeat demons."

Just as Sapphyre is about to speak, Talon squeezes the small hand which is still in his grasp and says, "I will travel with Sapphyre and Lymer." He looks at Sapphyre, who smiles softly and then to Ashon, expecting opposition to his proposal.

Ashcon is about to speak when Ka'alshene cuts him off. "The idea is sound, but I worry we will not have time. If Drak'thonn attacks with demons, then we need Sapphyre here, not on the eastern seaboard."

Sorenthor takes control of the conversation once again. "The armies that have amassed along the northern border of the Myth Mountains are orcs and dreggans, correct?" Ka'alshene nods and Sorenthor continues. "According to prophecy, the final battle that will take place will be between Ashcon and Drak'thonn and there are allusions to otherworldly creatures, which we can now assume means demons. There is no mention of massive armies. The orcs and dreggans will be attacking the kingdom in preparation for world domination if Drak'thonn emerges victorious. I don't believe we need to worry about demons joining their ranks."

He stands up and paces while continuing to voice his thoughts. "I believe Drak'thonn's demons will be at his side when he faces you, Ashcon. Just as you will have Skken, Sapphyre, Talon, and Lymer with his wizards as your comrades, he will have warlocks and demons as his."

Skken looks to Sorenthor and asks, "When will the battle take place?"

"That is not certain, although it is inevitable."

Ashcon says, "I say we dictate the schedule then." All eyes turn to the runestar as he continues. "If we all must be present for the battle to take place, then let us set our own timetable."

Sorenthor smiles as he sees where Ashcon's line of thinking is going. "What do you have in mind?" he asks.

"Ka'alshene, you must go and meet with the prince regent. Afterwards, you can try once again to muster the help of the dwarves of the Myth

Mountains." The high priestess nods. "Lymer, Sapphyre, and Talon will travel to the Wizards Consortium." The three all nod to him as well. "Then Skken and I will enter the Demon Realm and rescue Katrivus." Sorenthor is about to object when Ashcon holds up his hand. "The battle cannot take place without me, Sorenthor. If I'm not here, Drak'thonn and his demons cannot win."

Skken finishes his runestar's thought. "When we all finish our objectives then we will face Drak'thonn. And when we do, we will have the knowledge and forces necessary to defeat him."

The Lost Seeker takes his seat once again and says, "I will keep Katrivus's body safe." Sapphyre smiles to Sorenthor. "Now that I know your true identity, Sapphyre, I will be revisiting prophecy regarding your coming. There may be information in scrolls I have not yet read that can aid us."

A silence fills the room as they all contemplate their latest charges. Just as Sorenthor is about to suggest retiring for the night, Sapphyre gasps so loud that all eyes turn to her and Talon jumps to his feet in alarm.

She looks at Talon and says, "I am fine," to which the young seeker relaxes a bit. "We have a problem, however," she continues. "A Demon Lord has entered our realm."

Lymer is the one who gasps now and they all look at the little wizard, who has lost all color in his face. "Demon Lords did not even come into play in the War of the Sanctum. Are you sure, Sapphyre?"

"I am."

Sorenthor stands up and exclaims, "That does it then. At first light, Sapphyre, Lymer, and Talon will make east to meet the high wizard. Ka'alshene, you will –"

She cuts him off with a hand. "I will depart this evening. The attack from the orcs and dreggans is imminent."

Sorenthor nods to the high priestess and says, "Very well. I will prepare Ashcon and Skken for their journey into the Demon Realm. Let us retire and reconvene on the morrow."

They all nod and rise, walking into the main chamber of the library where they exchange hugs with Ka'alshene, who leaves to head to Thorenn.

Doors appear all around the circular chamber and Sorenthor announces, "Rooms have been prepared. Until tomorrow." He then proceeds to walk up the spiral staircase leaving the others on the ground floor.

Ashcon and Skken turn to the room closest to them and enter while Lymer takes the room immediately to the right. Talon hugs Sapphyre, turns to his left, and opens the door to his chambers for the night. As he turns back to close the door, Sapphyre steps forward and blocks his way.

The young seeker steps back and allows Sapphyre to enter. She smiles at the stunned young man and stops briefly at his side to give him a lingering kiss on the lips. Talon closes his eyes until he feels her mouth leave his and then turns to see Sapphyre walking deeper into his room. As he is about to speak, Sapphyre lets her gown drop to the floor and, without turning around, slides into Talon's bed.